RETURN TO
KING SOLOMON'S
MINES

STEVE BARLOW &
STEVE SKIDMORE

USBORNE

First published in the UK in 2012 by Usborne Publishing Ltd., Usborne House, 83-85 Saffron Hill, London EC1N 8RT, England. www.usborne.com

Cover illustration by Sam Hadley.

The name Usborne and the devices ♀ ⊕ are Trade Marks of Usborne Publishing Ltd.

A CIP catalogue record for this book is available from the British Library.

ISBN 9781409521433   FMAMJJASOND/12 00632/1

Printed in Reading, Berkshire, UK.

In the winter of 1934–5, the rise of totalitarian governments in many parts of the world is gathering pace. Hitler has declared himself fuehrer of a German empire, which he boasts will last for a thousand years. But the focus of world crisis has shifted to Africa, where Italian leader Benito Mussolini has ambitions of his own.

This is the new Scientific Age, when discoveries simultaneously promise a bright future and threaten global disaster. But there are powers in the world older than science, and just as deadly...

1 EXERCISE

Salisbury Plain, Wiltshire, United Kingdom
December 1934

The Bedford three-ton truck bounced, wallowed and slid over the rutted, snow-covered track. A particularly severe jolt brought Luke Challenger's head into sharp contact with one of the stanchions that supported the canvas roof. He swore violently and rubbed at his thatch of straw-coloured hair.

His cousin Nick Malone, who had been lifted out of his seat and slammed back into it, gave a low moan. "My backside just shook hands with my brainbox."

"I thought," Luke shot back, "you kept your brains *in* your backside."

"Oh, har-har."

"Quiet there!" The voice, like its owner, was thin and spiteful. Luke glowered across the back of the truck at Cadet Sergeant Warren. He was fed up with the way Warren (who was only a year older than him and Nick) threw his weight about. His fists clenched, not for the first time, with the desire to flatten the Cadet Sergeant's sharp nose across his weaselly face. "No talking in the ranks! Do you hear me there, Challenger? Malone?"

The question was completely unnecessary, and Nick's response was sarcastic. "Faith, Sarjint, I hear youse loud and clear, so I do!" he bellowed. Warren had once made the mistake of making a snide comment about Nick's Irish father. Since then, Nick had needled the Cadet Sergeant by speaking to him in an outrageous "faith and begorrah" accent. Ignoring Warren's glare, Nick continued, "Only, strictly speaking, aren't we only in the ranks when we're on parade, at all, at all?"

"That will do, Malone." Warren knew he was being made to look foolish, but when he had complained that Nick kept talking to him in an Irish voice, their instructor Lieutenant McNeil, who didn't like Warren either, had merely said, "I expect that's because he's Irish, Cadet Sergeant," and Warren hadn't dared bring the matter up again. So Nick (who was, in fact, only half Irish) continued to bait Warren with impunity.

The truck jerked again and Luke let go his handhold on the vehicle's side to grab at his rifle as it slipped from his lap. He cursed again, but silently this time. He and Nick had only joined his school's army cadet force in a fit of boredom, and because the alternative was extra Latin homework. The school's aim in running the cadet force was that pupils would use it to prepare for a career in the regular army. Luke and Nick had no intention of doing this, and they had not foreseen the amount of spit and polish – not to mention the endless, repetitive drill – that being a cadet would involve; nor that they would find themselves being shaken to bits in the back of this rattletrap truck, on their way to an exercise on a fog-bound Salisbury Plain in the dead of winter.

Warren, having realized that in trying to victimize Nick he was on a hiding to nothing, turned his attention to another target. He directed a savage grin at a huddled figure sitting near the tailboard of the truck, where the icy draughts from the flapping canvas sides were at their worst. "How are you getting on, *Sally*? Is it cold enough for you?" One or two of his cronies in the squad sniggered.

The cadet Warren had addressed looked up. His sharp nose and prominent cheekbones might have appeared forbidding but for the warmth of his dark eyes; and his voice, though unexpectedly deep, was pleasant. "In the highlands of my country, we often have temperatures similar to this, Sergeant, but thank you for your concern. And my name is Salim – Salim Menelik. I believe I have mentioned this?"

Warren exchanged grins with his cronies. "I'd stick with 'Sally' if I were you. What sort of a name is 'Menelik'? It sounds like some sort of lollipop."

"It is pronounced Men-err-lick, not Many-lick, Sergeant, and it is a very interesting name. Very ancient. My family can trace its roots back to King Solomon and the Queen of Sheba. Their son Menelik was the first Emperor of Ethiopia, and one of our more recent Emperors was Menelik II. Of course, Haile Selassie is Emperor now, my father is a relatively junior member of the royal family…"

Warren's temper had been rising during this recital. "I'm not interested in your stupid family!"

"Are you not?" said Salim mildly. "Personally, I find the study of family history very interesting. For example, your own ancestors rose to power by constantly changing sides to suit their own interests. One was a Royalist until Charles I was beheaded, and became a Roundhead while Cromwell was Lord Protector, but when Charles II came to the throne – hey presto – suddenly he was a

Royalist again! And your own father—"

"You leave my father out of this!" Warren surged out of his seat, fists balled.

But Luke and Nick, having watched the flush of rage flood across Warren's ratlike features, were instantly on their feet between their Cadet Sergeant and his intended victim. Warren's cronies eyed each other uncertainly; both Luke and Nick had a well-earned reputation for being handy in a fight, while the cronies were more at home persecuting small fry than standing up to anyone who could take care of themselves.

Warren gave Luke a savage glare. "Lay a finger on me, Challenger, and I'll have you on a charge."

The prominent jaw Luke had inherited from his grandfather jutted menacingly forward. "Try bullying anyone in this squad, *Sergeant*, and I'll knock your ruddy block off."

"Ah, now, oi'm sure the Sarjint wouldn't be after assaulting a man under his command." Nick's mouth was creased in an easy-going smile, and his voice was jovial, but there was no hint of friendliness in his eyes. "Him bein' sich a fine upstanding gentleman and all."

The stand-off might have gone on indefinitely but for another jerk from the truck that sent the three would-be combatants staggering back to their seats. The rest of the journey passed in sullen silence.

Luke gave Salim Menelik an appraising look. The young Ethiopian had only arrived at the school the previous September. At fifteen years of age, he was a year below Luke and Nick. If they had any impression of him at all, it was of a small, slightly roly-poly figure sitting under a tree and reading a book while most of the other boys were playing rugby. But the way he had stood up to Warren had taken courage, and the ease with which he had got the better of his older opponent showed quickness of wit.

Luke frowned. It had also almost certainly guaranteed young Menelik a bed in the school sickbay. Visibility out on the plain was down to a few yards. Once the exercise had started, what was to stop Warren and his thuggish friends cornering Salim and taking their revenge? Luke resolved to keep a close eye on his Ethiopian schoolmate for the rest of the day.

At length, the Bedford clattered to a halt and the tailboard dropped down. Luke and the other members of his squad clambered stiffly out of the truck, shouldering their rifles and packs. Nick struggled to force his unruly black curls into place beneath his forage cap.

Several other trucks were parked nearby, their tyre-tracks tracing dark, muddy curves against the snow. The winter-withered grass and scrub of the plain lay under a covering of snow which, at no great distance, merged indistinguishably into fog. Salisbury Plain, the traditional training ground for the army, spread out unseen for miles in all directions: a ragged landscape of sick-looking vegetation, tank tracks and shell holes. Luke shivered. What a place for a walk!

Lieutenant McNeil was speaking to one of the other squad leaders from Luke's school, Ashleigh House. Spotting the new arrivals, he came over, casually returning Warren's crashing salute. "There you are, Sergeant," he observed without enthusiasm. "For the purposes of this exercise, you and your squad are on the blue team." Luke fingered his blue armband as McNeil held out a folded slip of paper. "In there, you'll find a map reference. You do have a map with you, I take it?"

Warren saluted again. "Yes, sir!"

"Well done. At that reference point, you'll find a hut with a red flag flying from the roof. Your objective is to take possession of the flag. The red team from Saint Gilbert's school will be defending the position." Despite his loathing for Ashleigh House, Luke scowled at the mention of his school's hereditary enemies. "Now, obviously, this is not a live-fire exercise. You are carrying rifles for authenticity, not to use them – in any case, they aren't loaded, so nobody is going to be shot today. If a member of the defending team catches you unawares, he will say, 'Halt, you are my prisoner.' And if one of your opponents thinks he has a clear shot at you before you can take one at him, he will say..." Lieutenant McNeil took a scrap of paper from his breast pocket and read it. "'Bang-bang, you are dead,'" he said tonelessly.

The boys of Luke's squad grinned and nudged each other. Luke and Nick, who, alone among all their schoolmates, had actually been under fire on a number of occasions from enemies determined to kill them, remained poker-faced.

McNeil held up a smoke grenade. "You've all been issued with these. They will be used in the same way as explosive grenades – so if, for example, you manage to land one near a gun position manned by your opponents, that position will be marked down as destroyed. Once you've pulled the pin, for goodness' sake don't forget to throw the thing or you could get a nasty burn. To make the whole thing more realistic there'll also be a few whizz-bangs going off. There will be marshals stationed across the battlefield to ensure fair play. Oh, and by the way, the regular army is doing a tank exercise in another part of the range."

One of Warren's cronies looked alarmed. "Tanks, sir?"

"Yes, Hobbs, but don't worry. You may hear them, but they shouldn't be coming over here."

Hobbs gulped. "What if they do, sir?"

McNeil looked amused. "Well, I wouldn't try to attack one single-handed if I were you. It's a lot harder than you are. Give it a wide berth, is my advice." Hobbs looked relieved. "The trucks will pick you up from the hut at 4.30 pip emma." Catching Hobbs's blank look, he added with a sigh, "That's p.m. to you, Hobbs. Any questions? Very good – carry on, Cadet Sergeant."

"Sir!" Warren threw another salute. As McNeil turned away, Warren opened the paper and took a map from his pack.

"Eastings first," Nick reminded him helpfully. "You read the numbers off the bottom of the map—"

"Shut up, Malone, I know that!" Warren hardly seemed to glance at the reference. He merely jabbed a finger at the map. "There. That's where the flag is." He considered briefly. "All right, we'll divide into four teams of three. Challenger, Malone and—"

"Menelik," Luke put in smoothly. "He's coming with us."

Warren gave Luke a hard stare. "I decide who goes with whom."

"Fine. Then do yourself a favour and decide Menelik is going with me and Nick, because that's what's going to happen."

Warren gave the Ethiopian boy a sideways look. "Well, if you really want to play nursemaid to a—"

Luke glowered at him. "To a what?"

Warren's only reply was a leer so full of derision that Luke stepped forward, but his fist had hardly begun to move before Nick caught it. "Leave it. Too many people around – and McNeil."

Luke fought back the impulse to wipe the smirk from Warren's face. "One of these days..."

"But not today, Challenger." Warren pointed at the map. "Take the sunken road, here."

Luke glanced at the map. "But that takes us miles from the objective."

"It should be safe, then. No chance of you blundering into red team patrols and getting caught. Don't worry, when *we've* captured the flag we'll save you a cup of tea. As you've so far to go, you'd better get moving."

Luke turned without a word and set off into the fog. Nick gave Salim Menelik a nod. The Ethiopian set off in Luke's footsteps, with Nick bringing up the rear.

As the voices of the attacking party faded behind them, Salim fell into step beside Luke. "Don't think me ungrateful," he said, "but I can look after myself, you know. I'd prefer to fight my own battles."

Luke gave a non-committal grunt. He could believe that Menelik would stand a chance against Warren by himself, but Warren and two of his bully-boys? He doubted it. He walked on, snow crunching beneath his boots.

Nick patted their new companion on the shoulder. "Don't mind him. He's just sulking because he couldn't bust Warren on the snoot. Speaking of Warren, what were you going to say about his da?"

"My father suspects that during the Great War, Warren Senior supplied arms to people in North Africa who weren't exactly on Britain's side."

Nick whistled. "Warren's old man is something in the War Office, isn't he? No wonder he didn't want you bringing that up." He gave Salim a sidelong look. "Is your father really a prince?"

"Yes, a very minor one. 147th in line for the throne, I believe, which makes me 148th."

Luke turned. "Do you think you two could pipe down while we're trying to make our way silently through enemy lines?"

Nick gave him a grin. "You'll be wanting to get your hands on that flag, then?"

"Yes, before Warren gets hold of it – and if I do, I'll damn well make him eat it!"

From time to time they heard muffled explosions – Lieutenant McNeil's promised "whizz-bangs" – as they tramped through the snow and wavering tendrils of mist. Luke was slightly surprised at the ease with which their new companion kept up with the pace he set; Salim Menelik might look a trifle on the podgy side, but he was light on his feet and seemed to have plenty of stamina.

After half an hour of wading through snow and between frost-laced clumps of gorse and heather, they came across a deeply rutted track running between banks of earth. Luke checked his copy of the map and took a compass from his pack to sight along it. "This is the sunken road, all right," he whispered. "We follow it for a mile; then we head north towards this strip of woodland—" He broke off as the roar of a diesel engine broke out, somewhere in the mist.

"What's that?" asked Salim.

Luke listened intently. "A tank – a Brigadier Mark III, or I've never heard one. It's a Challenger Industries model – one of my dad's."

Salim looked surprised. "Challenger Industries?"

Nick nodded. "Luke's da is head of one of the biggest armaments companies in Britain. Did you not know?" Salim shook his head. Nick turned to Luke. "That's all right then – it's one of ours."

"We'd better keep out of its way, all the same," replied Luke as the engine settled down to a steady roar. "According to McNeil, it shouldn't be over here anyway."

Nick shrugged. "It's probably lost. Not really surprising in all this murk."

"Where's it coming from, do you think?" Nick and Salim pointed in different directions and Luke shook his head. "Hard to tell in the fog." Out in the mist, the tank's engine revved and they heard distant squeals and rattles as it began to move on its caterpillar treads. "Oh well, it shouldn't bother us if we don't bother it. Come on." Luke set off down the road.

As they walked, the snow became deeper, the banks of earth to either side of the road rose higher and the noise of the tank grew louder. Luke and his companions had hardly covered a hundred yards before the ugly, squat vehicle loomed out of the mist, also occupying the sunken road and coming directly towards them.

"We'd better climb up the bank a way and let it through..." Luke got no further. He watched with stunned disbelief as the tank ground to a halt and its turret swivelled until the gun barrel was pointing directly at the three cadets. There was a roar like the end of the world, and Luke threw himself to the ground as a fountain of mud and earth erupted a few yards behind him.

Luke stared wildly around. To his relief, Salim Menelik was struggling to his feet, seemingly none the worse for wear; and Nick was spitting out the mouthful of snow he had inadvertently taken in his frantic dive.

The tank creaked back into motion. With one accord, Luke, Nick and Salim scrambled up the bank to their left. Their feet slipped on the snow and stalks of the grass beneath slithered through their clutching hands. Another explosion close behind them spurred them on, and a split second later they were over the bank and tumbling down the other side to lie, gasping, in a patch of snow-powdered broom.

Nick swore violently. "I don't believe this!" He turned to Luke, his usually good-natured face twisted in fury. "We're being shot at – again!"

Salim stared at him. "Again? What do you mean, again?"

"No time to explain." Luke's voice rose above the roar of the tank's engine as it set off in pursuit. "Run!"

2 FOG AND SMOKE

Three figures stumbled across the bleached landscape.

Their flight was taking its toll. The muscles of Luke's legs were trembling with the effort of running through the yielding, clinging snow. His lungs ached from the strain of breathing great gulps of cold, damp air. Glancing from side to side, he could see that Nick and Salim were in no better shape.

He cursed inwardly. They couldn't hope to outrun a tank! Luke guessed that they had only managed to outdistance the lethal machine so far because, even with its caterpillar treads, the steepness of the earthen banks along the sunken road had obliged the driver to follow the track until these obstructions had flattened out. But at the speed the tank could move, it would not take long to catch up with them. The sound of its engine and the chattering of its treads followed them, rising and falling in the swirling fog but always on their tail, a constant threat.

Even so, they could not keep ploughing through the snow indefinitely. There was no shelter from the tank on the open plain; their only chance was to find woodland too dense for the cumbersome vehicle to penetrate. Luke dropped into a crouch and checked the map.

Nick and Salim stopped and turned. "Come on!" gasped Nick. "There's no time to hang about."

"And there's no point in running around like headless chickens either," retorted Luke. He pointed. "Over there – there's a thicket maybe a couple of hundred yards away. Not a big one, but we can hole up for long enough to get our breath."

Nick nodded and turned in the direction Luke had indicated. Their pounding feet sent up flurries of snow as they ran on. A little further than Luke had predicted, the skeletal limbs of leafless trees appeared, clawing at the mist surrounding them. Luke and his companions dived beneath their branches and rested on their haunches, gasping for breath.

Nick gave Luke a glare. "'If we don't bother it, it shouldn't bother us.' Hah!" When Luke made no reply, he gave his rifle a disgusted look. "Why are we still carrying these things? Without ammo, they're just dead weight. We don't even have bayonets." Lieutenant McNeil had forbidden the use of the sharp blades on the grounds that some overenthusiastic cadets might forget that their opponents were not straw dummies, and do each other serious damage.

"We may as well hang on to them," said Luke. "After all, they're the only weapons we have – we can always whack people with them if all else fails."

Salim nodded agreement. "In any case, if we go back to Lieutenant McNeil without our rifles, he will put us on a charge."

"Oh, that's got me really scared," said Nick bitterly. "There I was, worrying about being blown to pieces, when all the time I should have been fretting over being put on a charge if I lost my rifle. Silly me."

"What gets my goat," said Luke, "is that we're being hounded by a tank that my own father designed and built."

"Yes," said Nick, "but who's driving it?"

"I think," Salim said gravely, "it is unlikely to be the

British Army. The way the tank opened fire on us – that was deliberate. It was no accident."

"You're right, there," said Nick. "I'd bet a pound to a pinch of horse manure it's been hijacked by the Sons of Destiny."

Salim gave him an owlish stare. "The which of what?"

"They're a secret society," Luke told him brusquely. "They've been after me and Nick for a couple of years now, and I can't think of anyone else who wants to kill us enough to come after us in a tank."

Salim was nonplussed. "But who are—"

"There *really* isn't time to explain." Luke turned his attention back to the map.

Nick peered over his shoulder. "Where do we go? Back to the trucks?"

Luke shook his head. "They won't be there any more – McNeil said they'd be picking us up from the hut."

"So he did. Well, how about if we head north-east? There's no cover, but if the rest of our squad are making a beeline for the hut, we should come across them at some stage. The tank will have to give up then."

"I wouldn't count on it," Luke told him. "Have you asked yourself how the tank crew knew where to find us?"

"They couldn't have known," said Nick. "We didn't

know where we'd be going ourselves until..." He broke off as light dawned.

"Exactly. Until Warren told us to take the sunken road."

"Warren! I'll murder him!"

"You'll have to get in the queue."

"But Warren wasn't supposed to know exactly where the exercise was taking place until McNeil briefed him when we arrived here," Salim pointed out.

"Then whoever planned the exercise must have told Warren beforehand to send us on that road – it doesn't matter," said Luke. "The point is, we can't trust Warren – and in any case, I don't want to be responsible for leading that tank straight towards the rest of our lads." He tapped at the map. "We'll go this way, through the marsh – with any luck, the tank will get bogged down and..." He turned a stricken face to the others as the sound of the tank's engine began to grow louder. "We have to go! Now!"

"What's the big rush?" demanded Nick. "Even if the tank's coming this way the crew don't know we're in here..."

"Yes they do!" Luke cursed himself for a fool. "We've left tracks in the snow! All they have to do is follow them. And the tank might not be able to get in here but its shells can!" The words were hardly out of Luke's mouth before the crash of the tank's gun sounded close by, followed immediately by the whine of a shell passing overhead and an explosion of leaf litter in the centre of the thicket, followed by the creak and crash of falling trees.

Luke sprang to his feet, yelling, "Come on!" and led a mad dash through the thicket.

For a few yards, the trees thinned and Luke caught a glimpse of the tank as it ploughed through the snow, following the edge of the woodland. Evidently the crew spotted the fugitives, because its engine roared and it came racing up the shallow slope towards them. Luke and his companions hastily turned back into the trees – and a moment later, the tank burst into the thicket, skittling saplings to left and right. Luke dived to one side to avoid being run down, and looked up in time to see the tank rear up as it mounted a fallen tree. Its belly resting on the broad trunk, its treads screeched as they scrabbled ineffectually for purchase. Luke ducked as the vehicle's machine gun opened up, sending twigs and splinters dancing where its bullets struck. He glanced up to see Nick and Salim beckoning him from the far side of the thicket. Running in a crouch to dodge the fire from the chattering machine gun, he hastened to join them.

Nick was gleeful. "That should slow them down a bit."

Luke was less optimistic. "It'll buy us some time, but not much. The tank won't stay stuck for long. We need to get to the marsh – once we're there it'll be harder for the crew to pick up our trail, and if the ground's wet enough, the tank may not be able to follow us anyway. Or if it tries, with any luck, it might get bogged down." Luke led the way out of the trees and down a slope dotted with scrawny bushes and shell holes.

Once again, the mist claimed them. It was impossible to see further than a few yards. Luke slowed and glanced left and right. "Where is that blasted marsh? We should be in it by now."

Nick, who had drawn a couple of steps ahead, suddenly plunged through the blanket of snow, disappearing up to mid-thigh in a splash of dirty water. He swore violently and turned to Luke with a disgruntled expression. "I think I've found it."

Wading through the marsh was more tiring and infinitely more uncomfortable than their tramp through the snow had been. The freezing water squelched in their boots and trickled disgustingly down their legs at every step. Luke was again impressed at the stoicism shown by Salim; the young Ethiopian must have been unused to such terrain, but he struggled on without complaint.

The creaking and groaning behind them rose to a crescendo, then died away. The roars of the over-revved engine settled down to a less frantic note, which then receded. Luke guessed that the tank had succeeded in freeing itself, which was bad news. However, it didn't seem to be pursuing them. Had the crew given up? Or did they have another plan in mind?

Luke and his companions were exhausted by the time they reached the end of the marsh. They lay flat on their bellies in the snow – they were so wet and cold by now that this hardly mattered – and Luke checked his map again. "There's a series of gullies up ahead. If we can get through them, we're not far from the hut. Can anyone hear the tank?" Nick and Salim shook their heads. "It could be anywhere. Blast this fog." Luke took a deep breath and concluded, "Come on, then. Keep a sharp eye out."

The marshland had given way to higher ground criss-crossed by a network of trenches, around eight to twelve feet deep, their bottoms deeply rutted and dotted with pools of muddy, ice-flecked water.

The first of these lay directly across the line of their march. With Luke leading the way, they slithered down the steep bank into it, their scrabbling feet dislodging stones and earth. Suddenly, and shockingly close, an engine coughed into life. With a roar, the tank loomed out of the mist to their right, an olive-green juggernaut. The fugitives scattered as the gun fired again, blasting a hole in the side of the gulley that started a miniature landslide.

Luke led Nick and Salim in a breakneck race along the floor of the trench, with the tank at their heels. Just as it seemed they would be crushed beneath the vehicle's pounding, chattering treads, a side gulley opened to their right. Luke swerved into it, the others followed, and the tank rumbled past, its gunner unable to turn in time to get another shot in before the vehicle's momentum had carried it beyond their refuge.

The weary cadets scrambled out of the gulley. Nick and Salim lay gasping on the snow, but Luke settled into a crouch, listening hard. The tank's engine was idling. It seemed to have come to a standstill. Luke peered into the mist; he could just make out the turret, a couple of feet below the rim of the trench.

Luke broke into a run. Startled, Nick and Salim followed. When he reached the edge of the trench, Luke didn't hesitate. He leaped into space. One booted foot landed on the tank's turret hatch with a satisfying *CLANG!* as he used it as a stepping stone to the far side of the gorge. Nick and Salim followed suit: *CLANG! CLANG!* Luke turned momentarily to see the tank commander open the hatch, stick his head out, and stare around with a comically startled expression.

For the moment, they were safe from pursuit. Nick

and Salim were laughing like maniacs at their exploit, but Luke was consumed with anger. He was tired of being chased and shot at – and he'd had an idea.

He stopped the others. "I've had about enough of this." He took off his pack and tipped out a couple of the smoke grenades they had been issued to "destroy" enemy gun emplacements. Then he kneeled in the snow and began to untie his boots.

Nick stared at him. "Blisters?" he asked.

"Bootlaces," said Luke shortly. "An old squaddie who had to fight tanks in the Great War told me about this trick." He tied one end of each lace around the narrow neck of a grenade as he continued, "They used to do this with explosive grenades, but it should work with these. The driver's hatch is right beneath the gun barrel on a Mark III."

Nick was nonplussed. "What's that got to do with anything?"

"You'll see." Luke knotted the loose ends of the laces together. The result was an improvised bolas. He stood up, swinging it from his left hand. "All right. This is the plan..."

A few minutes later the fog began to lift. The tank commander, with his head and shoulders out of the vehicle's turret hatch, was scanning the open wasteland that lay beyond the gullies. Spotting a movement off to his left, he signalled to his driver. The tank's engine roared as Nick broke cover, running pell-mell across the snow towards a distant pond. The commander pointed and bellowed an order to follow.

Nick continued to run towards the pond. The tank had almost caught up with him when Salim appeared out of a shell crater to its right, waving his arms and hallooing like a maniac. As the commander turned to stare at this apparition, Luke rose from a gorse bush on the tank's left. He pulled the pins from the smoke grenades with his teeth, whirled them around his head for a moment, and then let go. The jury-rigged missile spun through the air until the laces snagged on the tank's gun barrel, winding around it until the grenades hung just before the driver's position. Then they exploded.

The tank driver and commander were instantly blinded by dense smoke. Just before he reached the pond, Nick dived out of the way as the vehicle thundered past, swerving from side to side. Coughing, his eyes streaming, the tank commander flapped at the choking fumes still belching from the grenade.

As the worst of the smoke cleared, the commander strove to peer ahead. He gave a hoarse cry of alarm and rasped out an urgent order. It came too late. The tank barrelled into the pond at full speed, sending up great jets of spray and a tidal wave of dirty water. Its engine coughed and died.

As the tank crew baled out from the vehicle's smoke-filled interior and splashed into the roiling water, Nick sprang forward, the light of battle in his eyes. "Come on, let's get them!"

Luke grabbed at his arm. "Calm down. We're still unarmed, remember, and those men will have guns – pistols at least." Even as he spoke, a sharp crack sounded from the direction of the tank. Luke and Nick ducked, but Salim, who had been standing just behind them, gave a gasp and crumpled to the ground.

"He's been shot!" Luke stooped down. The young Ethiopian lay on his back, his head resting on a mound of snow that cradled it like a pillow, eyes closed. There was no obvious sign of blood. Searching for a wound, Luke tore open his companion's tunic. He caught momentary sight of a medallion etched with two interlocking triangles set inside something that looked like a gearwheel. He brushed it to one side in order to feel for a heartbeat – and Salim blinked and sat up. Luke rocked back, startled. "Are you all right?"

"I think so." Salim sounded slightly bewildered and his eyes had an odd, glazed look, but Luke noticed that his hand closed protectively round his medallion, and hid it away at the first opportunity as he buttoned up his tunic. "Yes, I believe I am fine. Thank you."

"I thought you'd been hit."

"Evidently not. What happened to the tank crew?"

Nick swung round towards the pond. "I can't see them – but they must still be out there, somewhere. We'd better get over to the hut and meet up with the others, smartish." He reached down and hauled Salim to his feet. "Can you walk?"

Salim picked up his rifle. "Yes – I'm fine. Honestly."

They set off at a smart pace through the clearing fog, listening out for the tank crew – but all was quiet. They'd made it to within two hundred yards of the hut, from which the red flag was still flying despite Warren's boast, when a cadet with a red armband stepped out from behind a bush, pointed a rifle at them and, in a rather shamefaced manner, said, "Halt – you are my prisoners."

Nick flung an arm round the startled cadet's shoulders. "Excellent! Is there any tea going?"

Luke felt weak with relief. "Well, it looks as if we've made it, Sally..." He hurriedly corrected himself. "Salim, I should say."

The Ethiopian inclined his head with grave courtesy. "Please feel free to call me 'Sally' – all my friends do." He smiled and held out his right hand.

Grinning, Luke shook it.

Nick let out a whoop of sheer delight. "Hey, do you realize what we've just done? Only taken on a tank, three of us – unarmed – and given it a good thrashing. You just wait until the rest of the lads hear about this. We'll be heroes!"

3 HOLIDAY PLANS

Kingshome Abbey, Wiltshire:
Headquarters of Challenger Industries
The next day

"**E**xpelled?" Sir Andrew Challenger's wheelchair rocked back alarmingly as his roar rattled the windows. "What d'you mean, you've been expelled?"

"Sent home," said Luke helpfully. "Sacked. Given our marching orders. Told to buzz off and not come back, to put it in a nutshell."

"I know what 'expelled' means, blast your eyes." Luke's father controlled his breathing with difficulty. "You've just told me that you were chased halfway across Salisbury Plain by a bunch of homicidal maniacs in a tank. How, exactly, did that result in your being expelled?"

"The school didn't believe us," explained Luke. "The army reported the tank missing just before the exercise started: the Head reckons we must have pinched it, gone for a joyride, fired off a few rounds for sheer devilment and then put it in the pond and scarpered."

"He wouldn't even listen to us," Nick put in hotly. The injustice of their treatment still rankled.

"Well, you two do have something of a history in that regard, dear." The voice came from a walnut cabinet that stood on the right-hand side of Sir Andrew's desk. "One might almost use the term 'record'. Wasn't it only last month that you stole General McGuffrey's Rover when he came to your school to present the prizes on speech day?"

"Quite right, Nanny." Sir Andrew gave the box a grateful nod. Nanny was Challenger Industries' Head of Security. Sir Andrew's only contact with her was through this voice link and her actual identity (not to mention her exact connections to the official security agencies) was a closely guarded secret. Luke's father gave him a ferocious glare. "What d'you say to that, eh?"

"Not 'stole'," protested Luke. "Borrowed. And we took it back." Honesty compelled him to add, "Eventually. He didn't need it while he was jawing away to the lower school and sending them all to sleep, anyway. And we didn't do any damage. Nick even did some tinkering with the engine and cured a knock in the tappets. I don't see the old buzzard had anything to complain about..."

"Be that as it may, dear, you can't altogether blame the school for viewing your version of events with some scepticism." Nanny's tone was gently reproving.

"But we didn't deny we'd taken the car," Luke pointed out, "or try to put the blame on anyone else."

"Very creditable," said Sir Andrew with heavy irony. "But I seem to recall your Headmaster saying that that was the last straw; if the two of you stepped out of line again, he'd have you out of his school like a shot."

"But we didn't step out of line!" Luke protested.

"So you say." Sir Andrew's beard bristled. "How do I know you didn't take the tank? We only have your word for the whole taradiddle about a rogue crew."

"That's not entirely true, Sir Andrew," said Nanny. "We can corroborate Luke's story to some extent. Several soldiers from mechanized regiments were reported missing in the days leading up to the attack: a tank commander, a driver, a gunner and a loader – all from different units, but together they would make up a full tank crew. It's reasonable to assume that they were controlling the tank. Last night we picked up one of them – the loader, a Private Hicks, trying to board a ferry at Dover."

"And didn't you ask him what he'd been up to?" demanded Luke.

"We would have done, dear, but by the time the local police called us in, he was dead. A cyanide capsule. He did have a tattoo on his wrist, though. I'm sure you can guess what it was."

"A snake coiled around a spear," said Nick promptly. "The sign of the Sons of Destiny. We knew they'd be behind this."

"Well, the two of you have caused them quite a lot of trouble one way and another," said Nanny happily. "You put a stop to their diamond-mining operation in South America eighteen months ago, getting rid of the traitorous Lord Roxton into the bargain." Luke nodded. Lord John Roxton, his grandfather's friend and Luke's godfather, had been a daring and highly experienced explorer and adventurer; he had also proved to be a double agent within British Intelligence and a murderer whose victims had included Nick's father. Luke glanced at his cousin. Nick's expression was withdrawn – any reference to his father's killer upset him, though he and Luke had been present when Roxton met his death in a blazing Zeppelin on the Lost World.

"And last summer," Nanny continued, "you kept their

top assassin Kasumi Mochizuki from getting her hands on the secret of atomic power. I think you've given them quite a few reasons to try to blow you to smithereens."

Nick nodded. "I'm only surprised that Mochizuki woman wasn't driving the tank!"

"If that's the case, there's no reason for the school to expel you!" protested Sir Andrew. "It cost me enough to get you in there. When they read the report from your previous school, I had to build a blasted library for them before they'd agree to take you on!"

"I mentioned that," Luke told him. "The Head said he'd rather give all the books back and take the place apart, brick by brick, with his bare hands, than have us on the premises for a minute longer. He even told Salim he'd have to leave at the end of term. I think the old misery was a bit upset."

"Not as upset as he'll be by the time I've finished with him!" Sir Andrew gripped the wheels of his chair as if they had done him a personal injury. "I'll get on to the governors. You'll be back in that school by nightfall."

"We're not going back," Luke told him. "We did nothing wrong, and they wouldn't give us a fair hearing. I'm not sorry they chucked us out – we've been wanting to leave the place since we turned fourteen anyway..."

"Unfortunately," grated Sir Andrew, "they won't let you into Oxford unless you complete your schooling, no matter how much I offer them. D'you think I'm *made* of libraries?"

"We've been through all this before. I am *NOT* going to university—"

Luke was interrupted by the arrival of Bateman. Sir Andrew's major-domo was as quiet and softly-spoken a man as can be imagined, but his height, bulk and gravity ensured that he would never enter a room unobserved. He bent down and spoke into Sir Andrew's ear. The Head of Challenger industries directed a smouldering glare at Luke as he listened to the message; but when Bateman had finished, he merely said, "We'll pick this up again later," and allowed his hulking manservant to wheel him from the room.

As the door closed, Nanny said, "Tell me more about the incident" – ("'Incident' she calls it!" muttered Nick) – "with the tank, Luke dear. You said this boy Warren told you to take the sunken road."

"That's right," Nick cut in before Luke could speak. "And strangely enough, the little snake had disappeared by the time we met up with the rest of the squad, and nobody's seen him since."

"Apparently, he had to go home quickly," said Nanny non-committally. "Something about a family emergency."

"He'll have a ruddy emergency to deal with when I catch up with him," retorted Nick.

"I daresay, dear. Have you given any thought as to *why* the Sons of Destiny should have gone to so much trouble to put you out of the way yesterday?"

Luke and Nick exchanged puzzled glances. "You said it yourself, Nanny," Luke pointed out. "We've put a spanner in their works a couple of times. What's more, they think I'm going to be the next Head of Challenger Industries – not that I am, I've told my father that often enough. The Sons of Destiny are backing Hitler, Stalin and Mussolini to start a war with Britain, so any damage they can do to our armaments industry is good news for them."

"That's all very true, Luke dear. But I don't think it altogether explains what happened yesterday. The plan was certainly put together in a hurry to make an attempt at what we might call a target of opportunity. I'm just not at all sure that you and Nick were that target."

"What?" Luke and Nick exchanged startled glances. "Then who was?"

"Well, the two of you weren't alone, dear, were you?"

"You mean – *Sally*?" Luke was thunderstruck. "You're joking!"

"Not at all, dear. As I've had occasion to remind you before, Nanny knows best. Young Master Menelik was the only one of you who got shot, after all."

"I thought that was an accident – that they were really

aiming for one of us." Nick's brow furrowed. "I really don't know what happened there. If Salim wasn't hit, why did he fall? But if he was, what happened to the bullet?"

"Perhaps it was deflected by that medallion you told me about?"

"I don't think so," said Luke. "It didn't look damaged at all – and surely it would have been. But why would the Sons of Destiny want to get rid of Salim anyway?"

An exasperated sigh sounded from Nanny's cabinet. "Luke dear, you do have an unfortunate tendency to look on anyone younger than you as insignificant. In fact, Salim Menelik is an important person in his own right, and his father considerably more so. Tell me, what do you know about Ethiopia?"

It was Nick who answered. "Well, it's also called Abyssinia, it's in Africa and, according to Salim, its ruling family is descended from King Solomon. Oh, and it said in this morning's paper they're having some trouble with Mussolini at the moment."

"A masterly summation, Nick dear," said Nanny, with studied patience. "If you'd read a little further, you'd have discovered that Signor Mussolini – *Il Duce*, as he calls himself these days – is amassing an Italian army on the Ethiopian border. Last month, his forces clashed with local troops, and his air force has recently bombed

Ethiopian villages. There's little doubt that Mussolini plans to add your young friend's country to his African empire; and you can be sure that the Sons of Destiny are backing him to the hilt.

"Salim's father is currently in the Sudan, where the Sultan is holding an unofficial peace conference to try to resolve the dispute. Ras Menelik – Ras is one of their words for 'prince' – is a forceful and eloquent advocate for his country."

"But if he heard that his only son had been killed in England," said Luke slowly, "he'd be knocked for six – and he probably wouldn't like Britain very much."

"Quite. As for why the Sons of Destiny are so keen that Mussolini should succeed in Ethiopia – you'll remember their obsession with the Spear of Destiny?"

Nick nodded. "Of course. They think that anyone who gets hold of it will rule the world."

"Very good, dear," said Nanny in exactly the tone she would have used if Nick had just successfully completed his potty training. "And King Solomon's Mines?"

"That was in a book…" Nick's brow furrowed with the effort of memory. "Yes, by H. Rider Haggard. I read it when I was a kid. All about some explorers looking for treasure and someone's long-lost brother. Pretty good, actually, lots of fighting and lions."

"Thank you for that thoughtful critique." Nanny

sounded pained. "My reason for mentioning it is that our intelligence sources indicate that the Sons of Destiny believe the legendary King Solomon's Mines really exist."

"Hang on," said Luke slowly. "I thought *King Solomon's Mines* was a work of fiction."

Nick gave a hollow laugh. "Well, we know all about fiction, don't we? The Lost World was supposed to be fiction, until we found it again. Everyone thought Captain Nemo's submarine was fiction until we recovered it from the Java Sea."

"All right, but what's all this got to do with Ethiopia?" demanded Luke. "Solomon was King of Israel, wasn't he?"

"Yes." Nick's voice was excited. "But according to the book, King Solomon's Mines are in Africa."

"So if Sally's family really are descended from King Solomon..."

"Exactly, dear. The Sons of Destiny are searching for the Mines, which they believe are located in Ethiopia. And for some reason, they seem to think your young friend Salim – or his father – might be an obstacle to their plans; hence your little difficulty with them yesterday."

Ignoring Nick's snort of outrage at this description of their latest brush with death, Luke said, "But why are they so interested in these Mines?"

"Because they seem recently to have got the idea into their heads that in the Mines they will find the key to ultimate power…"

Understanding dawned on Luke. "The Spear of Destiny – they think that's where it's hidden? In King Solomon's Mines?"

"Exactly so, dear."

"And they think," said Nick, "that if they can get their paws on it, they'll be cock of the walk."

"Inelegantly put, dear, but that's what it amounts to."

Without hesitation, Luke said, "Then we have to stop them."

"Of course," said the plummy voice musingly, "Nanny wouldn't dream of encouraging such young people as you and Nick to undertake such a dangerous task. On the other hand, you have shown great resourcefulness in dealing with the Sons of Destiny in the past, and if it should happen that you found yourselves in Ethiopia anyway…"

"My mother is in Ethiopia," said Luke thoughtfully. "Digging up the remains of Early Man, I think. I'm sure she'd appreciate a visit. Salim is going back there, too, as soon as term finishes. He said we should call in and see him if we were ever in East Africa."

"Oh, I don't think we should leave a thing like this to chance, dear," said Nanny smugly. "In fact, I've booked tickets for all three of you on the Imperial Airways flight to Khartoum leaving from Croydon on Wednesday. I have a strange feeling that Salim Menelik is more likely to arrive at his destination alive if the two of you are travelling with him..."

The study door slammed open. "Now what have you done?" Sir Andrew entered the room like an avenging angel. "Do you know who I've just been called out to see? Sir Percival Warren. He's head of the War Office purchasing department, and he's just cancelled an order for two hundred of our anti-aircraft guns because he says you" – he stabbed a finger accusingly at Luke – "have been bullying his son."

Luke was speechless.

"Well, enough is enough!" roared Sir Andrew. "I can't send you back to school, and I'm not having you hanging around here – you'd ruin me in six months! What I'm supposed to do with you, I don't know..."

"Perhaps," said Nanny in her most butter-wouldn't-melt voice, "Lady Challenger...?"

"That's it! Brilliant!" Sir Andrew threw back his head with a shout of triumph. "Your mother can look after you. You can spend Christmas in Ethiopia with her, and I hope you like it!" Roaring with laughter, Sir Andrew wheeled himself out. Another cry of "Christmas in Ethiopia!" echoed down the corridor.

Luke patted the walnut cabinet on his father's desk. "Nanny, you're a genius."

"Of course, dear," said the comfortable voice. "Nanny knows best."

4 SOUTH

Over the Pyramids of Giza
One week later

Luke stared out of the window as the ungainly HP42 airliner, all four engines bellowing, clawed its way into the dawn sky. Below him, the great pyramids of Cheops, Chephren and Mycerinus cast long shadows across desert sands that glowed like a sea of rubies in the light of the rising sun. In the distance, the dark ribbon of the River Nile streamed away to the south. The aircraft, wings flashing silver in the growing light, turned to follow it.

"What a way to travel," complained Nick. "All the way from Paris to Brindisi by rail, for pity's sake..."

"That's because Mussolini won't let Imperial Airways fly over Italy," Luke told him.

"I know that – and the flying boat from Athens was all right, but now here we are in this contraption! It's just a motorized box kite. The Americans and the Dutch are building aeroplanes that look like they belong in the twentieth century, and the best we British can come up with is something that looks as if it was thrown out of the Great War for being too old."

"These things may look clumsy," said Luke, opening a battered copy of *King Solomon's Mines*, "but they're reliable. Nobody's died on one yet."

"Well, I don't want to be the first." Nick peered at the maps spread out across Luke's lap. "Are you still trying to work out where the Mines might be?"

Luke sighed and put the book down. "Yes, but the book is really short on detail. According to Rider Haggard, Allan Quatermain's expedition set off from Durban in South Africa for some place called Sitanda's Kraal, which doesn't appear on any map I can find. All he says about the place is that it's on the Lukanga River, where it meets the Kalukawe River, which I also can't find. There *is* a Kafue River, so maybe Haggard got the name wrong, or used another name from a different language.

"But in any case, even if we could pin down Sitanda's

Kraal, that's only the start of the journey to the Mines. After that, Quatermain and his party had to go north across a hundred and twenty miles of desert before they came to the mountains that surround the kingdom of the Kukuana tribe. That would put the Mines somewhere in Northern Rhodesia. The problem is, Nanny says the *you-know-who* think the Mines are in Ethiopia, and Ethiopia is nearly two thousand miles to the north of anywhere Sitanda's Kraal might be, not a hundred and twenty." Luke raised his hands in a gesture of despair. "I really need to talk to an old Africa hand – someone like Uncle John."

Nick scowled at the mention of the name. "Well, you can't talk to Roxton because he's dead, and good riddance."

Luke silently cursed himself for mentioning his godfather.

"I'm a young Africa hand," said Salim Menelik from behind his book. "Why don't you ask me?"

"I didn't know you were listening," said Luke.

"I didn't mean to, but it's difficult in an aeroplane this size not to hear a conversation taking place in the next two seats, especially when both of you are shouting over the noise of the engines."

Luke grinned in spite of himself. "All right. What do you think?"

Salim put down his book and steepled his fingers. "A few things spring to mind. One is that if I were writing a book about my adventures in search of a fabulous mine full of treasure, and if I had any thoughts of ever going back to the mine to get my hands on as much gold and as many precious stones as I could carry, I'd be very careful not to let every Tom, Dick and Harry know exactly where that mine was."

Nick was startled out of his brooding silence. "But Quatermain tells the story in the book and he must have told it to Rider Haggard – why? If he knew Haggard was going to write it up, and he wanted to keep the Mines a secret, why tell his story at all?"

"For money, perhaps? It was a very successful book. But whether Quatermain misled Rider Haggard about the location of the Mines, or whether Haggard himself was in on the deception, makes no practical difference. The Mines cannot be in Rhodesia. King Solomon never came to this part of Africa."

"But isn't there a ruined city in Southern Rhodesia called Great Zimbabwe that Solomon is supposed to have built?"

Salim looked Nick straight in the eye; his voice was so soft that Luke and Nick had to strain to hear him over the steady drone of the engines. "So the Rhodesian government – the *white* Rhodesian government – would like historians to think. It is not in their interests that the world should believe that a city of such great splendour could have been built by native Africans, so they claim it must have been built by Solomon, or the Arabs – or the Man in the Moon. The truth, nevertheless, is that Great Zimbabwe was built by black Africans. Solomon never went there."

"All right." Nick was thoroughly discomfited by Salim's vehemence. "Sorry."

"On the other hand," Salim went on in a much lighter tone, "Queen Makeda of Sheba ruled an empire that stretched from the Upper Nile to the Red Sea from her capital in Ethiopia. She met – some say, married – King Solomon of Israel. So there is good reason to believe that King Solomon came to Ethiopia and that his Mines – if they exist at all – may be found in my country."

"I suppose you have deserts in Ethiopia?" said Luke, checking his maps.

"Lots of deserts," agreed Salim.

"And mountains?"

Salim nodded happily. "Stacks of mountains."

"Sounds promising." Luke began to fold away maps. "All right, we'll take your word for it. The Mines are in Ethiopia. As soon as we can, Nick and I plan to slip away from my mother and look for them. Are you with us?"

"That depends," Salim replied seriously, "on what my

father wants me to do when I get back. And on what you might do if you did find the Mines."

Luke stared at him. "How do you mean?"

"Well, apparently what Allan Quatermain did when he found them was start a civil war."

"That wasn't Quatermain," said Luke indignantly, "that was Ignosi. He went along with Quatermain's expedition as their guide, but it turned out that he was the rightful ruler of the Kukuana people—"

"And, with Quatermain's support," Salim broke in, "this 'rightful ruler' led an uprising that claimed the lives of twelve thousand men."

"But it got rid of King Twala, who'd killed Ignosi's father and taken the throne when he was just a kid. And he – Twala, I mean – was a bloodthirsty tyrant. Then there was the old witch woman – what was her name?" Luke clicked his fingers. "Nasty piece of work, went round sniffing out so-called traitors and had them killed, claimed to be hundreds of years old...Gagool, that was it. If Quatermain had just sat on his hands, Twala and Gagool would have won, and Ignosi would have died."

"But Ignosi only rebelled against Twala because he knew Quatermain and his friends were there to back him," said Salim. "And did Quatermain support Ignosi because he was the rightful king? No. He did it because he was afraid of Twala – and he wanted the treasure."

"Now you're making him sound like Lord John Roxton," said Nick grimly. Luke said nothing.

"And suppose you did find gold and diamonds," said Salim. "To whom would they belong? Quatermain's party found diamonds in the Mines, and shared them – amongst themselves."

"I see what you mean," said Luke. "All right, Salim. The diamonds belonged to the Kukuana, and Quatermain was wrong to take them. But I'm not interested in diamonds. Mind you, the Sons of Destiny are – they were digging them up on the Lost World to finance their friends Hitler and Mussolini. If one of their people – Kasumi Mochizuki, for instance – finds the Mines, she'll be very clear about who the diamonds belong to, and it won't be the people of Ethiopia.

"Maybe Quatermain was too quick to stick his nose into other people's business. But I'm not Quatermain and I've no intention of starting any wars. One thing I will say, though – if the Spear of Destiny is in King Solomon's Mines, I'm going to do my best to make sure the Sons of Destiny don't get their hands on it, and that's flat. If we do find the Mines, and the treasure – then as far as I'm concerned it belongs to your people."

Salim leaned back and folded his hands on his stomach. "Good."

"So, do you know where the Mines are?"

Salim shook his head. "I haven't a clue."

"Then what have we just been arguing about?"

"You asked me if I'd help you find the Mines. If we get the opportunity to search for them, the answer is yes. I will think about where we should start." Salim closed his eyes and appeared to go to sleep.

Luke felt a mixture of anger and grudging respect. He'd just been told off in no uncertain terms by a boy younger than himself, and normally his response would have been to tell Salim to shut up and, if necessary, dot him one. But he had a horrible feeling that Salim was right; and if he had tried to shut Salim up – or dot him one – he would merely have been demonstrating that everything he had said was true.

Nick was evidently having similar thoughts. "You know," he said in a voice as low as the noise of the engines would allow, "I never thought of Allan Quatermain and his friends like that. How they acted in the book, I mean. It was just a good story. But what they did was exactly what Roxton would have done – gone in mob-handed and bullheaded, foxed the natives and grabbed the loot. And he would have thought that was all right, because he was civilized and they weren't."

"That depends what you mean by civilized. I don't think Uncle John ever was. Civilization should be about living together, showing a bit of give and take, and he never did that. The whole idea that the most civilized people are the ones with the most money or the biggest guns – if that's civilization, I reckon it's overrated." Luke said no more. But he thought a great deal.

Salim did not wake as the plane made its short scheduled stop at Wadi Halfa, seemingly oblivious to the bustle of refuelling and the coming and going of passengers. Luke found his own eyelids growing heavy, and was only dimly aware of the aircraft taking off again.

When he woke some hours later, he found to his surprise that the day seemed to have become darker instead of lighter. An angry red haze stretched out across the desert.

The chief steward emerged from the flight deck. "Ladies and gentlemen," he announced, "we seem to be heading into some bad weather. There is no cause for alarm; however, we recommend that you use the seat belts provided..."

Luke fastened his seat belt and glanced at his fellow passengers. Some of these seemed to be farmers, businessmen and diplomats who had done this trip many times before and fastened their buckles with competent clicks, their expressions resigned. Parents of young families fussed over their children and each other. Towards the back of the cabin a party of schoolchildren, evidently boarders on their way home for Christmas, exclaimed and giggled as they got their seat belts mixed up with those of their neighbours…

Then the aeroplane pitched violently, and the giggles turned to yells and screams. The harassed steward tried simultaneously to restore order and keep his footing as the floor twitched and rocked. Soon there was a rustle of paper bags, followed by desperate retching.

Luke had the stomach of an ostrich, but even he was taken aback by the violence of the plane's movement. He glanced at Nick who, looking decidedly green about the gills, mouthed, "Sandstorm." Luke nodded and fought down a wave of nausea. Only Salim seemed undisturbed; he slept on, his hands rising and falling gently on his stomach.

The airliner danced and lurched like a drunken aunt at a wedding. Its engines alternately roared and whimpered. With her great biplane wings and three tail fins, the HP42 looked like some fantastic ship from the age of sail, and now she began to behave like one, soaring and wallowing as though being lifted on Atlantic breakers. Struts, wires and spars creaked and groaned as the wings flexed. The engines shot out bright blue and yellow flames. And now the desert sand came seeping into the cabin. The air became hot and smelled of brimstone. More and more passengers, succumbing to airsickness, were reduced to extremities of misery, wretchedness and fear.

Then, between one moment and the next, the plane flew out of the storm. Luke gave a sigh of relief that turned into a hacking cough as he tried to clear sand from his throat. He looked out again. The sky was clearing, and the sun falling towards the horizon as the aircraft dropped towards a range of low hills. Beyond them, the desert gave way to settlements of brown mud-walled houses huddled around courtyards, to picketed groups of camels, to the city itself.

The aircraft seemed to float over the timeless landscape, as slow and serene as the clouds high above. The crowded streets and huddled courts and bazaars of the capital of the Sudan spread out beneath them like an exotic carpet. There was the Governor's palace, and over there, dotted with the stately swanlike sails of feluccas, the Nile, which they had been following since leaving Cairo, nine hundred miles and thirteen hours behind them. This was where the great river split into its twin tributaries, with the White Nile winding away to its source of Lake Victoria far away to the south, while the Blue Nile began its lazy turn to the east and the highlands of Ethiopia.

The HP42 landed beside the golf course and bumped to a halt outside a number of tired-looking huts with corrugated iron roofs, fronted by paths marked out in whitewashed stones. Flags – one green with the crescent moon and stars of the Kingdom of Egypt, the other a Union Jack – fluttered bravely from poles outside the largest of the huts.

"Are we there yet?" Salim awoke instantly as the plane's door opened. He peered out of the window, spotted the flag, and turned to give Nick and Luke a great, beaming smile.

"What a pleasant journey. Welcome to Khartoum."

5 ELSA

Khartoum
Later that evening

"**H**onestly, Luke, you are the limit!"

Luke batted his mother's hands away. "I know how to knot a tie, thank you."

"You never even wear a tie if you can help it."

"That doesn't mean I can't put a knot in one." Glaring into the fly-specked mirror, Luke completed the knot. The instant he took his hands away, the tie unravelled to hang limply from his collar. Luke regarded it with loathing. "I don't see why we have to go to this stupid party anyway."

Absent-mindedly, Lady Harriet Challenger began re-knotting Luke's wayward neckwear. "Darling, we've been through this. I have to go because the stupid party, as you call it, is being put on by the Sudanese government, and since they're very nicely allowing me to dig up their ancestors, I'd be rude and ungrateful if I didn't. And you and Nick have to go because there's a lot of unrest in the city at the moment and I'm not letting you out of my sight. There!" Lady Challenger patted the perfect knot she had created, stepped back and eyed her son critically. "You still look like a scarecrow. Wearing a blazer and flannels to our Governor's reception, for goodness' sake! Why didn't you bring evening dress?"

"In the first place because I thought I was coming to Africa, not Buckingham Palace, so I packed clothes I thought would be suitable for the climate; and in the second place, I don't *have* any evening dress."

"Even in Africa," Lady Challenger said primly, "one must keep up standards."

Luke couldn't deny that, on this occasion, his mother was practising what she preached. Her normal working outfit – boots, jodhpurs, an open-necked shirt and a waistcoat with so many pockets that the keenest fisherman would have thought them excessive – had been replaced for the occasion with an elegant pearl-grey satin gown with butterfly sleeves, and her mass of red curls had been dressed with far more attention than usual. She was even wearing make-up. "You look – er – very nice," he managed.

His mother was startled. "Well, thank you." She gave her son a tentative smile. "I'm sorry I wasn't there to meet you at the airport."

Luke shrugged. "I expect you forgot." He felt rather hard done by. He hadn't seen his mother in over a year, and he and Nick, who had about half a dozen words of Arabic between them, would probably have still been trying to get through immigration and find their baggage if they hadn't had Salim with them.

"I didn't forget," said Lady Challenger indignantly, "I just lost track of time." She looked anxiously around the room. "Oh, where did I put my handbag? I *meant* to be at the airport, but Elsa and I don't come to Khartoum very often – it's such a long way from the dig – and when we do, I like to get as many things sorted out as possible." She kneeled by the bed and lifted the skirts of the counterpane to look underneath. "I was in the pharmacy buying medical supplies – where *is* that dratted bag?" Luke picked up the bag, which was lying prominently on the room's only table, and passed it to her. "Oh, thank you. Well, I was in the pharmacy and I couldn't get the stupid man to understand that I wanted sulphanilamide, not sulphur—"

"Who's Elsa?" interrupted Luke.

"What?"

"You mentioned Elsa. Who is she?"

"Oh – Elsa Fairfax, my assistant. She's a treasure. So organized and efficient. I don't know what I'd do without her." Luke could well believe it. His mother, though skilled and painstaking when she was digging up ancient bones, was notoriously scatterbrained when it came to mundane details such as remembering to pick people up from airports, or to eat. "She's supposed to be meeting us in the lobby…" She broke off, pressed a hand to her temple and closed her eyes.

Luke eyed her with concern. "Are you all right?"

"Oh, just a bit of a headache."

"You ought to rest," said Luke. "You know you're always working too much."

"Nonsense!" Lady Challenger looked up and picked an invisible speck of dust from her son's sleeve. "I'll be fine. Now, are you ready?"

"I suppose so."

"Then wipe that scowl off your face. I'm afraid you'll just have to make an effort to be civilized for once." Lady Challenger offered her arm; glumly, Luke took it.

Moments later they descended the staircase of the Grand Hotel into an atmosphere that, despite the ceiling fans, was hot and stuffy. The lobby was dotted with coffee tables and low sofas, many of which had already been colonized by well-dressed Europeans drinking cocktails and prosperous-looking Sudanese men sipping coffee and smoking hubble-bubble pipes. As Luke's mother led him towards the hotel's reception desk, a girl stepped forward to meet her – and Luke was suddenly aware of nothing and no one else.

She was what Nick would call a "stunner". Her fair hair – a deep gold colour, unlike Luke's untidy thatch of straw – flowed around her head like a lion's mane. Her eyes were amber, set in a finely-boned face with skin as smooth as porcelain but the colour of desert sand. She was wearing a plain, light blue dress with a flared skirt – a garment so at odds with the current fashion as to make her appear young, though Luke guessed she was about his own age.

"Elsa! There you are!" Harriet Challenger took her protégée's arm. "This is my son, Luke."

"Hello." If Elsa Fairfax was enchanted to meet her employer's son, she gave no sign of it.

"Er – hello." Luke felt that his collar had suddenly shrunk by two sizes and his shoes grown by three. He held out his hand. Elsa looked at it for a moment; then she touched it as if it were something the cat had brought in and returned it to its owner. Turning from Luke in clear dismissal, she said to Harriet, "I think the car is here."

"We're still waiting for Nick – I hope he won't be long…" Lady Challenger spotted a mop of dark curls making its way between the heads of the growing crowd. "Oh, there he is!" She waved. "Nick!"

As his mother repeated her introduction, Luke was both amused and annoyed to see his cousin's hand automatically shoot to his tie. Nick was capable of turning on his particular brand of lazy, good-humoured charm in an instant. Luke watched it flow over Elsa with all the effect of a wave dashing itself against a rock. She seemed, if anything, even less impressed by Nick than she had been by Luke. Nick looked discomfited, and Luke felt a little happier.

"I'll go and tell the driver we're ready, shall I?" said Elsa and, without waiting for an answer, she turned on her heel and headed for the doors.

Lady Challenger beamed after her. "Marvellous, isn't she?"

Luke, who found himself feeling uncomfortably hotter than the temperature in the room could account for, said, "I don't think she likes us much."

"Oh, nonsense." His mother dismissed this with a wave. "She's just a bit shy with strangers. Shall we?"

Nick crooked his arm and inclined his head. "Lady Challenger – may I have the pleasure?"

Harriet Challenger took his arm and raised her

eyebrows at her son. "You see, Luke? That's how it's done." Nick escorted her out in fine style leaving Luke to trail behind, feeling a little foolish and, for the moment, not entirely friendly towards his cousin.

The Hispano-Suiza H6 that the Governor General had sent to collect them had seen better days, but Nick was enchanted by its classic lines and would undoubtedly have preferred to spend the evening tinkering with its all-aluminium straight-six engine than making small talk with foreign dignitaries. Still, he strove manfully to chat to Elsa, who swatted away all his conversational openings as though they were annoying insects. Luke, whose experience of girls was more limited and who never bothered with polite conversation, sat in silence, occasionally casting glances at Elsa's striking but unresponsive profile as she managed, while remaining perfectly composed and polite, to give the impression that if Nick were suddenly to drop dead, it would be fine with her.

Luke was relieved when the car drew up outside the Governor's Residence. The building was lit up in fine festive style, and the laughter and chatter of the guests reached out to draw the new arrivals in. He paused to take in the scene as his mother and Elsa, showing a great deal more animation now that she was free of the boys' company, drew ahead.

Nick gave a low whistle. "What a corker."

Luke gave a shrug, failing to meet his friend's eye. "Cold fish, I thought."

"A corker, all the same." Nick gave Luke a satirical grin. "You can't fool me. I saw the looks you were giving her. Gawping like a constipated bullfrog."

"I was not gawping!"

"Go on, admit it. Smitten, that's what you are."

Luke snorted. "Rot!"

"Whatever you say. Just prepare yourself for disappointment, when she succumbs to my boyish charm."

"Your boyish charm doesn't seem to be having much effect so far."

"Ah, she's just playing hard to get. I'll have her eating out of my hand by the end of the evening." Nick patted his cousin on the shoulder and set off for the door with a carefree whistle. Luke watched him go, seething inwardly. Then his sense of irony nudged him in the ego and he gave a wry smile. All right, maybe he was "smitten" with Elsa – but she showed no signs of returning his interest, and he thought Nick's self-confidence was misplaced. It seemed to Luke that Elsa was more likely to break Nick's fingers than eat out of his hand. Feeling more cheerful, he headed for the door.

In the entrance hall of the Governor's Residence,

Nick was shaking hands with a slim, distinguished-looking man of medium height. His face was careworn and Luke guessed that he was younger than he looked. He was dressed in an immaculate white tunic with an embroidered hem and a bright scarlet sash over his left shoulder.

Nick glanced over his shoulder and beckoned Luke across. "Luke – this is Salim's father."

Ras Menelik shook hands with Luke, but his expression was one of slight puzzlement. "Luke Challenger – delighted, of course, but...have you seen my son?"

"No, sir – I've only just arrived."

"That is odd. Salim was given a message a few minutes ago – that you were in the garden and wanted to speak to him."

Nick and Luke exchanged a glance. Luke said lightly, "Probably some mistake."

"Yes, but we don't want to leave him standing out there all on his own," said Nick, with the slightest emphasis on the final four words.

Luke nodded. "We'd better go and find him, sir. Please excuse us." As Ras Menelik's attention was claimed by another party of newly arrived guests, Luke drew Nick aside. "I don't like the sound of this – whoever's been sending Salim messages, it wasn't us."

Nick nodded. "Nanny said we were to get him here alive, but that won't do any good if he gets knocked on the head the minute he arrives."

"It could be nothing. But let's keep our eyes and ears open, all the same." They slipped through the front door and round the side of the brightly lit house, into the garden.

Despite the hot, dry climate of the Sudan, successive governors of Khartoum had gone to great lengths to create something like an English garden around their official residence. There were trees, shrubs and flower beds, arbours with elegant wrought-iron seats, and statues on stone columns. Nick and Luke threaded their way across moonlit lawns, avoiding gravel paths and staying close to hedges to avoid being heard or seen, straining their eyes to see their way in the dim light.

At length, as they slipped along an avenue of carefully trimmed bushes, they heard quiet voices from somewhere ahead. Redoubling their precautions, they ran silently across the manicured grass. As they approached the source of the voices, they flattened themselves against a yew hedge.

Peering cautiously round the side of this barrier, Luke found himself staring into a small garden with flower beds around its edges, and a star-shaped lily pond in the middle. A fountain in the shape of a stone fish surrounded by capering nymphs spouted a jet of water that fell pattering onto the floating lily pads.

There were two people on the far side of the pond. Luke recognized Salim, who was wearing a tunic and sash almost identical to that of his father. As Luke took in the scene, his friend spoke. "You still haven't told me why you brought me here."

"I require your medallion." The voice belonged to a woman wearing a loose-fitting kaftan over white trousers. She was holding some kind of knife or dagger at arm's length; its point hovered a hair's breadth from Salim's throat. Her face was expressionless, implacable. Her eyes, pitch black and merciless, were as cold and empty as the void between the stars.

Luke drew back sharply. In his ear, Nick whispered, "Who is it? Who's trying to get Salim's medallion?"

Luke drew a shuddering breath. "Kasumi Mochizuki."

6 ILL MET BY MOONLIGHT

Nick let out an involuntary hiss. "What's *she* doing here?"

Luke shook his head. His mind was racing. Salim was in more trouble than he'd ever imagined. Mochizuki was the Sons of Destiny's top assassin, trained as a samurai in the foremost school in Japan; skilled, unpredictable and lethal. Why she wanted Salim's medallion, he could not guess, but he knew that she would go to any lengths – including, if necessary, murder – to get it. What's more, she obviously knew that Luke was in Khartoum. The fake message she had sent to lure Salim into the garden had supposedly been from him.

Mochizuki's hatred of Luke was both professional and personal. Her twin sister Amaya had died during a confrontation with him on the Lost World, and just last summer he had thwarted her own attempt to wrest the secrets of atomic power from Captain Nemo's derelict submarine, the *Nautilus*. She would kill him without a thought. And he had little confidence that he and Nick, even acting together, could overcome her; not, at any rate, in time to save Salim.

He was still trying to decide what to do when Mochizuki spoke again. "Luke Challenger. You should not have run so fast. Your breathing betrays you – and your friend. Will you not join us?"

Luke exchanged a glance with Nick and took a deep breath. Further concealment was pointless. He could no longer hope to surprise Mochizuki – his only hope was to needle her into making a mistake. He stepped from concealment, followed by Nick. Mochizuki watched their approach with hooded eyes. The wicked three-bladed *sai* dagger she was holding at Salim's throat did not move a fraction of an inch.

"What a surprise to see you here," said Luke pleasantly. "Did you sail your submarine up the Nile?"

Mochizuki's eyes glinted. "I am no longer an officer

of the Imperial Japanese Navy, as you are no doubt aware."

Luke hadn't been, but he wasn't surprised. Having deposed the Commander of the submarine on which she was serving and then allowed herself to be provoked into a fight with a German U-boat which had severely damaged her vessel and resulted in the loss of the *Nautilus*, it would have been astounding to find that the former Captain Mochizuki had escaped punishment from her government. "Too bad. So why are you here?"

"About my masters' business." Mochizuki held up her arm, allowing the sleeve of her tunic to slide to her elbow and reveal on her wrist a snake-and-spear tattoo.

"So the Sons of Destiny want Salim's medallion," said Luke. "I wonder why?"

Mochizuki gave a mirthless smile. "If you do not know, it is no business of mine to enlighten you – and if your friend Malone continues his futile attempt to circle round behind me," she continued without a pause, "I shall instantly take this little princeling's life as well as his medallion." Nick abandoned his stealthy progress and glared at the Japanese assassin.

Mochizuki stared Salim straight in the eye. "Give me the medallion. I shall not ask again."

Calmly and deliberately, Salim clasped his hands behind his back. "Take it. I shall not prevent you."

A quick thrust with the knife would slit Salim's throat. Luke held his breath, expecting Mochizuki to strike. But perhaps even she could see that killing the son of a foreign dignitary in the grounds of the Governor's Residence would lead to more trouble than was necessary. Holding the dagger in readiness, she reached out. Her hand closed around the medallion.

There was a crackle. A blue flash, like a miniature bolt of lightning, erupted from beneath Mochizuki's fingers – so intense that the bones of her hand were clearly visible. The assassin's knife flew wide as she was flung back like a rag doll, arms and legs flailing, to land with a crash on the gravel pathway around the pond.

Luke charged, but he had hardly covered half the distance between himself and Mochizuki before the assassin was on her feet, her face twisted into a snarl. She snatched a razor-edged throwing-star from a pouch at her belt and hurled it at Salim. From the corner of his eye, Luke saw the deadly weapon fly towards its intended victim – and at the last moment, arc away to decapitate a stone nymph in the centre of the pond. Mochizuki gave a shriek of frustration, and Luke threw himself into the attack.

His opponent dropped into a *zenkutsu* fighting stance to meet it. She narrowly evaded Luke's flying drop kick and launched a furious counteroffensive. Luke was forced back, barely managing to block a flurry of punches, kicks and chops, any one of which, had it landed, would have left him disabled and defenceless. He attempted to retaliate with an elbow strike, but his opponent dodged it easily and responded with a stamp that raked painfully down his shin and left him limping. Mochizuki danced back out of reach. She stood with her back to the lily pond. Her initial assault had been intended merely to soften Luke up. Grinning like a death's head, she prepared to end the unequal contest with a blow that would break Luke's jaw, splinter his skull or stop his heart. He steeled himself to meet it.

At that moment, the water behind his assailant erupted. Scattering water and lily pads in all directions, Nick rose from the pond like an avenging Neptune. His fist, clutching the severed stone head of the unfortunate nymph, swung in a vicious arc. Before she could react, it slammed into the side of Mochizuki's head, and sent her sprawling.

As Nick dragged himself over the side of the pond, Luke spotted two shadows moving purposefully towards them from the far side of the garden. Moonlight glinted on edged weapons. He spun Nick round and pointed. "Come on – she wasn't alone." Grabbing Salim, who seemed not to have moved since Mochizuki's attempt to seize his medallion, they beat a hasty retreat.

Finding a side door to the house open, they slipped through and bolted it behind them. Luke led the way down a stone-floored corridor to a small lobby where they halted, panting. He patted Nick squelchily on the shoulder. "Brilliant! How did you do that?"

Nick coughed and spat out a piece of waterweed. "I slipped into the pond after she tried to get Salim's medallion and swam across – well, crawled, mostly. I reckoned that way I could get close enough to give her what for, she wouldn't see me under the lily pads – then that stone head thing fell right into my hand." Nick turned his attention to Salim. "What happened back there? When she touched your medallion?"

Salim seemed dazed. In a shaky voice, he said, "I do not know…"

Luke fought to bring his breathing under control. "So what do we do now? Tell the Governor there's a trained killer in his garden? Get him to turn out the guard?"

"No." Salim's voice had regained its strength. "There would be an outcry – the reception would be ruined. The peace conference must be given every chance to succeed. We must stay silent – that is what my father would wish."

Luke held his friend's gaze for a moment and then nodded. "All right – but you'd better find your father and tell him what's happened."

"Very well," said Salim. "We should both get back to the reception before we're missed."

Nick spread his arms, dripping extravagantly. "And what about me? What do I do?"

"My father will send someone to help you find dry clothes," Salim assured him.

"Fine," said Nick, struggling out of his jacket. He held it at arm's length and wrinkled his nose. "I reckon that's about it for this outfit, anyway."

7 INTRIGUE

As Luke stepped back into the entrance hall, he was caught up in a wave of new arrivals who propelled him into the main reception room and deposited him, feeling like a stranded fish, beside a lavishly decorated Christmas tree. This reminded him, with something of a shock, that it was less than a week till Christmas Day.

The Governor's reception was going with a swing. He, Nick and Salim had evidently not been missed – at any rate, not enough to cause serious alarm – and he realized that their encounter with Kasumi Mochizuki, though it seemed to have taken at least an hour, had in fact only lasted a few minutes.

He was surrounded by noisy chatter as people tried to make themselves heard over the din of their neighbours' conversation and music from a palm court orchestra. A uniformed waiter thrust a tray of drinks under his nose and Luke selected a tall glass filled with ice and a liquid that turned out, unexpectedly, to taste strongly of mint. Out of the corner of his eye he saw Salim approach his father, still at his station by the door, and draw him aside. Then he looked rather helplessly round the throng of people he didn't know.

He felt a soft tap on the shoulder. A voice said, "Hello, dear, we heard you were in town." Luke turned, and found himself facing two women who could not have been more dissimilar. One, tall and angular, with angry eyes and a determined jaw, was wearing a severely cut old-fashioned gown. The other was small and plump, and dressed in layers of chiffon patterned with so many flowers that she looked like a small meadow.

It took Luke a moment to place them. Then – "Dottie! Lottie! I thought you were in Brazil."

Dottie, the plump one, gave him a friendly, vague smile. "Of course, dear, that's where we first met you. But after your visit, your father decided to send our brother George to look after his company's interests in the Sudan."

Luke was puzzled. He remembered that fat, flustered, ineffectual George Partridge had been no use at all when he and Nick had needed his help on their way to the Lost World. "I didn't think Challenger Industries had any interests in the Sudan."

"It doesn't, dear. That's why your father sent George here."

"George is an ass," observed Lottie.

"I'm sorry…" Luke began.

"Oh, we don't mind," said Lottie robustly. "This is a perfectly decent country. There's plenty of ridin' to be had, and huntin' and shootin' – even fishin', though the Nile isn't exactly the Tay…"

"Quite, dear." Dottie laid a pudgy hand on Luke's arm. "Anyway, it's lovely to see you again. We've already had a quick chat with your dear mother before she was whisked off to meet more important people, with that sweet child Elsa Fairfax…"

"Do you know anything about her?" asked Luke. Dottie shot him an uncharacteristically penetrating glance, and he said hurriedly, "I mean, my mother just said Elsa was her assistant, but I've hardly met her – I was just wondering…"

"Clive Fairfax's girl." It was Lottie who answered, in her usual clipped tones. "Captain in the 21st Lancers. Damn good horseman." Luke grinned to himself; Lottie

Partridge judged everyone by how well they rode. "He was killed in India but his people had settled here and Elsa came to join them when her mother died a couple of years later – I suppose she's been here since she was four or five. Speaks Arabic better than I do English, and Amharic too – that's the Ethiopian lingo, Lord knows where she picked that up, but it's one of the reasons she's so useful to your mother. Good looking gel – usually has a swarm of boys round her like flies round horse apples..."

Dottie fluttered. "Really, dear."

"Don't be such a prude, Dottie. Anyway, she doesn't seem to care for them much – the boys, I mean. Sensible gel in my opinion."

Dottie seized Luke's arm in a firm grip. "Now, dear, we must introduce you to some people. Who don't you know? Almost everyone, I suppose. You simply must meet the Governor General, he's a dear, and I'm sure he'll want to introduce you to the Sultan..."

She was interrupted by a roar of laughter. A gigantic man, almost seven feet tall and broad in proportion, seemed to explode into the centre of the gathering. He wore a white suit with a sumptuously embroidered waistcoat and, around his waist, a flamboyant sash. His red face was surrounded by black whiskers and he wore a white fedora hat, which he now took off to wave to all sides. "Ras Menelik," he bellowed. "My dear old friend! Sir Charles, such a pleasure, and your lovely wife – *deliziosa! Signore, signori!* Charmed...delighted...*molto contento*..." He was immediately surrounded by a chattering crowd, mostly of women, and his extravagant gestures and gales of laughter seemed to make the room twice as crowded as before.

Luke stared at the newcomer. "Who on earth is that?"

"That," Lottie told him disapprovingly, "is Count Claudio Gentile."

"And who," said Luke, "is Count Claudio Gentile?"

"He's with the Italian delegation at the talks, dear." Dottie gave the white-suited giant a look of simpering admiration. "Such a *virile* man."

Lottie snorted. "Act your age, Dottie! Anyway, the blighter's a complete fraud – a mountebank – a charlatan."

"He is not! Signor Mussolini thinks a great deal of him..."

"Signor Mussolini is a fool – and so are you."

"Oh, Lottie, you are such a *beast* sometimes!" Her eyes brimming with angry tears, Dottie pushed past her sister, heading for the ladies' cloakroom.

Lottie watched her go without concern. "Don't worry," she told Luke, "she'll have a little weep and come straight back here. Silly old baggage – she thinks the sun shines out of Gentile's...well, never mind. She keeps pestering me to call on him, but I won't. The man's nothing but an adventurer. He calls himself a count, but he's nothing of the kind. Do you know what he did before Mussolini took him up?" Luke shook his head. "He was a circus strongman. He used to prance around in a leotard and tights, lifting things. Apparently," Lottie continued in a whisper that could be heard halfway across the room, "he used to get three or four *painted hussies* to sit on a bench, and then he'd lift it above his head. Disgraceful." Luke tried to give the appearance of being shocked by these revelations, and failed dismally. "And before that, from what I hear, he used to perform in the *music halls*," Lottie went on, as though she was announcing that Gentile ate boiled babies for breakfast. "I've even heard that, at one stage of his life, he was a *wrestler...*"

"Signora Partridge!" Luke spun on his heel to find Gentile bearing down on Lottie with his arms spread wide, beaming all over his enormous face. "Why do you and your enchanting sister never come to see me, heh? I shall start to think maybe you don't like me."

Lottie stared him down and announced in ringing tones, "I *don't* like you, Gentile. You're a quack."

There was consternation among the guests who heard this remark, but the giant showed no sign of being offended; on the contrary, he threw back his head and roared with laughter. "Dear lady, what do you take me for?"

Lottie gave him a hard stare. "I don't know what you are, or what you're doing here, and that's a fact. But one thing I am sure of – you're no peace envoy."

Gentile gave an indulgent chuckle. "We shall see. But who is your young friend?"

Lottie looked as if she would have liked to refuse to answer, but common politeness demanded an introduction. "This is Luke Challenger."

"Luke…?" Gentile's eyes widened in wonder and gratification. He seized Luke's hand and pumped it as though Luke was his long-lost brother. "My dear sir – such a pleasure. I know your father!" Lottie gave Luke a warning glance and took herself off. She needn't have bothered. Luke was already on his guard. The Italian's bonhomie was much greater than the situation warranted, and a little too studied to be real.

"You know my father, sir? Really?" Luke managed to retrieve his hand. "When did you meet him?"

Gentile dismissed this with a wave. "Well, when I say 'know', I mean in the sense of 'have corresponded with' – I have invited him to Rome many times, but alas, he does not travel."

No, he doesn't, thought Luke, *and particularly not to*

Mussolini's Italy. Sir Andrew Challenger might have many faults, but deliberately providing armaments to fascist dictators wasn't one of them.

"No, I have never met your father – in person, as it were," said Gentile, "but it remains my ambition. Sir Andrew Challenger is a great man. But you, his son – you have quite a reputation of your own, you know."

"Really, sir?" Luke did his best to keep his expression and voice neutral. His exploits in search of the Lost World discovered by his grandfather, and last summer's search for Captain Nemo's fabulous submarine, the *Nautilus*, were certainly enough to have established the reputation Gentile was speaking of, but they were hardly common knowledge. Only two organizations were fully aware of those events: the British Intelligence Services, and the Sons of Destiny. And Gentile was obviously not a British agent.

But had the Italian just blundered in revealing a link with Luke's enemies, or had the remark been made deliberately? Was this some sort of test? Luke had an idea that Gentile was a lot shrewder than he appeared: that the larger-than-life bluster, intended to give the impression that the self-styled Count was merely a buffoon, was a smokescreen.

Gentile was speaking again. "Why, yes. And tell me – is this your first time in Africa?"

"I came to British East Africa once." Luke decided to try a bit of gentle prodding. "On one of my mother's digs. I was very young. I don't remember much about it, except that I was very frightened of snakes." Did Gentile's look of polite enquiry flicker for an instant, or had Luke imagined it? "I wouldn't go to sleep until my mother assured me that one of the diggers would be outside the door of my tent all night, to keep them away. With a spear." This time he was sure. Gentile might be a good actor, but he'd make a terrible poker player. "Snakes and spears – that's all I remember from my first visit."

Gentile gave him a disarming grin. "What a delightful story. You must come and visit me; I'm sure we would have much to talk about." Luke thought so too, but somehow he didn't think he would find any discussions with Gentile either cordial or comfortable. "Well, I regret I must leave you for the moment. The negotiations over a possible peace treaty with our Ethiopian friends have reached a very delicate stage. I really must go over some of the details with my fellow delegates – 'off the record', I think your English phrase is. I'm sure we'll meet again before I leave."

"I'm sure we shall."

Gentile bowed and moved away. Instantly, Nick appeared at Luke's elbow. "What was all that about?"

"I was just having a chat with the Count, about snakes, and spears and other things…" Luke took in Nick's costume and gaped. "What on earth are you got up as?"

Nick was dressed to kill in a splendid uniform. "Nice, eh? It's Salim's father's military rig-out – he didn't think he should wear it at a peace conference, so he's lent it to me. Do you like the sword?" He drew a sharp looking cavalry sabre half out of its scabbard.

"Stop fooling with that thing, you'll cut yourself."

Nick shot a glance at Gentile's ample back and beckoned Luke into the nearest thing the room had to a quiet corner. "Is he really with…?"

"The Sons of Destiny? I'm not sure – but if he's not actually with them, he knows all about them, I'd take an oath on that."

"Lottie Partridge just lugged me away from Elsa and bent my ear for a couple of minutes about what a bad lot she thinks he is…"

"Hard luck."

"What?"

"About being dragged away from Elsa."

Nick ran a finger round his collar. "Actually, I didn't mind. I thought I'd knock her dead with the uniform, but she just turned her nose up. I'm starting to find her pretty hard work, to be honest. Stop smirking."

Luke hastily rearranged his features. "I wasn't smirking."

"I know a smirk when I see one. If you think you can do any better with Elsa, be my guest. I like girls who smile at least once in an evening and occasionally notice I'm in the same room as them." Nick cast another glance at Gentile, who was talking to Salim's father. "What are we going to do?"

"About what?"

"Him!" Nick jerked his head at the Italian just as Ras Menelik, who looked very put out about something, bowed stiffly to Gentile. The Count returned the bow and walked away.

"I don't know," said Luke. "Keep an eye on him, as much as we can – but he's an official of the Italian government. We'll have to tread carefully."

"Well, I think we—" Nick broke off as a hand tugged at his sleeve, and turned. "Oh, hello, Dottie. How's my best girl?"

"Now then, Nick, none of your nonsense." For once, Dottie was impervious to flattery. "Luke, dear, I'm afraid you'll have to leave – your mother isn't very well."

Luke gazed at her in alarm. "What's wrong with her?"

"Oh, I'm sure it's nothing – the heat – it *is* frightfully stuffy in here..."

"Where is she?"

"Over here, dear." Trotting in order to stay ahead of Luke's long strides, Dottie led him and Nick to a chaise longue on which his mother was sitting, looking rather pale, while Lottie Partridge took her pulse with one hand and rested a hand on her brow with the other.

"Well," she announced, "you're definitely running a temperature. I daresay a dose of liquid paraffin will set you right."

"For goodness' sake, Lottie dear, she isn't a horse."

Lady Challenger gave Luke an apologetic smile. "Sorry to be a bore, Luke."

"Don't be silly. We'd better get you back to the hotel, and call a doctor."

"I don't need a..." Harriet Challenger tried to get up and sank back onto the chaise longue with an expression of surprise. "Well, perhaps I do. I'm feeling a little giddy..."

Elsa Fairfax appeared. She looked concerned, but her voice was calm. "There aren't any cars, I'm afraid – they were told to turn up in an hour. There are a couple of horse-drawn carriages outside..."

"The very thing!" Lottie was instantly enthusiastic. "Bit of fresh air will do you the world of good."

Ras Menelik and Salim pushed their way through the crowd. "Lady Challenger," said Salim's father with his customary grave courtesy, "I am so sorry to hear that you are indisposed."

Harriet made an effort to rally. "Please don't concern yourself. A momentary weakness."

"Indeed, I hope so. But I have two carriages at the door, and I would be honoured if you would allow me to escort you back to your hotel."

"But surely you should be here, at the reception? I don't want to put you to any trouble."

"No trouble at all." Ras Menelik cast the briefest of glances at the door of the Embassy, where Count Claudio Gentile was making his theatrical farewells, and his lips tightened. "As for the reception – I have just been given news by Count Gentile that makes any further talks with the Italian delegation purposeless. The carriages can return later for my staff. I believe I have concluded my business here."

With Luke and Nick supporting Harriet on either side, Lottie clearing the way, Dottie fussing behind, and Salim, his father and Elsa bringing up the rear, the little party made its way to the doors in the wake of the Italian's entourage. A few people waved vaguely; otherwise their exit caused hardly a stir.

By the time they reached the carriages, Gentile's party had already disappeared into the night. Ras Menelik called the drivers and guards to him and gave them their instructions in a calm, authoritative voice. He turned to Luke. "Perhaps Lady Challenger would be kind enough to travel with my son and myself in the first carriage, and Mr. Challenger with Mr. Malone and Miss Fairfax in the second?" Luke would have preferred to stay with his mother, but he didn't want to waste time arguing; in any case, as Ras Menelik was doing them a kindness, it was only polite to agree to his arrangements. He and Nick helped his mother into the first carriage and joined Elsa in the second. As soon as they were all seated, the little party set off.

"Has she been like this before?" Luke asked Elsa.

"I don't know." Worry was making Elsa more forthcoming. "I haven't been with her very long."

Luke lapsed into silence, which remained unbroken as the carriages made their way through the darkened streets.

Nick gave him a nudge. "Why d'you suppose we have armed guards?"

Luke glanced at the guard who was sitting next to the driver. He hadn't noticed that the man was carrying a battered but serviceable Lee-Enfield rifle. "I don't know – my mother did mention unrest in the city. Something to do with the peace talks, I suppose…"

He got no further – because at that point, the whole world exploded.

8 ENCOUNTERS WITH CAMELS

When Luke came to his senses he was lying on the packed earth surface of the road. The carriage was on its side. One of the horses lay unmoving. The other was trying frantically to get to its feet.

Luke's ears were full of a dull roaring. The struggling horse was clearly neighing and whinnying in distress, but he couldn't hear it. A bomb, his fuddled mind concluded. That's what had damaged his hearing. Somebody had thrown a bomb – or it had been planted by the side of the road, waiting for them.

Dazedly, he looked around. Nick was lying not far away, bleeding heavily from a cut on his temple, his borrowed uniform torn and dusty. Elsa was picking herself up. The coach driver was lying in the road groaning; the guard was spreadeagled beside him, but a glance told Luke that he had caught the full force of the blast and was beyond help. His rifle was lying at his side.

There was no sign of the other carriage.

Luke took a deep breath and willed his quivering limbs into action. Sounds began to return as he staggered to his feet. He heard a scream – and turned to see two white-robed figures running towards him, howling as they raced to the attack. One was carrying a scimitar and the other an ancient Brown Bess musket.

Luke's bewilderment was instantly dispelled, to be replaced by cold fury. He stepped forward and reached for the guard's rifle; but his clutching fingers never reached it.

Elsa had got there first.

As the closer of the attackers dropped to one knee and sighted along the barrel of the musket, Elsa snatched up the rifle, took aim and fired in one fluid movement. Blood spouted from the man's shoulder. He screamed and dropped his weapon. The swordsman skidded to a halt beside his fellow assassin, clearly wondering whether to continue the attack. But as Elsa swung the muzzle of the Enfield in his direction, he decided against it and hauled his wounded colleague's arm over his shoulder. They turned together and stumbled away as fast as they could go.

Luke stared at Elsa, who had lowered the rifle. "Good shot." His voice sounded tinny and far away.

He had to strain hard to hear her reply. "Good shot, my foot! The sights on this thing must be off – I was aiming for his heart."

"Oh – right."

Luke saw to his relief that Nick was now on his hands and knees. He helped his friend to his feet.

Nick's eyes were wide and his speech slurred. "Thanks – whoa!" His knees buckled. "Sorry – m'blasted feet don't want to work…"

"All right." Luke hooked Nick's arm over the side of the upturned carriage. "Listen – stay here…"

Nick shook his head. "Wha'…?"

Luke bent down and bellowed into Nick's ear, "Stay here – I'm going after the other carriage!"

"Righ'…" Nick patted Luke weakly on the arm and sat down abruptly in the dust.

Luke hesitated – but he was sure the Sudanese authorities would be along in a minute to find out what had caused the explosion; the attack had happened close enough to the Governor General's Residence for the blast to have been heard there. The police could take care of Nick. The carriage carrying his mother, not to mention Salim and his father, had obviously survived the explosion because it was nowhere in sight: either its driver had panicked, or the horses had bolted. There was no telling where it was now – and if there were more thugs armed with muskets and swords out there in the darkness, its passengers could still be in terrible danger. His *mother* could be in danger – Luke felt an emptiness in the pit of his stomach, which was instantly filled by a seething rush of anger. Not for long, if he had anything to do with it!

He turned to ask Elsa Fairfax to look after Nick – and realized that she was no longer there. He peered into the darkness, and in the dim moonlight could just make out a slim figure running up the road in the direction they had been travelling. Cursing, he set off in pursuit.

It took him some time to catch up with Elsa, who was pounding along in determined fashion, holding the luckless guard's rifle at port arms. Luke grabbed at her wrist. "Where the hell are you going?"

Elsa skidded to a halt and threw his hand off. "To find your mother."

Luke made an impatient gesture. "Give me the gun."

"Go and get your own gun! I don't suppose you know how to shoot anyway."

Luke was stung. "I got top marks in my cadet squad's rifle training."

"I can put a bullet through a gazelle's heart at two hundred yards."

Luke spread his arms helplessly. "It could be dangerous."

Elsa worked the bolt on the rifle to send a round into the breech. "Oh, it will be!" She set off again, only to come to a halt a few steps later, cursing. Hopping first on one leg, then the other, she tore off her shoes and hurled them into the night. "How can anyone run in these stupid things?" She set off again.

Luke drew alongside. "You can't run any distance in bare feet!"

She shot him a disdainful glance. "Why not? Africans do it all the time."

"All right – it's your funeral."

Elsa's grip on the rifle tightened. "I don't think so."

The road rounded a corner. Luke had drawn a couple of yards ahead. Hearing a startled grunt, he turned round just in time to see Elsa crumple to the ground, the rifle flying from her grasp.

Luke swore. Blast Elsa! He knew she couldn't run barefoot. Then he realized that the girl wasn't moving.

She hadn't tripped. Something had brought her down...

A baulk of timber landed in the road, kicking up dust. Luke stared at it. Then a giant figure stepped out of the shadows.

Count Claudio Gentile had removed his hat and his jacket, waistcoat and sash. He stood at his ease, and rolled up his shirtsleeves. "Signor Challenger. Once again – a pleasure."

Luke glanced at Elsa. "You've killed her!"

Gentile shrugged. "*Forse*. Perhaps. We have matters to attend to, you and I. I did not wish her to interfere."

The rifle was lying where Elsa had dropped it. Luke made a dart for it – but once again, he wasn't quick enough.

Gentile, moving with unexpected speed for such a big man, scooped up the gun and casually aimed it at Luke, who stepped back. The Italian gave him an outrageous wink. Then he hoisted the rifle and wedged it behind his bull neck with one hand on the butt and the other on the muzzle. He closed his eyes. His brow furrowed with effort – and he heaved. After a moment's straining, the rifle's stock splintered and the barrel bent into a horseshoe.

As it did so, Luke stepped forward and punched Gentile in the solar plexus with all his strength.

The Italian's stomach muscles were as hard and unyielding as a steel breastplate. Luke swore and wrung his hand. Grinning, Gentile threw the ruined rifle at his feet. "So! Makes it fairer, yes?"

There was movement in the darkness. Luke glanced to left and right. Half a dozen Sudanese men wearing *jellabiya* robes and turbans, and carrying swords and wicked-looking *jambia* curved daggers with serrated blades, stepped out of hiding.

Gentile gave Luke a wolfish grin. "But not *too* fair!"

Luke turned on his heels and ran.

Gentile bellowed an order, and his hirelings burst into a chorus of bloodthirsty yells and charged. The Italian giant's laughter rang in Luke's ears as he pounded across open ground, hurdled a ditch, and found himself running alongside a wire fence. An opening appeared on his left, and he dived through it.

Now he was running along a sort of lane, with wire on either side. There were other structures as well – rudimentary shelters of rough timber frames with corrugated iron or thatched roofs. All around him the night air was full of soft grunts, gurgles and rumbles. For a moment, Luke couldn't make out what was causing these. Then, from out of the darkness, came a long, guttural roar of complaint, and Luke understood. He was in the camel market.

Luke glanced back. His pursuers were not yet in sight. Without hesitation, he threw himself full length and rolled to his right, squirming under the bottom strand of wire to fetch up against something that felt like a hairy sack full of coat hangers. The camel whose midriff he had just butted gave a bark of surprise, which became louder when Luke slid over its back to the other side.

As silently as he could, Luke patted the beast's neck. "Sssh – good camel," he breathed. He peered through the hairy gap between the creature's neck and hump as three of his pursuers raced past. "Good camel – woah!" Luke ducked just in time. Irritated beyond endurance by the intruder who had disturbed its night's rest, the outraged camel spat. A good quart of semi-digested stomach contents sailed over Luke's head. As the camel bellowed a further protest, and before it could work up another disgusting missile, he slipped away.

He moved from pen to pen, the rumbling and gurgling of the camels' formidable digestion masking the noise of his progress. The powerful odour of the beasts assailed his nostrils, threatening to make him sneeze. Once or twice, he caught sight of his pursuers stalking him through the lanes between the pens.

Luke considered. Clearly he was in no great danger of discovery at the moment, but hiding in the camel pens wasn't a good long-term strategy. To begin with, as soon as the sky became light, Gentile's men would find him.

More urgently, while he was pinned down here, he couldn't do anything to help Elsa – assuming she was still alive – or his mother. Luke ground his teeth in frustration.

He took a close look at his immediate surroundings. The pen had a gate, loosely fastened with string. The camel beside him was wearing a halter, and its forelegs were hobbled. An idea occurred to Luke, and a grin slowly spread across his face. He slid a hand into his trouser pocket and brought out a penknife...

A couple of minutes later, four of Luke's pursuers had met on the far side of the market. Having clearly missed their quarry, they were engaged in a vigorous debate about what to do next. Their discussion was interrupted by a rhythmic drumming of pounding feet, which grew closer and closer...

The men roared with fright and scattered as a camel came hurtling out of the darkness towards them. Luke sat perched on its hump with one leg crooked over its neck, hanging onto the creature's makeshift reins for grim death. Like a railway engine, the camel had taken some time to get going; but now that it was moving, there was something unstoppable about its rolling, stiff-legged gait.

In seconds, Luke had torn through the small knot

of his pursuers. Their cries and curses faded behind him as his mount stampeded away from the market. He had ridden camels before, in Australia, but those had mostly been well-trained, docile beasts with comfortable saddles and proper reins. Now he had no saddle, he had no idea whether this beast was trained at all – and there was another problem... Luke hauled on the reins, which seemed to have no effect, and cursed. "Where are the brakes on this thing?"

The surface beneath the camel's feet turned from soft sand to packed earth. Somehow, it had found a way back to the road. It thundered on through the night. Luke dimly wondered whether it would carry him far into the desert to die of thirst. He decided that wouldn't be a problem – the miserable creature would have shaken him to death long before that.

Eventually, his frantic tugging had an effect, though not the intended one. The string rein broke, and with a roar of despair, Luke slipped from the camel's back and landed heavily on the ground. Relieved of its unwelcome burden, the creature quickly came to a halt. Then, perversely, it wandered back to Luke as he lay winded and groaning, gazed down at him with its long-lashed eyes, and gave a rumble of enquiry.

Another shadow fell across Luke. "Resourceful, Signor Challenger."

Luke swore. Blast the camel! With the whole of the Sudan to choose from, why had the idiotic beast carried him straight back into the clutches of his gigantic new enemy?

Gentile chuckled. "I suppose Signora Partridge took great delight in telling you that I was once a *lottatore* – a wrestler?" The Italian giant shrugged. "Well – she was right!"

He reached down, grabbed hold of Luke's lapels, hauled him to his feet – and enveloped him in a bear hug.

Luke had already been fighting for breath from his fall. As Gentile's arms tightened, the remaining air burst from his body in an explosive gasp. In vain he kicked and writhed in a desperate attempt to break free. But Gentile was as strong as an ox; he threw back his great head and laughed as his victim struggled. Luke's arms were pinned to his side, blows from his threshing knees and feet seemed to have no effect. He tried a feeble headbutt and was rewarded with a squeeze that made his ribs creak. He couldn't breathe. He was suffocating in the Italian's grip. The camel watched the struggle with an air of detached interest.

As his consciousness ebbed, Luke dimly realized that the camel was practically looking over his shoulder. Calling on reserves of strength he did not know he had, he buried his face in Gentile's barrel chest and kicked out as hard as he could – backwards.

His feet caught the camel full in the throat. The startled beast gave an affronted gurgle – and spat.

Gentile roared and released his grip. Luke slid from his grasp and found himself on hands and knees, gasping for air, as the Italian clawed at the clinging, foul-smelling cud that now covered his head and shoulders. Luke hauled himself upright, gathered all his remaining energy, and launched a flying side kick that connected with the point of Gentile's jaw. The Italian's head snapped back and he went down as if poleaxed.

Once more, Luke hauled himself upright, ready to resume the contest. To his dismay, he saw that his opponent, though groggy, was far from beaten. Gentile lumbered to his feet, wiped blood from his mouth and barked a command. A score of armed men stepped from the shadows behind him, weapons raised.

Luke muttered, "Oh, *rats!*"

He was defenceless. The odds against him were overwhelming, and he was too winded to run. There was no way out. He drew himself up, glaring defiantly at his attackers, and waited for the end.

9 NIGHT FLIGHT

The clattering sound of galloping hoofs arose from the surrounding darkness, rapidly coming nearer. Luke's would-be murderers paused, uncertain. He risked a glance in the direction of the noise, and Gentile, seeing his momentary distraction, roared another command at his men and threw himself into a charge – only to be bowled over by a horse that thundered out of the night. With a screech, the giant Italian went down beneath its flailing hoofs. His hirelings scattered.

Luke gaped as the creature skidded to a halt. Elsa

Fairfax, knees clamped behind the horse's shoulders like a champion bareback rider, hauled on the reins as the excited beast reared and plunged. Nick slid from its back willy-nilly and staggered towards Luke with a curious, bow-legged gait. "Are you all right?" he demanded.

Luke stared past him. "Where did you get the horse?"

"I cut it free from the carriage and came looking for you, but I found Elsa first. That girl rides like a lunatic!"

Luke glanced at Elsa. Blood from her head wound had run down her neck and shoulder, creating a stain on her blue dress that looked like tar in the moonlight, but her fighting spirit was clearly undiminished. He turned his attention to Gentile, who was struggling to his feet, spitting out a mouthful of dirt and clutching at his left arm. He gave Luke a glare of pure hatred and roared, *"Dahama!"*

Luke's assailants, who had fallen back in consternation at the horse's sudden appearance, howled a blood-curdling battle cry and charged. Elsa urged her mount forward. "He's telling them to attack!"

"I'd never have guessed!" Luke helped Nick scramble onto the horse's back. He followed with a desperate leap, landing on the point of the unfortunate beast's croup as Elsa yelled and dug her heels into its ribs. The horse neighed and surged forward. Luke came within an ace of tumbling backwards across the overloaded mount's hindquarters as it went from a standing start to a gallop in half a dozen strides. He regained his seat and glanced over his shoulder, ducking as some of the pursuing party slid to a halt, raised their muskets and fired. Bullets drilled the air around them, but in the darkness the ancient weapons were not accurate enough to hit a moving target.

Elsa threw a glance at Nick, who was clinging to her waist with a death grip. "Do you have to hold onto me quite so hard?"

"Yes!"

"I thought all Irishmen could ride!"

"I'm only half Irish!"

Luke was aware that the horse's stride was becoming uneven. The poor creature had not had a good evening. It had been nearly blown to bits, then tethered by its harness to a wrecked carriage, and now it was being galloped hard with three people on its back. He risked another backward glance. The faster of their pursuers were still in sight.

Over her shoulder, Elsa yelled, "Any minute now, we're going to founder!"

"I know!" Luke stared ahead into the darkness. In the

distance, a glow of oil lamps cast a golden haze across the night. He pointed. "What's that?"

"A market – the night *souq*."

"Can we get there?"

"We can try!"

In the event, they were a quarter of a mile short of the *souq* when the horse stumbled. Fortunately for its riders, it skidded to a halt on its knees. Luke, Nick and Elsa tumbled from its back and were on their feet and running in a few seconds. The relieved horse regained its feet and limped painfully to the side of the road to crop at a patch of dried grass. Seeing their mount's fall, the pursuers let out a yell of triumph and redoubled their efforts. They were hard on their quarry's heels as Luke, Nick and Elsa tore into the night market.

The scene was one of frenetic activity. Traders yelled and gesticulated, drawing attention to the wares on their stalls that littered the narrow street, displaying every conceivable variety of goods. There were stalls selling cloth, brightly-coloured beads and the embroidered pillbox hats worn by Sudanese men. There were vegetable stalls, grocery stalls, stalls piled high with baskets of dates and cowrie shells. The uprights holding up shade canopies were festooned with shoes, sandals and leather goods. Trestles groaned under the weight of pots and pans, brass ornaments and pottery lavishly decorated in red, black and gold. Shoppers milled around, eyeing the wares or haggling vociferously with stallholders. Others sat at tea stalls, laughing and chatting with friends. Smoke from cooking fires floated through the living tide like the threads of an exotic carpet. The whole scene was illuminated by the mellow glow of oil and paraffin lamps, against which insects incontinently battered themselves, casting dancing shadows over the crowd.

Luke and his companions burst onto this scene like a bombshell. Startled market-goers hardly had time to protest about the sudden appearance of the fugitives before they were shoved aside, battered, trampled and overwhelmed by their yelling pursuers.

Luke's mind was racing. Nick and Elsa seemed to be feeling the effects of their injuries, and he wasn't in mid-season form himself. They couldn't hope to outdistance Gentile's men. Their only chance was to slow their enemies down. He acted instantly on the thought, dodging behind a stall loaded with bowls and baskets of peas, beans and other dried pulses. A quick heave – and their pursuers suddenly found themselves skating on thousands of small, round, shifting seeds that scattered across the road and rolled beneath their feet like ball bearings.

With the yells of the outraged stallholder ringing in

his ears, Luke ran on. Perhaps they had gained enough distance to be able to hide. But as he caught up with his companions, another dozen or so thugs appeared in the road ahead. Nick and Elsa skidded to a halt so suddenly that Luke nearly barged into them. Yells from behind them indicated that at least some of their pursuers had overcome the vegetable skidpan Luke had created.

Elsa pointed down a side alley. "This way!" Luke and Nick followed as she pelted up the narrow passage. The ground rose as the alley climbed the flank of a hill. The stalls were sparser here, and at the end of the alley was a shop selling rolls of carpet and matting. Luke and Nick exchanged a glance – and a grin.

Their pursuers charged into the alley, to be met by a positive flood of rolling carpets. They stumbled and tripped; those that managed to hurdle the first wave of carpets found themselves tripping over the second. Their curses and threats echoed between the narrow walls. Luke and Nick gleefully hurled more and more carpets, adding to the confusion, as the shopkeeper tried ineffectually to stop each of them in turn, before giving up, moaning and wringing his hands.

"Come on!" Elsa was beckoning them from another alleyway that led diagonally down to the main street. As she turned to run, Luke sent a final carpet tumbling to join the chaos, grabbed Nick by the arm, and followed.

They emerged into the main street just in time to see Elsa brought to bay by a giant of a man wearing black robes and wielding a huge scimitar. They watched in horror as the grinning giant raised the great curved sword for a stroke that looked set to cleave Harriet Challenger's assistant in two.

There was no time for thought. Luke realized that he was standing next to a spice stall. He grabbed the basket nearest to hand, and hurled its contents full into the face of Elsa's assailant. The man's head and shoulders were enveloped in a dark red cloud.

The results were unexpectedly dramatic. The giant screamed, dropped his sword and clawed at his eyes. Elsa darted back out of reach. Startled, Luke sniffed at the basket. Chilli powder! No wonder Elsa's attacker had lost interest in chopping her into bits. Luke leaped over the grovelling swordsman and sped away through the market with Nick and Elsa pounding in his wake.

Hearing a stifled cry from Elsa, Luke glanced back. The girl was limping badly. He slowed his pace. "What is it?"

She shook her head. "Something in my foot – a nail, a thorn – I don't know…"

Luke cursed under his breath. "Get her out of here," he told Nick. "I'll try and lead them off." Nick nodded and, ignoring Elsa's protests, hauled her arm across his shoulder for support. Luke halted and glanced around as the sounds of pursuit came nearer.

A group of thugs burst out of an alley to his right. Luke sidestepped, barely evading their rush, and a sword sliced the air beside his ear with a noise like tearing paper. He spotted a cart piled high with furniture parked under the eaves of one of the shops lining the street. He sprinted towards it, scrambling over chairs and cupboards until, with a convulsive leap, he landed chest-first against the wall of the building with his forearms hanging over the parapet. He swung his legs, his feet scrabbling at the adobe wall, and hauled himself up, tumbling onto the roof just as his pursuers opened fire with their muskets.

Luke picked himself up and ran. From the noises behind him, he knew that at least some of his pursuers were following him onto the roof. He came to an alleyway; without stopping to consider the distance across it, Luke launched himself into space. He landed on the opposite roof, rolled and came up running. Despairing screams behind him indicated that one or more of his enemies had failed to make the leap.

Luke raced on, leaping from rooftop to rooftop. Now, at last, he seemed to be gaining on his enemies. Their cries were falling further and further behind.

At length, he came to a square where a fire-eater was

performing to an appreciative crowd. Spotting a shade canopy below him, Luke made a rolling dive from the roof onto the canopy and slid off it, landing with a thud among a knot of startled spectators.

He had hardly clambered to his feet when someone alighted, as nimble as a cat, right behind him. Luke cursed inwardly. His belief that he had shaken off all his pursuers was evidently misplaced. The man who had followed him was slim and wiry, with a scar down one cheek. He grinned at Luke and raised a wicked-looking cutlass.

Luke backed slowly away. The man followed. Spectators scattered at the sight of the sword. Luke found himself in the cleared area around the fire-eater, just as the performer blew on a flaming wand to send a prodigious sheet of flame into the night sky.

Luke watched from the corner of his eye as the fire-eater, who had his back to him, took a mouthful of paraffin. As he raised the wand to his lips, Luke tapped the man on the shoulder, and instantly dropped into a crouch.

Startled, the fire-eater turned, simultaneously spraying a mist of highly inflammable fuel. The spray passed over the wand and instantaneously burst into flames, which roiled around the hapless swordsman. The man's screams echoed round the square as Luke made his escape.

Unfortunately, the pause had given his other pursuers time to catch up. A horde of screaming thugs poured into the square behind him. Bullets struck the walls to either side of the street as Luke redoubled his efforts to outdistance his enemies. But he was tiring. His legs felt increasingly leaden, his breath came in tearing gasps. The fox had given the hounds a good run, but the end of the chase was in sight. He hoped that Nick and Elsa, at least, had got away.

He rounded a corner – and skidded to a halt. Before him stretched two lines of African troopers in immaculate khaki uniforms; the front rank was kneeling, the rear standing; both ranks held rifles shouldered and ready to fire. A British officer stood to one side of his men. Beside him, apparently undamaged, was a carriage from which Salim, his father and Luke's mother were gazing on the scene with obvious concern. By the door of the carriage, drooping but alive, stood Nick and Elsa.

The officer called out, "I say, you there – would you mind awfully ducking down for a moment?"

Luke threw himself face down into the road just as his pursuers came pouring round the corner. Confusion arose as those in the front tried to back-pedal and those in the rear, unaware of the new threat, piled into them with cries and curses.

The officer ordered, "Single round, Sergeant. Fire when ready!"

The Sergeant gave the order. The rifles crashed in perfect unison. A few of Luke's assailants screamed and fell, but apparently the rest of the bullets had been aimed high. The surviving thugs broke and fled.

As Luke, half-dazed, struggled to his feet, the officer strolled across and offered his hand. "Agnew of the North-East Africa Rifles. Hope those blighters didn't give you too much of a scare. You look about all in. Would you like a cup of tea?"

10 CONFERENCE

The Governor General's Residence, Khartoum
The following day

The council of war took place in the Governor General's drawing room. The hawk-nosed, sharp-eyed man who ruled the Sudan in the name of the British Empire may well, in Dottie Partridge's words, have been a "dear": but at this moment he looked like a vulture robbed of his breakfast carcass. He sat behind an elegant writing table, fiddling with a paper knife. Lieutenant Agnew stood at his left shoulder.

Nick was sporting a head bandage, which he seemed to feel gave him a rather dashing air. The doctor who had stitched Elsa's head injury had proposed shaving off a good deal of her blonde mane until she had told him what she would do to him if he tried it. He had wisely settled for a narrow strip either side of the wound. Elsa, evidently more self-conscious than Luke had thought her, was wearing a headscarf to cover this disfigurement. She also had a bandaged foot from which the doctor had removed a rusty three-inch nail. He had administered a tetanus injection in a place that made Elsa sit rather uncomfortably, with most of her weight on one side of the chair.

The other members of the conference consisted of Salim and his father and, looking pale but composed, Harriet Challenger. Declaring that she felt much better following a night's sleep, she had insisted on being present. She sat on an uncomfortable settee with Luke, holding his hand; which Luke found both embarrassing and oddly comforting.

The Governor General surveyed the assembled company. "So," he said, "if I have the story right, this bomb or grenade or whatever it was went off after the first carriage had gone past: so that the guard and the horse on the side of the second carriage nearest the blast were killed."

"Undoubtedly a mistake on the part of the bombers," said Ras Menelik. "Beyond question, I was the intended target."

"Hmmm." The Governor General gave Salim's father a narrow-eyed stare. "Are you certain of that? We have just heard that, earlier in the evening, your son was held up at knifepoint, in the grounds of this very residence."

"By an opportunistic thief, I am sure."

"An odd sort of thief!" The Governor General turned to Luke. "A Japanese woman – Mochizuki, you said her name was? Formerly a captain in the Imperial Japanese Navy?" Luke nodded. "What on earth was she after?"

Luke said nothing. By unspoken agreement, neither he nor Nick nor Salim had mentioned Mochizuki's attempt to seize Salim's medallion. Not one of them could explain what had happened when she tried, even to himself, let alone anyone else. Luke strongly suspected that any attempt to tell the Governor General what had really happened in his garden would result in him and his friends being regarded as liars or madmen.

Fortunately, the Governor General did not press the matter. "The situation here in the Sudan is complicated enough without some Asiatic hellcat causing even more trouble. How on earth did she get into the country in the first place? And how has she managed to disappear? You'd think a Japanese woman in the Sudan would stick out like a sore thumb!"

"Oh, that's easy." Catching the Governor General's

glare, Luke hurriedly added, "I'm sorry, sir, but she'd only have to put on a *burqa* – lots of women here wear them – and how would you ever know her from one of the locals?"

"Good lord!" Agnew was evidently thunderstruck by the very idea that a Japanese woman might dress in the all-enveloping Islamic veil. "I say, sir, there's something in that, you know."

"I daresay. We might have caught the blasted woman if Mr. Challenger had seen fit to inform me immediately that a serious offence had been committed in my own garden!"

"That was my fault, sir," said Salim promptly. "I asked Luke to keep quiet until the reception was over. I did not want my foolishness in allowing myself to be lured into a trap to jeopardize the peace conference."

"A wasted effort, as it turns out," said the Governor General sourly. "To return to the bomb outrage: I gather the driver of the carriage carrying Your Highness, your son and Lady Challenger lost his head and whipped up the horses. Eventually, you managed to prevail upon him to bring you back to the Residence where Lieutenant Agnew, having heard the blast, was assembling his men. Hearing reports of a disturbance at the *souq*, you and he arrived there just in time to meet Mr. Malone and Miss Fairfax, and disperse the rabble pursuing Mr. Challenger."

He turned his full attention on Luke. "And you say that Count Gentile attacked both you and Miss Fairfax."

Luke nodded. "Yes, sir."

"A member of the Italian peace delegation assaulting British subjects. That would create the devil of an international incident – if we could find Gentile." The Governor General turned to Agnew. "I don't suppose he's turned up?"

"Not a sign, sir. All the Italian Embassy will say is that he's been recalled to Rome. He seems to have vanished into thin air."

"Probably just as well," growled the Governor General, "from a diplomatic point of view."

"He had already informed me," said Ras Menelik in low, angry tones, "that his government was not prepared to consider any of the submissions I had made to him at the peace conference. That is why I left your very excellent reception earlier than I had intended."

"From which," said the Governor General, "we can infer that he expected you to react as you did, and had laid his plans accordingly. So we can add murder and attempted murder to his crimes."

"I imagine you might have some difficulty connecting Gentile with the bombers, Your Excellency," said Luke's mother.

"Quite possibly; as we cannot find him, the question

does not arise. But for Gentile to get his hands on a bomb, arrange an ambush and recruit a bunch of ruffians to make sure no one survived it, and then to disappear so completely, he must have backing from a powerful organization. And so we come to the Sons of Destiny, and their recent interest in Ethiopia."

Ras Menelik waved a hand dismissively. "I'm sorry, Your Excellency, but my enemy is Mussolini. It is now clear that the Italian government only agreed to unofficial peace talks to stall for time. *Il Duce*'s army is poised to invade my country. I must do everything in my power to prevent that invasion from happening, and I cannot allow myself to be sidetracked by a bunch of crack-brained fanatics on some ludicrous quest. My son has told me that these people seek King Solomon's Mines. Let them. The Mines are a myth, a fairy story. They can search until they are blue in the face and they will find nothing."

Luke glanced at Salim. While his father was speaking, his young friend's face had been expressionless. But at the mention of the Mines, Luke thought Salim gave him the ghost of a wink.

"My course is clear." Ras Menelik looked troubled. "I must return to Addis Ababa at once and report to the Emperor. However, it seems that my staff and I will be in grave danger on the journey. I have already survived one assassination attempt, which the British authorities here failed to prevent, and I see no reason not to expect more."

The Governor General looked ready to breathe fire, but his voice was calm as he said, "I have already apologized for that lapse; the situation here is volatile and we had no prior intelligence of the attack."

"Nor will you, I expect, of the next one." Ras Menelik made a conciliatory gesture. "Let us not quarrel. I am apprehensive, not on my own behalf – the Emperor has many advisors he can call upon – but on my son's." Salim opened his mouth to say something but a stern look from his father caused him to close it again. "I had planned to take Salim with me when I returned to Addis Ababa, but that would be extremely unwise in the current situation. Nor would I wish to leave him here, where he knows no one."

"Might I make a suggestion?" said Harriet. "Perhaps Salim could come to the Omo Valley with me. He would be with Nick and Luke, whom he knows – and Elsa, of course – and in his own country…"

"But at the opposite end of it from the Italian forces waiting to invade," said Ras Menelik slowly. Luke waited with bated breath. If Salim's father agreed to this proposal, it would greatly increase the chances that he, Nick and Salim would be able to slip away from his mother and search for King Solomon's Mines. "And, if war should come," Salim's father concluded, "my son would be within a day's ride of the Sudan or British East Africa, where he would be safe."

This time, Salim could not remain silent. "If war comes, I do not want to be safe!" he said fiercely. "I want to fight, to defend my country."

"Many young men will do that," said his father bleakly, "and many will die. Some must survive to lead our people in the future, whatever this current crisis may bring. Your time will come; you have said enough." Salim's mutinous look showed that he did not consider that he had said enough by a long shot, but he subsided.

Ras Menelik turned back to Harriet. "Lady Challenger, thank you for your very kind offer. I accept." Luke gave a mental sigh of relief. "I shall leave for Ethiopia this evening. Hopefully, the assassins will follow, and my son – and your party – will no longer be in danger."

"Lieutenant Agnew's men will escort you as far as the border," the Governor General put in.

Ras Menelik inclined his head gravely. "Thank you."

"My steamer is heading up the Nile in two days," said Harriet. "You can send an escort to collect Salim" – ("I am not a parcel!" muttered Salim, earning himself a frown from his father) – "from my camp when the situation is calmer."

"That will serve excellently." Ras Menelik stood. "I have many arrangements to make. Please excuse me."

When the diplomatic pleasantries had been observed and Ras Menelik and Salim (still looking mutinous) had left, the Governor General addressed his remaining guests.

"I'm afraid," he said, "that I – and another interested party – have more to say on this subject; however, there is no need to burden Miss Fairfax further with matters that do not concern her."

Elsa bristled. Luke's mother said calmly, "Elsa is my assistant and she knows everything I know. There's no point shutting her out. I'll probably forget half of what we're going to talk about anyway – but she won't."

The Governor General thought for a moment. Then he nodded, and stood. "Very well. Please will you join me in the library?"

Posting Lieutenant Agnew at the library door with an instruction to "See that we're not disturbed", the Governor General led Luke, Nick, Elsa and Harriet into the book-lined room. On the desk that occupied the centre of the floor stood a walnut loudspeaker cabinet that looked identical to the one that graced Luke's father's study. Their host indicated it with a wave of the hand. "I believe the interested party I mentioned wants to have a word with you."

"Hello, everyone," said a plummy voice.

Luke stared at the cabinet. "Nanny?"

"No need to sound so surprised, dear." The voice sounded faint and crackly; Luke realized that Nanny was speaking over a long-distance telephone line. "Nanny is watching you, of course. That's what Nanny does." The voice became businesslike. "Sir Charles has given me a full account of your escape from that ruffian Gentile and the amiable Captain Mochizuki." The Governor General nodded. "He believes, as I do, that Gentile's attack was bungled. The bombers were aiming for the first carriage and hit the second because the detonation of the bomb took longer than expected. But we are also convinced that Ras Menelik was not, as he believes, their intended target."

Luke remembered Nanny's interpretation of the attack on Salisbury Plain. "You still think the bombers were after Salim?"

"Yes."

"Why?"

"We don't know. After that business with the tank, our first thought was that the Sons of Destiny were trying to get at Ras Menelik by harming his son, but more recent intelligence indicates that they have been making extensive enquiries about your young friend – about *him*, specifically, not about his father. The inescapable conclusion is that Salim Menelik himself is their ultimate target, but we don't know why."

Luke couldn't resist a dig. "I thought Nanny knew best."

"She does, dear," said Nanny sharply, "when she is in full possession of the facts. But I'm afraid on this occasion I'm at a bit of a loss. Everything suggests that the Sons of Destiny are throwing all the resources they have at finding King Solomon's Mines. They certainly believe the Mines exist, whatever Ras Menelik might think." Luke's ears pricked up. So Nanny had been listening in on their conference with Salim's father – that was interesting.

"The Sons of Destiny would support Mussolini's land-grab in Africa anyway," said the Governor General, "because they see the fascist governments of Italy and Germany as instrumental in their rise to power."

"Just so," said Nanny, "but there seems to be more to it than that. Our information is that they are actively goading Mussolini into invading Ethiopia, possibly in the hope that in the resulting chaos they will be able to find and plunder the Mines without interference. Presumably, as part of that aim, their first plan was for Captain Mochizuki to kill or kidnap Salim Menelik."

Luke said nothing. He was sure now that Mochizuki's aim had not been to kill Salim – she had had the opportunity to do so, and had not taken it – but to mention her attempt to seize his medallion would only complicate matters. Why, after all, would she do such a thing? It wasn't as if the medallion was made of gold or silver, or covered with precious stones. From what Nanny had said already, Luke was sure she would have no idea what the Japanese assassin wanted with an apparently valueless family heirloom. And he knew what she would say if he told her what had happened when Mochizuki had touched the medallion. *Luke, dear, isn't that a little far-fetched?* Despite the gravity of the situation, he grinned at the thought.

"When that attempt failed," Nanny went on, "they were prepared to sacrifice the cover they had crafted for Gentile, who had been successfully posing as a bona fide representative of the Italian government. Once again, you and Nick – and Miss Fairfax, of course – were merely in the way." Elsa started at the mention of her name and Luke wondered whether Nanny knew that she was in the room and, if so, how. "The only possible explanation for the Sons of Destiny's interest in Salim Menelik," Nanny concluded, "seems to be that they believe he can interfere with their plans to find the Spear of Destiny."

"Salim can?" said Nick. "How?"

"As I've already explained, Nick dear," said Nanny

with studied patience, "we don't know. There seems to be no rational reason why they should imagine any such thing."

"No," said Luke slowly, "but there may be an irrational reason. We're dealing with the Sons of Destiny, remember. They believe a two-thousand-year-old spear will help them rule the world. They may be good at cruelty, brutality and cold-blooded murder, but rational thinking isn't what they do best."

"The main thing," said Lady Challenger decisively, "is to keep Salim out of the clutches of those horrible cut-throats."

"Quite so," said Nanny. "Does Salim know where the Mines are to be found, I wonder?"

"I asked him that," Luke told her. "He says not."

"Then I believe that the plan Lady Challenger suggested for getting our young friend out of harm's way may be the best we can do at the moment, though I'm not sure that the assassins will follow Ras Menelik's party as he imagines."

Luke gave his mother an encouraging nod. If he, Nick and Salim were to go off looking for King Solomon's Mines, they may as well set off for the Omo Valley as planned. After all, based on their current information – or lack of it – the Mines were just as likely to be found there as anywhere else; and ever since Ras Menelik had accepted his mother's offer, Luke's brain had been buzzing with schemes for detaching the three of them from her party in order to begin their search.

Nanny was speaking again. "It really would make sense for the rest of you to start upriver as soon as possible, while the energetic Lieutenant Agnew's enquiries are forcing our enemies to keep their heads down – if Lady Challenger is sure she's feeling well enough to travel."

"Absolutely." Harriet stuck her chin out. "That turn I had last night was just a passing weakness. I'm much better now. I feel absolutely fine. Fit as a flea. There's nothing the matter with me at all."

11 UPRIVER

"**M**alaria!" boomed the doctor cheerfully as he closed his medical case with a snap. "That's what it is, all right. Not a shadow of a doubt."

Luke stared at him in horror. "But she was fine yesterday."

"You said she started feeling feverish a couple of nights ago?" The doctor nodded. "Classic symptoms – apparent recovery, then a relapse. All to do with the life cycle of the parasite; I won't bore you with the grisly details. I've pumped her full of quinine, so that should settle the little blighters' hash, but she's had a nasty bout and I'd like to keep an eye on her for a week or two."

"But we're supposed to be heading up to her dig this afternoon."

"Out of the question, I'm afraid. She can't travel in her condition and if she tries living in a tent at the back end of nowhere rather than here under proper medical supervision, I won't be answerable for the consequences. Anyway, the fever's subsided for the moment, you can see her now." The doctor collected his hat and bustled off.

Luke poked his head round his mother's bedroom door. Harriet looked up and gave him a weak smile. "Has he gone?"

Luke slipped into the room. "Yes."

"Thank goodness. I'm sure he's a very good doctor but his bedside manner is a bit overwhelming. Enough to make anyone feel worse."

"Are you feeling worse?" Luke asked her with some alarm.

Lady Challenger gave his arm a feeble pat. "No, darling, I'm better than I was, honestly."

"I was really worried about you last night," Luke said awkwardly. He wasn't used to talking like this with his mother. From his earliest years, his conversations with her had largely consisted of her asking him to "Pass me the one-inch camel-hair brush, will you, Luke?" and him replying "Here you are." Expressing concern made him feel embarrassed and on edge. It wasn't what a chap *did*.

He was also feeling guilty that when his mother had been shivering, sweating and mumbling delirious nonsense in the small hours of the morning, it had been Elsa, not himself, who had sat with her and mopped her brow. He tried to tell himself that nursing was women's work, but he didn't believe it. Luke hated illness, wasn't good at coping with it and had absented himself from his mother's sickroom as soon as he could. Elsa had shown no sign of reproaching him for his weakness but he found it hard not to feel resentful towards her even though – or perhaps because – he knew he owed her nothing but gratitude.

"The doctor said..." he began, and then stopped abruptly. His mother had fallen asleep. Luke awkwardly rearranged the coverlet beneath her limp hand and tiptoed from the room.

Nick and Elsa were waiting anxiously for news. Luke dealt with their questions about his mother's condition, and what the doctor had had to say about it. "At least," he concluded, "it's lucky the Governor General invited us all to move into his Residence before she was taken ill again. She'll be safer and more comfortable here than she would have been at the hotel."

"So what do we do now?" demanded Nick. "The steamer's waiting for us, our bags are packed. Do we go, or do we stay?"

"I know what my mother would say," said Luke heavily. "She'd say 'go', but she'd also insist on going with us, and the doctor says she must stay here until she's well enough to travel."

"Then she shouldn't go," said Elsa promptly.

"Nobody's saying she should," said Luke sharply. "But what about the steamer?"

"The steamer will go upriver on schedule," Elsa told him. "And all the expedition's supplies are on it – food, medicine, equipment, everything. If it doesn't get there, the diggers will leave."

"So we can send the supplies on with the steamer while we all wait here until Lady Challenger is fit to travel?" said Nick.

"No good," said Elsa. "Half the supplies will mysteriously disappear en route if there's no one there to keep an eye on them. Anyway, the site foreman, Hakim, knows his business, but he's hopeless at taking decisions. The whole dig will fall apart if there's nobody to tell him what to do. I'll go with the steamer, you two wait here."

"That won't do," said Luke. "You're forgetting about Salim."

"What about me?"

Luke, startled, swung around in his chair to see that Salim, who had moved to the Governor General's Residence when his father had left the night before, had come silently into the room at some time during the discussion. "It's not polite to eavesdrop," he said.

"It's not polite to talk about people behind their backs," replied Salim amiably. "How is your mother?"

Luke told him. "That's why we mentioned you," he went on. "Mother promised your father to take you to the Omo Valley with her, but it's obvious she can't travel. The way I see it is this: we all need to go to Ethiopia anyway. Once we're there, Elsa can go on to Mother's dig in the Omo Valley and carry on her work."

Elsa stared at him. "And what are your plans, may I ask?"

Luke took a deep breath. "To find King Solomon's Mines."

"Now just a minute!" Elsa was on her feet. "Lady Challenger didn't say anything about letting you go haring off looking for some mythical treasure."

"No," said Luke calmly, "we hadn't got around to discussing it. Unfortunately, it looks as though the decision is out of her hands." He turned to face Salim. By now, he knew his former schoolmate well enough to understand that he would resent any attempt to force him into a course of action. Salim did not know of Nanny's belief that he had been the real target of the bomb attack, but other than that he understood the situation just as well as Luke. "So, what will you do? Stay here? Go with Elsa to the Omo Valley? Or search for the Mines with me and Nick?"

"It's not up to him—" Elsa began.

"You've had your say," Luke told her sharply. "It's Salim's decision." Elsa folded her arms and glared at him.

Salim remained silent for so long that Luke was about to ask the question again when he said, quite shyly, "I promised my father – against my own wishes – that I would go with Lady Challenger. Since she is unwell, I will go with you – if you'll have me."

"We will," said Luke, "and welcome." He checked his watch. "Are we all packed?"

"I won't have this!" Elsa was in a fury. "I'll tell Lady Challenger about this Mines nonsense – she'll stop you!"

"She's in no condition to stop anybody doing anything," said Luke, "and if you tell her what we're planning, you'll only upset her for no reason."

"The Governor General—"

"The Governor General, as you saw yesterday, is in cahoots with Nanny, who has done everything short of order us to find the Mines."

Elsa looked as if she would have stamped her foot if only it wasn't still recovering from the nail. "Well, if you're going off on some hare-brained treasure hunt, I won't have Lady Challenger think I did anything to encourage you. You can take the steamer without me, so there!"

"Fine," said Luke. "Do you have any messages you'd like us to pass on with the mule train?"

"Oh!" Elsa stormed out.

Luke turned to Nick, who was grinning, and Salim, who was trying not to. "We'll need to be at the jetty in just over an hour. I'll let Sir Charles know what's going on and ask him to arrange for a nurse. If my mother wakes up before we go, I'll tell her what we've decided."

"And if she doesn't?" said Salim.

"Then I'll leave her a note."

"A note?" Salim looked troubled. "But she is your mother. You should not leave without saying goodbye."

"I don't see why not," said Luke quietly. "She would. In fact she has. Often."

And to that, Salim had nothing to say.

The following evening, the Nile steamer *Star of the Sudan* was chugging industriously southwards.

The steamer had a long, narrow hull that sat low in the water with scarcely three feet of freeboard. Its accommodation deck was oblong and made of wood covered in blistered and flaking paint. This was topped by a planking roof, which extended outwards to cover the side-decks. At the forward end of the top deck sat a squat, ugly wheelhouse, and from its middle rose a tall smokestack that belched out clouds of soot and ash. Beneath the semicircular stern, the propeller turned the turbid waters of the Blue Nile into dancing froth.

The steamer carried a crew of four – the captain, a morose Egyptian with a drooping moustache; his engineer and his stoker, both of whom Luke had hardly seen since the trip began; and a cheerful young Arab cook. Two armed guards completed the company; the Governor General had insisted on their riding shotgun on the river, and they were clearly not happy about it. They spent their time cleaning their rifles and speaking to no one.

The journey had begun the previous afternoon. Luke and the others had left the Residence while Lady Challenger was still asleep – a relief to Luke, who found it hard enough to argue with his mother when she was well and knew he would have found it next to impossible when she was ill.

Elsa had appeared at the jetty shortly after midday,

just as the gangplank was about to be raised. Luke guessed that she had decided to press on to meet the mule train alone; he wondered if she thought she could talk him out of the decision to search for the Mines, but she had made no attempt yet to do so. She had boarded the paddle steamer without a glance or a word at the boys, and had continued an angry silence as the steamer carried them upriver as far as the dam at Sennar. At this point it had been necessary to transfer their luggage and the archaeological expedition's supplies to this smaller vessel; a long, hot and exasperatingly slow business, which had forced Elsa into at least acknowledging the presence of the others, if only to order them to "Put that box over there!" or "Don't drop that – it's fragile!"

Once they were under way, Elsa, while remaining barely civil to her fellow passengers, had quickly established a partnership with the cook, Ali. As they approached sunset of their second day on the river, the sound of their chatter, along with enticing spicy smells, rose from the small galley on the deck below, where they were preparing supper.

Luke and Nick were sitting at a rickety table in the lee of the wheelhouse, out of the hot wind caused by their passage. The day had been oppressively warm, and Luke felt a sense of relief as the sun began to dip below the low hills to their right. He rose from his seat to lean on the rail, starting as the steamer's whistle blew a piercing blast. Some way ahead, a felucca adjusted its big triangular sail without haste to steer out of their way.

Luke had seen plenty of feluccas. He turned his attention to the western bank of the river. Neatly tended fields ran alongside the course of the Nile. Here and there stood waterwheels, worked by oxen or donkeys, which lifted water from the river and fed it into irrigation channels that spider-webbed across the fields, bringing life-giving water to the crops. But most of the waterwheels were still now, the farmers who ran them gathered round their evening fires.

Beyond the fields lay the desert, stretching some six hundred miles to the highlands of Darfur on the opposite side of the Sudan. All that emptiness, Luke thought. You could lose England in the desert many times over. As he watched, the farmland gave way to low hills on either side of the river. It was as if the desert was reaching out to claim the little ship and everyone aboard her. Luke suddenly felt very small, and very far from home.

Salim materialized at his elbow. "We shall be in my country by morning," he said happily.

Luke nodded. "Unfortunately, we'll also be leaving the river."

"Yes," said Salim. "I don't believe anyone has

succeeded in sailing down the Abay Wenz – that is our name for the river in Ethiopia – from Lake Tana. My people love the river, they regard it as holy – but they do not travel on it. The current is too strong, there are too many rapids."

"So where do we start looking for the Mines?" Luke asked him. "Do we meet up with the mule team from my mother's camp? And if so, do we go with it? Or head off somewhere else?"

Salim shrugged. "Perhaps we will find some information in the village where the mules are waiting. I do not know." Luke frowned. "Don't be downcast," Salim advised him. "I am a fatalist. Something will turn up to show us the way, I'm sure of it."

Luke grunted. He admired Salim's optimism, but he would have preferred a plan.

"All this talk of travel is making me hungry." Nick rose from his seat as Elsa appeared on the accommodation ladder from the lower deck carrying a loaded tray covered with a cloth. "I hope that's food you have there," he told her, "because I'm going to eat it."

Elsa set the tray down on the table. "Just some starters – not that you deserve them. Kofta and falafel with yoghurt and tahini dip."

Nick gazed at her with frank adoration. "You're wonderful. Will you marry me?"

Elsa gave him a hard-eyed stare. "You're joking, of course."

"I was serious!" protested Nick.

"So was I. Eat your kofta before it gets cold."

Nick sighed, took a meatball and dunked it in the bowl of dip. He lifted it to his lips – and paused halfway. "Hello!"

The chuntering of the *Star of the Sudan*'s ancient engine was suddenly overpowered by the sound of aeroplane motors. Luke followed Nick's gaze. A three-engined monoplane was approaching from the south-east.

"What is it?" he asked Nick. "An airliner?"

"I don't think so," said Nick slowly. "It looks like a Savoia-Marchetti SM79." Luke didn't doubt the identification; Nick's knowledge of aircraft was encyclopaedic. "It's a new type; only been flying for a few months. I didn't know they'd even started delivering it to the *Regia Aeronautica* yet..."

The aircraft turned to run along the river towards the *Star of the Sudan*. Luke stared at Nick. "Just a minute – are you saying it's Italian?"

"Certainly, it's Italian."

"And a bomber?"

"Probably."

"Like the Italian aircraft that dropped bombs on

Ethiopian villages a little while ago?"

Nick dropped his kofta and said, *"Hell!"*

Luke snatched open the door of the wheelhouse. "Captain!" he yelled. "That plane..." Belatedly, he remembered that the Captain spoke only Arabic and French. He pointed frantically at the approaching aircraft. *"L'avion – le bombardier!"* he managed.

The captain stared at him. *"Qu'est-ce que vous dites?"*

Luke could hear Nick was shouting down the accommodation ladder to Ali, the guards, and the unseen crew, while Elsa and Salim were staring at both of them as though they'd gone mad. He swore in frustration. "There's no time! We have to get out of here – abandon ship – *abandonnez le navire!"* The Captain gave him a disgusted look and turned back to the wheel.

The aircraft was thundering towards them. Luke grabbed Elsa round the waist and, ignoring her startled cry, vaulted over the rail. From the corner of his eye, he saw Nick do the same to Salim. He hit the dirty brown water, going a surprisingly long way down. Elsa fought him all the way. As soon as their heads broke the surface, and she had spat out a good mouthful of Nile water, she swore at him. "What on *earth* do you think you're doing, you...you *lunatic*?"

Luke hardly heard her. He stared at the steamer, which was still trundling along in the middle of the river, some distance upstream of them now, with its wake spreading serenely behind it. He looked up as the Italian aircraft passed overhead with a roar and watched in sick horror as a harmless-looking tube detached itself from the bomber and tumbled towards the vessel, hitting just astern of the smokestack.

The *Star of the Sudan* exploded into a fireball.

12 OASIS

The River Nile

Luke felt his hair crisp in the heat of the explosion. He ducked under the water for a few seconds. When he came up again, Elsa, her face contorted with grief and rage, struck out at him with clenched fists. "Ali!"

Luke blocked the blows with his forearms. "Are you mad?"

"You left him to die! You left them all to die!"

Luke remembered that Elsa had befriended Ali, the young cook. "I tried to warn them! You heard me. We barely got off in time ourselves!"

The only reply was another blow. Luke grabbed Elsa's wrist. "Stop splashing," he snapped. "Swim for the reeds. That plane will be back any minute looking for survivors." He thought for a moment that Elsa was too angry to understand him, but after a moment she turned away and struck out for the nearer bank of the river, where a narrow strip of reeds maintained a precarious hold between the water and the desert. Luke followed.

They had hardly reached the cover of the reeds before the aircraft completed its turn and came racing along the river at treetop height. Luke caught a glimpse of a Japanese face at the cockpit window, hungrily scanning the surface of the water. Mochizuki again! The bomber roared past and Elsa began to pull herself through the reeds towards the bank.

Luke grabbed her arm again. "Stay here. There's no cover away from the river and that plane may come back." Elsa gave him a look of pure loathing, but remained where she was.

The aircraft did indeed come back – twice. On its first pass, it banked so that the gunner in the turret behind the cockpit could open fire. Bullets hissed through the reeds and splashed into the water, though none came close to the spot where Luke and Elsa were hiding. Whether the gunner had really spotted something or was just firing at random in the hope of flushing out a target was unclear; but after a final pass, the aircraft turned off to the east and did not return.

They remained in the reeds for some minutes before Luke judged it safe to leave cover. He and Elsa splashed through the shallow muddy water, brushing reeds aside, to the bank. As soon as they were on dry land, Elsa turned to stare at the wreck of the steamer. "They're all dead," she said harshly. "Ali, the captain – everyone."

Luke sat down on the sand, feeling suddenly very weary. "They didn't understand. I tried to warn them."

"You should have tried *harder*!"

"How?"

"You could have explained to me, I could have told them in Arabic..."

Luke shook his head. It would have taken time to make the threat clear to Elsa, and longer to translate it to the crew – and even then, would everyone have dropped what they were doing and dived overboard? No, people would have hesitated, asked questions... "I told you," he said, "there was no time – if we'd hung around, we'd all be going down with *that*..." He pointed to the centre of the river where the remains of the *Star of the Sudan*, still burning fiercely, were settling with hisses and gouts of steam as the brown water doused the flames that had consumed the vessel and its crew.

Elsa, fists clenched, was weeping helplessly. "We should have done *something*…"

Luke wondered whether he should give her a hug, but decided that in her current mood this would not be welcomed; so he merely said, "We need to find Nick and Salim."

As it turned out, Nick and Salim weren't hard to find. They emerged from the reeds a hundred yards upstream of where Luke and Elsa had come ashore.

Nick squelched towards them. "Are you all right?" Luke nodded. Elsa seemed not to hear the question. Nick watched glumly as the last remnant of the steamer slid beneath the water with a final rush of steam. "We could have been on that."

"Elsa's upset about Ali," said Luke quietly.

"The cook?" Nick sighed. "Yes – he was a good sort, poor devil."

"She thinks we should have tried harder to rescue the others."

"If I'd twigged what that aircraft was up to earlier, we might have stood a chance." Nick shook his head. "There wasn't time. If we'd been any closer when the old *Star* went up, we'd be goners too."

Luke went over to Salim, who was looking in the direction the aircraft had disappeared. His face was working with fury.

"They dare," he growled, "they dare to come to Africa and bomb people who have never done them any harm, just because they can. I pray that one day I will have them in my grasp. Then there will be a reckoning."

Luke gave his friend an awkward pat on the shoulder. Salim looked startled, as though he had forgotten that he was not alone. Then he gave a weak half-smile. "At least the four of us are still alive – thanks to you and Nick."

Luke said nothing. He didn't think he deserved thanks. Was there anything more he could have done to save the crew of the *Star of the Sudan*? He knew the question would haunt him for a long time.

He and Salim rejoined Nick and Elsa. After a long silence, Nick said, "What now?"

"We keep moving," said Luke. "It's getting dark – the temperature will start dropping. We'll freeze if we sit around."

Nick nodded. "Which way do we go?"

"Along the river. Upstream."

"We're more likely to find a farm or something downstream," Nick pointed out.

"That's true – but the whole idea of this attack was to stop us. I for one don't want to give the Sons of Destiny the satisfaction of seeing us turn tail and leg it for safety." Salim and Nick nodded agreement; Elsa said nothing. "All right, then," Luke continued, "we've at least two days' march to where my mother's mule train will be waiting for us, but we may find a village along the way and at least if we follow the river we'll have water."

Salim cleared his throat. "I'm not sure that's the best plan, Luke. I've travelled this part of the river before. It takes a wide curve just here. We'd be better to cut off the loop – if we follow the river we'll have to walk half as far again to reach the same point."

Luke was dubious. "I don't fancy wandering off into the desert and going round in circles. We don't even have a compass."

"That's all right," said Salim confidently. "We'll be travelling at night, we can navigate by the stars."

"Are you sure? At least we know the river is flowing from the south – if we leave it, won't we lose all sense of direction?"

Salim looked puzzled. "I never lose my sense of direction. I always know where north is."

"Really?" said Nick. "Where is it, then?"

Salim pointed.

"Ah, well, that's easy, we're still beside the river…"

"That doesn't make any difference. Even in the middle of a featureless desert, I would know. Any African who has spent time in the bush would know."

"How?" persisted Nick.

Salim shrugged. "How do you know when and where it is safe to cross a busy road? That's the skill you need to survive in London – without it you would die. Here, you need to know how to get to the next oasis – or you will die."

"Salim is right." Elsa wiped her eyes and nose on a sleeve that was dripping wet already. Her expression said that, while she was prepared to co-operate with Luke, she had by no means forgiven him. "I've lived here a long time, my sense of direction is pretty good too. We can guide you across the desert."

Luke gave a helpless shrug. "Then we're in your hands."

Nick was still staring across the river, to the mass of rising bubbles that marked the wreck of the steamer. "Shouldn't we try to salvage stuff? Food, for instance?"

"Probably not a good idea," said Luke. "Even if the bomb left anything to find, we'd be diving in zero visibility – and there may be crocodiles about."

Nick glanced nervously at the riverbank and shuddered. "I wasn't really that hungry, anyway."

With Salim leading, they set off at a slight angle to the river which, after half an hour or so, disappeared from sight. Their clothes began to dry, but soon, as the last light disappeared from the sky, the temperature fell sharply; it was nowhere near freezing but even so, the contrast with the fierce heat of the day was stark. Luke found that his teeth were chattering as he walked. All the party were wearing light-coloured shirts and slacks, which gave little protection against the cold as they slowly dried. Luke was grateful that he hadn't kicked off his shoes in the water, but Elsa took hers off and carried them. She had lost her headscarf. After a while, she began to limp, though she did her best to disguise this. Her injured foot was clearly still painful, but she made no complaint.

They made two rest stops, about half an hour each; it was too cold to stop moving for any longer, though Luke's leg muscles increasingly protested under the continuing strain. The country through which they walked was nothing like the sand dunes of the northern Sahara; it was merely a featureless expanse of dusty khaki-coloured sand, which shifted beneath their feet. Luke could feel blisters developing as, in the pre-dawn light, Salim called a halt and pointed towards a distant thread of grey. "There is the river again."

Luke nodded. Salim had been as good as his word. "Well done."

"There is a valley on this side with a small stream – we can rest there."

"How far?" asked Nick.

Salim shrugged. "Two hours, maybe three."

Nick sagged and groaned. Elsa merely tightened her lips and limped on at once. Luke followed, giving the back of her head an unfriendly look. All he wanted to do was collapse in a heap; but he'd be damned if he allowed himself to show any human weakness before Elsa did.

The sun was up and it was already uncomfortably hot when they reached the oasis provided by the little valley. They drank from the stream and rested in the shade of the palms that lined the watercourse.

Luke was beginning to slip into an exhausted doze when he heard Nick say, "Luke – has it occurred to you what day it is?"

Luke forced himself to concentrate. "No," he said, "I'm afraid I've rather lost track of days. What day is it?"

"It's the twenty-fifth of December," said Nick. "Christmas Day. Happy Christmas, Luke."

"Happy Christmas, Nick." Suddenly, the two cousins were laughing like lunatics, crying with laughter. After a while they calmed down a little, then looked at each other – and burst into renewed guffaws. Salim regarded his helpless friends with a faint smile. Elsa rolled her eyes.

When their hysterical mirth had finally died down, Salim became businesslike. "We can set off again later this afternoon," he said. "If we keep going, we should meet up with the mules at around dawn tomorrow."

Luke, still giggling feebly, struggled to his feet. "We'll need to eat something, then," he managed. "I'll have a look around. There may be dates or—"

He got no further. With savage yells, twenty or more armed men burst onto the scene. Four of them were soldiers in Italian Army uniform, bearing rifles. The others were local tribesmen dressed desert-style in robes and headscarves, and brandishing swords and muskets. They surrounded Luke and his companions, weapons at the ready.

Luke raised his hands, being careful to make no sudden movement. From the corner of his eye, he saw that the others were doing the same. "Elsa," he said quietly. He didn't know what Elsa could say that might get them out of this situation, but there was clearly no possibility of defending themselves, and he knew he could not hope to make himself understood. "Elsa – ask them what they want."

"The troops want to serve *Il Duce*, Signor Challenger." The booming voice of Count Claudio Gentile seemed to fill the small valley. Luke turned slowly as the giant Italian made his way towards his prisoners. "And the others – they want money. They are poor, and we have promised them enough to feed their families if they would show us where any survivors of the steamer would be sure to go seeking water. We are benefactors, you see."

"Enough!"

Luke clenched his fists on hearing the hated voice. Following Gentile appeared the slim form of Kasumi Mochizuki. The Japanese assassin was wearing her tinted glasses; she looked cool and collected. "We are not here to talk."

Gentile gave Luke a mocking bow. "My associate is right. It was a good bout we had in Khartoum, Signor Challenger. I would have welcomed a rematch. *Tristemente*, it is not to be."

Mochizuki pointed at Salim and shouted an order in Arabic. "'*Kill them,*'" Elsa translated flatly. "'*That one first.*'"

Two of the tribesmen grabbed Salim's arms and shoulders, forcing his head forwards. The medallion Luke had first seen on Salisbury Plain slipped from his shirt to hang, spinning slowly on its silver chain, from his bare neck.

A third tribesman raised his sword. His intention was unmistakable. The terrible weapon's razor edge glinted in the sun as the executioner steeled himself to strike.

13 MEDALLION

Luke gathered himself to spring. He knew that the instant he did, the Italians and their allies would open fire, but he could not stand by and watch his friend being slaughtered. From the corner of his eyes, he saw Nick and Elsa tense themselves for action.

Then one of the tribesmen bellowed a command. Salim's would-be executioner paused, sword aloft. The tribesman pointed at Salim and launched into an impassioned speech. Slowly, the executioner lowered his sword. The men who had been holding Salim let go of him and withdrew. Salim straightened up and gazed around him with a look that was dignified, if not imperious.

Luke glanced at Elsa. From the corner of his mouth, he hissed, "What's going on?"

Elsa's full attention was on the tribesmen, who were now silent and seemed to be watching Salim warily. "The man doing the talking told the others to stop, to let Salim go – I didn't catch all of it – something about the medallion he's wearing…"

"What is wrong?" Mochizuki's angry voice cut through the silence like a whiplash. "Why do they hesitate? Gentile – *che succede*? What is happening? Order them to obey!"

Gentile looked worried. "I am not sure…"

"Give the order!"

Looking very unhappy, Gentile let rip with a stream of what Luke guessed to be Amharic. The tribesmen looked at each other and at Salim. Angry muttering arose. Gentile spoke again, more assertively. The muttering burst out into open disagreement. The tribesmen gesticulated angrily. Muskets were raised and pointed, not at Luke and his friends, but at Mochizuki, Gentile, and the Italian soldiers, who suddenly looked very nervous.

Elsa's quiet translation continued. "Gentile's insisting

that they follow orders – they say he did not tell them he expected them to make war on...I'm not sure of the word – a lord? A prince? A holy man...?"

Mochizuki broke the deadlock. Uttering a Japanese oath, she snatched a pistol from her belt-holster and aimed it at Salim. The response was instant. The tribesmen lifted their muskets to their shoulders and pulled the hammers back to full-cock so that they had only to pull the triggers to fire.

"Signora Mochizuki!" Gentile's voice was urgent and pleading. "Put...the...gun...down. *Prego*...please."

For a moment, it seemed as though Mochizuki would ignore the command. But the Japanese woman, though ruthless, was not stupid. The odds against her and her men were too great. Moving slowly and carefully, she lowered the gun and placed it on the ground. Then she backed away.

The tribesmen advanced. Salim gave a quiet order, and the advance halted.

Elsa rounded on him. "You can't tell them to let those murderers go! They sank our boat! They killed Ali and the others!"

"Be quiet." Salim's voice brooked no disagreement. "These are my countrymen, not yours. More deaths now will not bring anyone back to life."

The tribesmen continued to cover Mochizuki's party

with their weapons, but made no further aggressive move as the Italians and their Japanese leader backed slowly out of the valley. As they disappeared from view, the tribesmen slowly lowered their muskets. Salim gave another command and two men moved swiftly up the valley, taking advantage of whatever cover they could.

"They will make sure our friends do not return," said Salim.

Nick was staring around, his mouth open like that of a stranded fish. "Would someone care to tell me what just happened here?"

"I don't know," said Salim. "These men are of the Tigray people, from the north of my country. I will try to find out what they are doing here, and in the company of our enemies."

He turned to the tribesmen, who faced him with something very like apprehension. Starting with the tribesman who had halted his execution, they bowed respectfully, each placing the fingers of his right hand on the tip of his nose, on his eyelid, on top of his head, and to his beard.

"Well, they look a lot friendlier now, at least," said Luke.

"They look," observed Nick, "like a bunch of lower-school kids who've been caught smoking, hauled up before the Head, and are waiting to see just how much of a telling-off they're going to get."

"You're right." As Salim and the tribesmen began an earnest but muted conversation, Luke turned to Elsa. "Can you tell what they're saying?"

Elsa was frowning with the effort of following what was being said. "It's difficult – they're speaking so fast – they're certainly afraid of Salim – no, that's not quite right – 'in awe' of him would be a better way of putting it. They're using a very respectful form of address. They're apologizing for having laid hands on him – he's saying something like 'Don't mention it', but he's asking what they're doing so far from their homes..." In replying to this question, the tribesman who was speaking lowered his voice to such an extent that Elsa gave an exasperated shrug. "It's no good, I can't hear."

"Not to worry." Moving slowly, Luke sat down with his back to the trunk of a date palm. Their captors – if that's what they still were – watched him warily, but made no hostile move. "I'm sure Salim will tell us what they're jawing about when he can. In the meantime, I've been awake all night." He closed his eyes.

The sun was higher in the sky when he woke from a doze to find that the dialogue between Salim and the tribesmen was evidently reaching a conclusion. The atmosphere among the latter had clearly lifted to an extraordinary extent. There were smiles, a series of respectful salutations and expressions of mutual esteem, and Salim left his countrymen to join Luke, Elsa (who was wide awake) and Nick (who was sound asleep). Luke elbowed his cousin in the ribs and Nick woke with a start.

As the leader of the tribesmen issued orders to his men that sent them hurrying off on some errand, Salim said, "Well, that was interesting." He paused for a moment, evidently gathering his thoughts. Luke held his tongue. He was sure Salim would tell them what they needed to know without being asked questions which were likely to be more of a hindrance than a help.

"These men are from the border with Eritrea, which is one of the Italian colonies where their troops are gathering. Gentile was telling the truth, up to a point. Their harvests have been poor, and the Italians offered them high wages to act as guides and irregular troops for himself and the Mochizuki woman. They were quite prepared to kill me out of hand, as you saw."

"Then what changed their minds?" asked Luke.

"This," said Salim. He reached into his shirt and took out the medallion.

Elsa said, "That's the Seal of Solomon. Where did you get it?"

"I've always had it. It's passed down to the eldest son in my family, when he reaches the age of thirteen. It has been for generations. My father had it before me. I thought it was just a family heirloom, but it seems to be more than that. I'm sorry to say it's not me that has so impressed the Tigray – it's this." He held the medallion up by its chain and it spun slowly, catching the dappled light that fell through the palm leaves.

"Isn't that the Star of David in the middle?" asked Nick. "I thought that was a Jewish symbol."

"Well, Solomon was Jewish," said Salim. "The Tigray claim descent from Menelik I, the son of Solomon and Sheba, just like my own family. They say the Star is the symbol of Solomon's temple – and of his Mines."

Elsa snorted derisively. "You three have King Solomon's Mines on the brain."

"If you're not interested," said Luke pointedly, "no one's making you stay."

Elsa gave him a furious look and strode off to the mouth of the valley, where she stood looking across the river, arms folded.

Luke turned back to Salim. "Does that mean the… Tigray, did you call them?…know where the Mines are?"

"I'm not sure," said Salim. "They became very cagey when I asked about that. These people are just ordinary tribesmen, you understand. They know they were wrong to threaten violence to someone who carries Solomon's Seal, they're very apologetic, and they're not at all sure what to do next. They're also worried that Gentile and his soldiers may come back here with reinforcements, or their aeroplane might return to bomb us."

Luke sat up in alarm.

"Don't worry," Salim reassured him, "that won't happen for a while yet. Gentile and the Tigray met Mochizuki at the airstrip when she landed after bombing the steamer – apparently, Gentile and she had a furious row about something – and then they all rode here. But the horses belong to the Tigray, and when the men they'd left in charge of them saw Gentile and his people heading back alone, they drove the horses off into the desert; so Gentile and Mochizuki will have to walk back to their plane. Even so, the Tigray leader, Isaias – he's the one who stopped my execution – wants us to leave as soon as possible. While you were asleep, the man in charge of the horses came in to report that his riders were bringing them back now the Italians have gone. Isaias says we can have the ones our enemies were riding. He wants to take us to speak with a holy man – a priest – who lives a day's ride in that direction." He pointed to the east. "He says this man can tell us more about King Solomon's Mines."

Luke nodded as the tribesmen returned, leading horses. "Then he definitely sounds like someone we need to see."

Nick gave the horses a jaundiced look. "You did say a day's ride?" Salim nodded, and Nick groaned, rubbing his backside in anticipation.

Luke gave Salim a grin. "So, we're on the trail of King Solomon's Mines at last. You said something would turn up."

"Yes." Salim fingered his medallion with one hand and rubbed his neck with the other. "And I am very glad it did."

Salim pointed. "That is where we are going – up there."

Luke stared upwards. "Good grief."

He was looking at a building carved from solid rock halfway up a sandstone cliff. It reminded him of the ruined city of Petra which he had visited with his mother a few years ago. "Is it a church?" he asked.

"It is," said Salim. "There are many such churches in the land of the Tigray, though I did not know there was one so far south."

"And how do we get to it?"

"We climb," Salim replied, indicating steps set into the cliff. He dismounted and handed his horse's reins to one of the tribesmen, who took them with a bow.

It was now mid-afternoon of the day after they had left the oasis. Their journey across the desert had been uneventful. Once in the early evening, and again a couple of hours after sunrise the next day, they had heard the sound of aero-engines, but it had been distant and they had not caught sight of the Italian plane. Nevertheless, Isaias had led them through as many dried-up stream beds and into the shadow of as many cliffs as he could find in order to avoid any possibility of detection.

They had made two stops during the night, of about two hours each, allowing the horses to be watered and the travellers to get some much-needed rest. Nevertheless, Luke and his companions were saddle-sore and weary by the time they reached their destination. Nick, who by his own confession was not a good rider, had suffered most from the journey, but even Elsa (whose riding had been badly affected by the tetanus jab she had received a few days earlier) was wilting by the time they reached the sprawling village at the foot of the cliff.

Isaias approached Salim and spoke in a low voice. He seemed unhappy about something. They conversed for a while. Salim frowned, and his voice became insistent, but Isaias was evidently sticking to his guns. Eventually, Salim rejoined his friends, looking annoyed.

"I'm afraid this is awkward," he said. "Isaias says that the man we must speak to is a monk, and very holy – he lives in a cell at the side of the church. Women do not see him. In any case – Isaias says – what he will have to say to us is men's business." He gave Elsa an apologetic look. "I'm sorry, I couldn't persuade him otherwise. I'm afraid you'll have to stay here. The women of the village will look after you."

Leaving Elsa speechless with indignation, Salim led the way to the worn steps leading up the rock face to the church. The last Luke saw of her, Elsa was being led away by a group of village women, chattering and exclaiming over her; he guessed that European women were rare visitors to this isolated community. She turned to give him a smouldering glance before ducking through the doorway of one of the village's adobe dwellings.

The steep and uneven steps did nothing to soothe Luke's aching muscles, but at length they reached the church. Inside, the air was cool. As Luke's eyes adjusted to the dimness he saw that the walls, pillars and ceiling of the building were painted with images of saints (some of whom were on horseback), geometrical designs and animals – lions, monkeys, snakes and other creatures that seemed to be hybrids of familiar species. The decoration was at once entirely unfamiliar and strangely restful.

Isaias led them through the church, across a small courtyard overhung by the cliff face, to a door at which he knocked respectfully. After a short pause, a voice replied – evidently with an invitation to enter, because Isaias opened the door and ushered them in. Luke had expected their guide to join them, but Isaias closed the door behind them, remaining outside.

In the light of an oil lamp, which burned in a wall-niche, Luke saw that an old man was sitting on a low stool at the opposite end of the small room. His eyes were rheumy, his skin wrinkled and his sparse hair grey. He was dressed in an immaculate white robe.

He gave his visitors a smile of great serenity. "Welcome," he said in English. "My name is Giyorgis. Please be seated."

Luke and his friends settled themselves on cushions. "Thank you, sir," said Salim. "Please allow me to introduce my friends. This is Luke Challenger. This is Nick Malone. And I am Salim Menelik."

The old man's smile broadened. "I know," he said. "I have been waiting for you for a long time."

14 THE SPEAR OF DESTINY

Denebere Village, Ethiopia

Salim regarded the old man steadily. "I am sorry, I don't understand. How did you know I would come here?"

Giyorgis gave him an enigmatic smile. "It was foretold." The smile broadened as Salim, Luke and Nick exchanged confused glances. "Not that you yourself would come, and not exactly here; but it was prophesied long ago that in a time of great danger, one would appear to a member of my order, bearing the Seal of Solomon. The Tigray who found you" – ("That's one way of putting it," muttered Nick) – "know of the prophecy; that is why they brought you here. And you also bear the name of our great ancestor, the Emperor Menelik I. It is fitting."

"And this prophecy," said Salim carefully, "does it tell you what to do when the bearer of Solomon's Seal appears?"

The old man inclined his head gravely. "Certainly. To help the bearer of the medallion on his way, as far as lies in my power."

"That's what I wanted to hear," said Nick, brightening. "I like this prophecy."

Giyorgis continued, "Before I came here, I travelled widely. I was a soldier, a scholar, an adventurer. I lived in many lands. But at last, as I grew old, I came back to Africa and joined the Order of Solomon. We are the guardians of Solomon's treasure.

"The Mines of King Solomon have been hidden so long that they have passed from history and into legend, as their creator intended. But Solomon also knew that nothing can be kept secret for ever; that sooner or later, an enemy would come, so determined, so ruthless, that no concealment would prevail against him. Against that day he established our Order, so that the bearer of his Seal should have the knowledge he needs to find the Mines, and protect their treasures – if he can."

When Salim remained silent, Luke said, "What exactly are King Solomon's Mines?"

The old man regarded him steadily for a moment. Then he said, "Luke Challenger, you and your friend Nick Malone are not of our people. Before I speak further, I must know why you seek King Solomon's Mines."

Luke said, "Our enemies, the Sons of Destiny – the ones who ordered the Tigray to murder Salim – want something from the Mines. I want to make sure they don't get it. That's all." Nick nodded confirmation.

The old man nodded and turned to Salim. "And you – as the bearer of Solomon's Seal, have you taken these to be your companions? Do you trust them to hear all the secrets you must learn to discover the Mines and deal with what you will find there?"

"Both them," said Salim solemnly, "and Elsa Fairfax."

Giyorgis paused, apparently deep in thought. "The Order of Solomon forbids my revealing its secrets to women; but if it is your judgement that she is to be trusted, whether you share with her what you will learn today is a matter for you." He looked up. "Very well. In answer to your question, King Solomon of Israel came to Ethiopia as the consort of Queen Makeda of Sheba, whose empire stretched from the headwaters of the Nile to the Red Sea and beyond.

"Solomon's people were skilled in the working of precious metals, and he dug deep beneath the mountains – for gold, diamonds and other valuable gems. The gold made him the wealthiest ruler of his age. The caverns from which he had extracted it eventually ran deeper and further than any man can tell. To protect them, he created cunning traps and pitfalls to deny thieves. And in the largest cavern, he built a great Treasure House, of which his famous Temple at Jerusalem was only a pale imitation, a mere shadow.

"Legends say that Solomon enlisted the aid of demons to raise the Treasure House." Luke shifted impatiently in his seat, and Giyorgis gave him an enigmatic smile. "I do not say that this is so; I live under the protection of the Church, and it would not do for me to suggest that one of the great kings of the Old Testament had dealings with such creatures."

He turned his attention back to Salim. "I only mention the legend because the Seal, which you now wear, was supposed to give Solomon power and mastery over the creatures who emerged from the Well of Souls beneath the Treasure House. They took the stones that had been carved for its construction, and caused them to fly through the air and settle in their allotted spaces. In this way, the task of years was accomplished in a few hours."

"Bunk," said Nick quietly.

The old man heard him, but seemed to take no offence. "No doubt," he said quietly. "I speak merely of a legend." Nick blushed and examined his fingernails. "At any rate," Giyorgis continued, once more turning his attention to Salim, "the medallion you wear is very powerful, whether or not it can control demons."

"It seems to protect its wearer," said Luke, thinking of the deflected bullet on Salisbury Plain and what had happened when Mochizuki had attempted to take the medallion by force.

"Indeed so. And you saw its effect on the Tigray tribesmen."

"They were certainly a lot friendlier to us once they'd seen it," said Salim.

Giyorgis chuckled. "They were probably afraid that, having laid hands on you, you would turn them to stone where they stood." His mood became more serious. "All I know is that the medallion has power, more power than you – or even I – can guess. Guard it well."

Luke said, "You said something about a time of danger."

The old man nodded. "The planned Italian invasion." He smiled at their startled faces. "Our community is a long way from the world, but we are not totally unaware of what is happening around us."

Luke exchanged a quick glance with Salim, who indicated with a nod that he should go on. "We believe that our enemies – those who want to invade your country, and others – are looking for the Mines because they think that, hidden somewhere inside them, is something they want."

"The Spear of Destiny," said Giyorgis calmly.

Luke stared at him. "So you know about the Spear?"

"Of course. It is one of the Mines' greatest treasures. Or most terrible secrets, depending on your point of view.

"The Spear was already ancient beyond reckoning when it was presented to Solomon by Queen Makeda. Some say that the power of Solomon's Seal was linked to the Spear; Solomon, besides being a king, had the reputation of being a great magician in his day." Nick raised his eyebrows at Luke but said nothing. "Even then, legend said that he who wielded the Spear would defeat all enemies.

"When Solomon died, the Mines were sealed and their location became a closely guarded secret. But the history of the Spear continued. It was carried into battle by the Black Pharaohs of Nubia, who conquered the whole of Egypt. Later, it was wielded by the Assyrian king Sennacherib and his descendant Nebuchadnezzar, who conquered Jerusalem and destroyed the great temple that Solomon had built. Following that catastrophe, the Spear of Destiny was lost for five hundred years."

"Until it turned up in the possession of the Roman centurion Longinus, at the Crucifixion," said Luke.

Giyorgis nodded.

"And then it was rediscovered in Jerusalem three hundred years later by Constantine the Great, the first Christian Emperor of Rome. He decided the Spear would make a terrific holy relic and took it to Constantinople—"

"Ah, no." Giyorgis held up a hand. "You must forgive me; that is what is believed in Europe. But the Order of Solomon tells a different story. Constantine did indeed demand the Spear as a treasure to grace his new capital of Constantinople; but the Judean priests gave him a copy."

Luke regarded him steadily. "So the Sons of Destiny are right. Uncle Ned told my mother that they believe the Spear of Destiny that ended up in the Imperial Treasure House in Vienna is a fake."

"It is," said Giyorgis simply. "The real Spear of Destiny was spirited away by the priests, eventually to find a safe resting place in King Solomon's Mines, where no tyrant could find it and use its power to his own ends."

"And the Sons of Destiny know this?"

The old man spread his hands. "I believe so. How they came by the knowledge – through a renegade member of our Order, or perhaps through capturing and torturing one of my fellows – I cannot say. But I believe they know where to find the Mines."

"And why," asked Luke, "do they want to kill Salim?"

Salim regarded him with surprise. "I thought they wanted to kill my father – and you."

Nick gave him a grin. "If they wanted to get your da, they've made a pretty lousy job of it – but they've had four goes at bumping you off. They've not managed it yet, but you can't say they haven't been trying."

Salim was thunderstruck. "You know, that never even occurred to me." The look he gave Giyorgis was almost plaintive. "It's a good question. Why do they want to kill me?"

"They do not want to kill you," said the old man, "except in so far as your death would make it easier for them to grasp what they really want – the Seal of Solomon." Salim's hand flew to his medallion and he stared at Giyorgis. "If they have obtained their information through the Order of Solomon," the old man continued calmly, "they know of the belief that only Solomon's Seal can open the Mines." Salim shook his head in bewilderment, evidently struggling to come to terms with this new idea.

To Luke, on the other hand, the Sons of Destiny's attacks on his friend suddenly made sense. It didn't matter to them whether Salim lived or died, if all they wanted was his medallion. The tank crew on Salisbury Plain had no doubt been told to kill Salim, and anyone with him, and recover the medallion from his body. In Khartoum, Mochizuki had tried to snatch the medallion, and when she failed had tried to kill him. Then Gentile had tried a more drastic approach. But in that case, why...?

Nick had evidently been following a similar line of thought. "If the Sons of Destiny wanted to get their hands on Salim's medallion, how did it make sense for them to bomb the *Star of the Sudan*?"

As Nick raised the question, Luke had the answer. "Mochizuki has a habit of exceeding her orders," he said. "Gentile and whoever he's working for want the medallion to get the Spear; I'm not sure Mochizuki's that bothered. Maybe she only took on the job of finding the Mines to have another crack at us. I bet that's why they had a row when she met up with Gentile after she'd sunk the poor old *Star* – Gentile must have been worried that the medallion might be at the bottom of the Nile and he'd never get his hands on it. And when the Tigray led them to us, Mochizuki tried to have Salim beheaded – maybe, after her first attempt to snatch the necklace, she'd decided to take no more chances..."

"Or maybe she just thought it would make the medallion easier to get off," said Nick. "The clasp on those chains can be really fiddly." He caught Luke's frown. "Sorry. But anyway, Salim's medallion didn't look as if it was going to protect him there, did it? He was within an ace of getting a haircut right down to his Adam's apple."

"No," said Luke. "The medallion *did* protect Salim – by showing itself. In the situation, that was all it needed to do." Nick looked unconvinced, but Luke was sure he was right. Salim had seemed knocked for six after the medallion had deflected the bullet on Salisbury Plain, and after Mochizuki's attempt to seize it; whereas when he had escaped execution by the Tigray, he had shown no sign of distress. If the medallion could only protect its owner by drawing on his strength in some way, it made sense that the protection should take the simplest form possible.

Giyorgis gave Luke and Nick an appraising stare. "You are travelling with the bearer of the Seal, and sharing the dangers that befall him. You say your aim is to keep the Spear from your enemies. I confess to being puzzled. You seem to doubt that it possesses any mystical powers; if you do not believe that it will enable the Sons of Destiny to rule the world, why do you wish to keep it out of their hands?"

Luke had thought a good deal about this. "I don't know whether the Spear has any mystical powers or not. In fact, before Nick and I saw Salim's medallion in action, I'd have said I didn't believe in mystical powers of any kind. But the Sons of Destiny do, and the first step to ruling the world is to believe that you can. The Spear may or may not be mystical, but it's certainly powerful. If the Sons of Destiny can get their hands on it, they'll be confident they can do anything. And with Hitler, Mussolini and the Emperor of Japan on the rampage, they may turn out to be right. If we can stop them getting the Spear, we hit them where it hurts."

"In their self-belief," said Giyorgis.

Luke gave him a startled glance. "That's right."

The old man gave a slow smile. "You are a philosopher, Luke Challenger."

Salim looked stricken. "It seems, then, that we have played into our enemy's hands."

Giyorgis gave him an inquiring glance. "How so?"

"If they truly need Solomon's Seal to open King Solomon's Mines, I've obligingly brought it to them! I should have stayed away from Ethiopia altogether!"

"But the Sons of Destiny tried to get the medallion for the first time when you were still in England," Luke pointed out, "and they've been trying ever since. Sooner or later they'll succeed." He took a deep breath. "It seems to me that the only way we can be sure they won't get their hands on the Spear of Destiny is if we get to the Mines first, and destroy it."

Giyorgis inclined his head gravely. "The Order of Solomon is of the same opinion."

Salim was staring at his medallion in wonder. "There is a great deal about this that I do not understand."

Giyorgis gave a regretful half-smile. "I wish I could enlighten you further. Many secrets have been lost over time, even to my Order. We know, for instance, that once the way to the Mines is open, any intruders can expect to meet traps and pitfalls set by Solomon to protect his treasure, but we do not know how many there are, or their nature.

"However, what I can do, I will. I shall give Isaias detailed instructions on how to reach the Mines, and he and two of his men will guide you." Giyorgis looked troubled. "But I must warn you: once you reach the country around the Mines, you will have to deal with the Kukuana."

"They really exist?" said Luke.

"They do. The Order of Solomon traces its ancestry back to the Emperor Menelik I, and through him to Solomon and Sheba, creators of the Mines. But the

Kukuana are the tribe that live in the country around the Mines. They provided the labour that dug the shafts, tunnels and caverns, extracted the gold and carved the stones to make the Treasure House. They regard themselves as the guardians of the Mines, and long ago they rebelled against the rule of the Order of Solomon.

"Your countryman Allan Quatermain visited the Mines more than fifty years ago. He helped overthrow King Twala and restore the rightful heir, Ignosi, to his family's throne. After that, though Ignosi kept his promise to Quatermain to keep European traders and missionaries out of his country, he guided his people into more peaceful ways, and relations between them and the Order improved. But when Ignosi died, a dark shadow descended on the land of the Kukuana. Their visits to surrounding tribes ceased, and no one who crossed their borders since that time has returned."

"Dinosaur-infested plateaus; seas swarming with giant squid, rogue submarines and pirates – and now a country from which no one returns," said Nick. "We do pick all the fun places."

"Will the Kukuana acknowledge my medallion, as the Tigray do?" asked Salim.

The old man shrugged. "In Ignosi's day, yes. Now? I do not know." He looked each of his audience straight in the eye as he continued, "The Mines of King Solomon are perilous, and the journey to reach them is not one to be undertaken lightly. I will help you reach the Mines if that is your wish; but I must counsel you that if you continue on that road, you will walk with death every step of the way."

"That's grand," said Nick breezily. "He can carry our packs for us when we get tired."

Salim and Luke said nothing; they merely nodded.

Giyorgis raised a hand in blessing. "Then go with God."

15 TREK

"**W**ell?" said Elsa when Luke, Nick and Salim had collected her from the village women. "Did you have a nice time with your precious monk while I was being poked and prodded and fussed over by those old *hens*?"

Luke regarded her with annoyance. Elsa seemed to blame him for everything – his mother's illness, the attack on the steamer and now her treatment by the Tigray, none of which had been his fault. He had begun to consider Elsa Fairfax, attractive and spirited though she might be, as a thundering nuisance. He had never had an older sister, but he was sure that if he had, she would have been exactly like Elsa.

"I'd have thought," he said shortly, "that being left with the women, you might have had the sense to try and find out if they knew anything about the Mines…"

Elsa gave him a furious look. "Oh, would you? And what would have been the point of that? The men here don't tell their women anything. All they wanted to talk about was clothes and babies and cooking. They've been driving me mad! And why should I ask them about your stupid Mines? I don't want to go there!"

At this point, Luke should have sympathized, soothed Elsa's ruffled feelings and explained what they had learned from Giyorgis. But he was tired and on edge. It hadn't been his decision to keep Elsa out of the meeting with the old priest. He could understand her anger at being left with the women of the village – but then, Elsa seemed to be angry at everything, pretty much all the time, and this was getting on his nerves. Luke had had enough of her; his Challenger temper was on the point of boiling over. So it was particularly unfortunate that Elsa chose this moment to say, "So, if you've quite finished fooling around listening to fairy stories, can we be on our way now? Did you ask the people here to help us find your mother's mule train? Or didn't you have the sense?"

Luke exploded. "We are not going to find the mule train. We're going to King Solomon's Mines – and you can go to blazes!"

Even Elsa looked taken aback by the vehemence of Luke's outburst. Nick kept his expression carefully neutral. He had long ago learned that the only way of dealing with Luke in this mood was to let him get everything off his chest.

Salim stirred uncomfortably. "Luke, perhaps we should tell Elsa—"

"No!" Luke was seething with rage. "If she doesn't want to come with us, I don't see why we should tell her anything. If she knows our plans, she'd probably just get herself captured by Gentile and Mochizuki and blab the whole shooting match!"

"I would not blab!" stormed Elsa. "And I wouldn't get captured in the first place!"

A small crowd was gathering. The men of the village muttered disapprovingly at the sight of a girl asserting herself, while the women peered out of windows and doorways, giggling delightedly at Elsa's temerity and her companions' discomfiture.

"Nobody asked you to come to the Mines anyway," Luke pointed out. "Finding them is our show, and it's pretty certain to be dangerous—"

"Too dangerous for a *girl*, you mean?"

"If you like!"

"So what's your plan? To go sniffing after these mythical Mines and leave me in the lurch?"

"We wouldn't be leaving you in the lurch. The people here will see you safely to the mule train, you can go on to the dig and wait for my mother there."

"While you go swanning across deserts and mountains with Salim, when your mother promised to look after him…"

"Salim isn't a kid, he's chosen to come to the Mines with us."

"You're supposed to be trying to keep him out of danger, not taking him into it."

"Talk sense! Salim will be in danger wherever he is while the Sons of Destiny are looking for the Mines. But don't worry, *you* won't be if you don't come with us."

Elsa fumed. "How dare you! Do you think I'm scared to go with you?"

"I don't know and I don't care. Stay here or go on to the dig, it's all the same to me."

"And when your mother finds out that you left a poor defenceless girl to fend for herself among strangers," Elsa said, with heavy irony, "do you think she'll be happy?"

With an effort, Luke mastered his anger. Elsa had a point. Harriet Challenger would blow a fuse if he dumped her precious assistant in the middle of nowhere. He glowered at Elsa and said nothing.

Elsa returned his stare for an uncomfortable length of time. Then she squared her shoulders, seeming to come to a decision. "Well," she snapped, "if you three are determined to make fools of yourselves, I don't suppose I can tie you up, and the men here would take your side if I tried to stop you, so I suppose I'll have to come with you. I can certainly shoot straighter and go further and faster on foot than the best of you anyway."

"I thought you were a poor defenceless girl?"

"We'll see about that, won't we?"

Later that night, as the boys sat around a fire, Salim said, "Luke..."

"No."

"You don't even know what I was going to say."

"Yes I do. You were going to say that now Elsa's decided she's coming with us, shouldn't we tell her what Giyorgis told us?"

"Something like that," admitted Salim.

"Elsa's dug her heels in every time anyone's even mentioned the Mines," said Luke. "Has she really changed her mind? Or does she just want to know where we're going so she can go sneaking back to my mother and tell her what we're up to? I reckon we shouldn't tell Elsa anything until she's proved she's really with us now." He gave the fire a moody poke and sparks danced into the velvet sky. "But you're the man with the medallion. It's up to you."

Salim shot an unhappy glance at Nick, who shrugged. He sighed. "All right, Luke. I won't say anything to Elsa for now. But I think you're wrong not to trust her."

Luke looked over his shoulder. In the light of an oil lamp, Elsa was chatting animatedly to the women of the village. For some reason, her change of attitude worried him. He poked the fire again. Flames leaped and crackled.

Two days later, it felt to Luke as though he and the patient, plodding camel on which he sat had been trudging through the desert for ever.

There was no animal life visible in the endless, dusty landscape. Occasionally Luke saw a set of smooth, curving marks winding across the parched sands, which he knew were the tracks of a snake; but no snake, not even a lizard, had appeared.

There were flies, though. They buzzed and bit, from time to time goading the camels into ill temper and their riders into furious despair.

The villagers of Denebere, poor as they were, had done their best to supply the travellers for their journey. Having escaped the wreck of the steamer with only the clothes they were wearing at the time, Luke and his companions were now dressed for desert travel in white robes with long scarves wrapped loosely around their heads and necks. Each carried a goatskin containing water, and a pack of food.

Their guides – Isaias, taciturn and still much in awe of Salim; Abele, weather-beaten and hawk-eyed; and Keshe, young and light-hearted – seemed to shrug off any discomfort. Salim rode his camel with evident enjoyment, clearly relishing the trip and looking at what scant diversions the landscape had to offer with interest. Elsa, too, seemed barely to feel the heat and rode her camel comfortably. But Luke found long-distance camel-riding painful and undignified, while Nick was clearly struggling to stay on his beast, which he cursed in low, savage tones throughout the journey: "You half-witted, hairy bag of old bones; you stinking, swaying, spitting spawn of Beelzebub; you evil-tempered, four-left-footed, ghastly, gurgling, galumphing gawdelpus…"

The Tigray were armed with their favoured daggers. In addition, Isaias carried his musket, Abele an ancient Lee-Enfield .303, probably a relic of the Great War, and

Keshe a Martini-Henry of even greater vintage. Giyorgis had, before their departure, unexpectedly presented Salim with a Mauser rifle – old, but carefully cleaned and maintained, seemingly a relic of his adventurous former life. Salim had thanked him diplomatically, but soon after their departure had pressed the gun on Luke. "You're much more likely to hit whatever you aim at," he had said. Elsa, who was clearly itching to get her own hands on the rifle, glowered over this exchange but said nothing.

The sun was low in the sky behind the travellers when they crested a small rise and saw a dark, jagged line stretched across the desert in the far distance. Isaias pointed to this and said something to Salim in Amharic. Salim nodded thoughtfully.

He turned to Luke. "He says those are the mountains that surround the land of the Kukuana." He asked Isaias a question and, on receiving the reply, went on, "Those two big mountains further west – the ones with snow on the peaks – are where Quatermain and his friends crossed into the country. They were following an old map made over four centuries ago by a Portuguese explorer, who claimed to have found the Mines; but he chose a poor road, and died in the mountains. In fact, Quatermain's party found his frozen body in a cave, and nearly shared his fate.

"Isaias says he will take us a different way, where the path across the desert is a little easier. Also, it is less likely to be watched."

Luke nodded. "I'd be amazed if the Sons of Destiny aren't on the lookout for us." He reached for his water-skin – and gave a grunt of dismay. "What the devil?" The skin was flaccid; a damp trail down the camel's flank showed where the water had flowed from the skin to be sucked up by the thirsty sand.

Nick let out a startled exclamation as he discovered that his own water-skin was similarly empty. A swift check showed that the same was true of Elsa's, Abele's and Keshe's skins. Only Isaias's and Salim's were still half full of the life-giving liquid.

Salim snapped a question at Isaias, who spread his arms wide in denial and spoke volubly.

Luke urged his camel alongside Salim's. "What is he saying?"

"I asked him how our water-skins come to be empty; whether they leaked because they were ill-made? He says that his people gave us the best water-skins they have, he is at a loss to explain how they have failed."

Nick stared at his friends in dismay. "So what do we do now?"

Elsa said, "We can't go on without water."

Luke's Challenger jaw set obstinately. "I'm not going

back." He nodded towards Isaias. "Salim, please ask him if there is any water up ahead."

Salim asked the question. On receiving Isaias's reply, he said, "Perhaps. There is a small oasis – in fact, the one where Allan Quatermain's companion Sir Henry Curtis found his brother. But in recent years, it has been drying up. The trees around it have died and he is not sure there will be any water at all there, now."

"If that's the only place there's even a chance we'll find water," said Luke, "then that's where we're going."

"Even if we travel all night," said Salim, "we cannot arrive there before dawn tomorrow. We will use all our remaining water on the journey; and what if the oasis is dry? We will be three days' march from Denebere with no water, and three days from the mountains if we press on."

"We would die in the desert," said Elsa flatly. "If we turn back now, we can just reach Denebere with the water we have."

Nick gave an unhappy nod. "That makes sense. Then we could sort out the water situation and come back..."

"Giving Mochizuki and Gentile almost an extra week to get to the Mines and find the Spear of Destiny," said Luke.

Elsa scowled. "I still think it would be suicide to go on."

"But admitting defeat to go back," said Nick. "I'm not a gambling man, but I'll risk a flutter now and then. I say we go on." Luke nodded, and turned to Salim. If he sided with Elsa, their quest to find the Mines would be over.

Salim considered for a moment. Then he pointed towards the north-east. "We had better be moving. We have a long night ahead of us if we want to find the oasis by dawn." He urged his camel forward. Luke and Nick followed suit. Elsa shook her head in exasperation, but at length she clicked her tongue and her camel followed the others.

They reached the oasis an hour after sunrise. It was already hot. Luke's tongue felt twice its usual size and he was light-headed with weariness. He was not encouraged to see that the oasis consisted of a few dead and withered trees and some dry, bleached grasses surrounding a small sandy depression. There was no sign of water. "What now?" he asked.

"Now," said Salim, "we dig."

Isaias dismounted and barked an order to his men. Abele and Keshe each took a tin plate from their packs and joined him in the centre of the depression. Isaias pointed, and the men began to scoop sand, flinging platefuls of it over the rim of the depression.

They all took turns. Isaias was scandalized that such an important person as Salim should take part in such demeaning manual labour, but Salim insisted, scooping sand with a will. They took half-hour turns, at first with three diggers working at once; then, with the hole narrowing as they went deeper, with two.

The hole was over four-feet deep when the sand began to grow damp. Another eighteen inches, and a little water began to appear in the bottom.

Luke scooped up a mouthful of water; it was muddy and warm, but did not smell or taste foul. He breathed a sigh of relief. "Well, it'll take some time to fill the water-skins, but it seems we won't be dying of thirst just yet."

After all the members of the party had slaked their thirst, Luke walked over to the camels and took the Mauser from its bindings. "We haven't seen any signs of being followed," he said, "but I don't want Gentile and Mochizuki jumping us again. I'm going to have a look around."

Nick nodded distractedly. He was already engaged in a discussion with Salim and Isaias about how they could ensure that the skins were properly watertight this time. Abele and Keshe were busy digging, and Elsa was rummaging in packs to find bread and dried meat for their breakfast and appeared not to have heard.

Luke trudged up a small hill. Taking care not to

show himself at its summit, he scanned the desert. He could see nothing moving in any direction. Further on in their line of march, the sand gave way to scrubland. Behind this lay the mountains surrounding Kukuanaland. They looked no nearer than they had the previous evening.

Once Luke had satisfied himself that there was no sign of their enemies, he began to take notice of his immediate vicinity. He realized that the summit of the hill was irregular, covered with humps and lines. Idly, Luke began to scrape away the covering of sand. Before long, he had uncovered a rectangular slab; either of stone, or mud brick baked so hard it might as well have been stone.

Startled, he looked around, and realized that the pattern of humps and lines extended all over the hill and beyond. At the foot of the slope, he could make out a pattern of squares, rectangles and parallel lines. As the picture swam into focus, he became aware that he was looking over the ruins of a city. The squares and rectangles were houses, stores and temples; the parallel lines, streets.

Intrigued, Luke walked down the side of the hill and along one of the dusty alleyways. Windblown sand drifted across the ruins. He came to a wide open space flanked by the remains of buildings on two sides, and realized that he was standing on a wide road that swept across the desert towards the distant mountains.

A regular shape alongside the road caught his eye. It seemed to be the base of a pillar, and as he looked more closely, he saw that carved on its stone surface were two lines that met in a point, like the top of a triangle. He rested the gun against the column, and began to scrape away at the sand.

A few minutes later, he had uncovered the carving: two interlocking triangles within a circle. The Star of David, Solomon's Seal, the same device that adorned Salim's medallion. Luke stood up and stepped back several paces to examine it. Could this mean that he had found a highway built by King Solomon, perhaps leading to the distant mountains and his fabulous Mines?

It was at this point that Luke heard a sound that chilled his blood – a low, coughing growl from right behind him. He turned slowly.

A lion crouched in the sand, barely ten feet from him. Its lips were pulled back in a snarl to reveal teeth like ice picks.

Luke backed away slowly. The lion's growl deepened and it shuffled forward, head low and belly to the ground, in the manner of all hunting cats, keeping the distance between them the same.

Luke risked a glance behind him. He was still several

paces away from his rifle. Could he reach the Mauser, turn, aim and fire before the lion was upon him? He knew he could not.

The lion tired of this waiting game. It shook its mane, gave a savage roar, and gathered itself to spring.

18 DESERT

Benishangul Region, Ethiopia

The lion bunched its powerful muscles and hurled itself at Luke. He threw himself to one side in a desperate bid to avoid the creature's leap – to no avail. With awesome agility, the great cat adjusted its flight in mid-air.

He heard a crack like thunder. Then the lion was upon him, its huge weight crashing into his body and skittling him over the sand. Luke closed his eyes and waited for the tearing of the beast's claws, the rending of its teeth, that would rip the life from his body.

Neither came. The great tawny body lay across his, unmoving. Luke opened his eyes. Inches away from his face, the lion's muzzle was still set in a snarl, but the single eye that faced him was cold and unseeing. Even as Luke watched, it began to glaze in death.

Elsa Fairfax stood about a hundred yards away on the small hill that he had recently vacated. As he watched, she lowered Abele's Lee-Enfield from its firing position against her shoulder and, with a curt "Don't move!" started down the hill.

Keeping the rifle trained on the lion, she walked steadily towards it until she was close enough to stir it with a foot. Only then did she lower her rifle, and say, "Sometimes they're shamming."

Luke pushed at the creature's body, which lay across him, heavy but unresisting. With Elsa's assistance he succeeded in rolling it aside, and struggled to his knees, sore, panting, but alive.

Elsa gave him a cold, hard stare. "You," she opined, "are not safe out."

Luke managed to gasp out the word, "Thanks."

Elsa regarded him steadily, and it gradually dawned on Luke that she was absolutely furious – not just angry or frustrated, as he had seen her many times before, but consumed with rage.

"You *never*," she told him through gritted teeth,

"go off alone like that. And you never, *ever* put down your rifle."

At any other time, in any other circumstances, Luke would have made an indignant response. But he owed Elsa his life, there was no question of it. He had been inexcusably careless, and he understood that her anger with him was not personal but professional – the anger of an expert who sees an amateur botch something so badly as to put himself in danger. He bowed his head and nodded.

Elsa turned away from him and crouched to examine the lion. When she spoke again, her voice was nearly normal. "Old male. Look at his back teeth – worn down to nubs. Kicked out of the pride when a youngster came along and fought him – see those claw marks on his flank? Starving without his lionesses to hunt for him – isn't that just like a male! He's probably been hiding out in these ruins, living off frogs and lizards until you came along. Only old lions turn man-eaters – you're the only prey stupid enough to wander within reach and too slow to run away."

Luke made no protest at this characterization. He'd been saved, now he was being lectured, and he knew that it served him right. "Thanks," he said again. "Er – how…?"

"I looked around and saw you were missing. I asked

the others where you'd gone; then I grabbed Abele's rifle and followed your tracks."

"Well, I'm glad you did. I—" Luke got no further. The rest of his companions appeared at the top of the hill, running towards him.

"What's happening?" demanded Nick. "Who fired that shot?" Luke and Elsa moved aside and he caught sight of the lion's body and skidded to a halt. "Hell's teeth!"

While Luke explained to Nick and Salim what had happened – taking care to admit his own carelessness and give Elsa full credit for the rescue and for her shooting, Isaias and the other guides engaged in furious mutual recriminations for letting one of their charges wander into danger. When Salim called a halt to this, Abele, a picture of wounded dignity, marched up to Elsa and held out his hands for his rifle. Elsa coolly slipped the safety catch on, handed it to him and folded her arms.

Luke stepped across to where he had left the Mauser and picked it up. He carried it across to where Elsa was standing and held it out to her. Elsa looked startled; but after a moment's hesitation, she took the rifle and, for the first time since he had known her, gave Luke a brief smile.

"It's a pity you had to shoot," Salim told Elsa. "If our

enemies are within earshot, that might bring them down upon us."

"I didn't have much choice," Elsa pointed out.

Salim gave her a half-smile. "You had no choice at all. I was making an observation, not a criticism."

"You can blame my stupidity for the fact that Elsa had to fire," said Luke.

"Well." Salim looked down at the body of the lion, then up to the distant hills. "It can't be helped now. Maybe no one heard the shot. Let us hope so. We'll rest up today and move on towards nightfall. We still have most of the desert to cross."

The day passed slowly. The Tigray had constructed sunscreens out of spare robes and scarves slung between the dead trunks of trees, and the travellers slept fitfully in their shade. Their guides, occupying the small hill Luke had found earlier, took turns to act as guard and lookout.

As the sun began to sink again, Luke opened his eyes from a doze to find Salim and Isaias deep in discussion. He waited for a break in the conversation, and then said to Salim, "That city down there – do you know its name?"

Salim shook his head. "Perhaps Isaias does." He put

the question to their chief guide and translated the answer: "He says there are many cities in the desert, all ruined, inhabited now only by ghosts." Salim listened for a moment, then continued his translation. "The people who built them disappeared long ago, no man can say how or why. The world turns, nations have risen and fallen, only the desert remains. For the days of the world are long, but the lives of men are short and pass as the sighing of wind among the reeds."

Luke thought this was more poetical than helpful. "But you saw the carving on the pillar. Was this one of Solomon's cities? And the road – could it be Solomon's Road?"

Salim spoke and Isaias replied. "He says it is possible. Solomon is said to have built many roads. But he does not know for sure." Salim gave Luke a faint smile. "You would like reassurance that the Mines are real: that we are not wasting our time on a wild goose chase. Don't worry. The Mines exist, I'm sure of it. And we shall find them." He stretched and checked the angle of the sun. "Speaking of which, we had better make ready to march."

Luke was tightening the straps that held his camel's saddle in place when Abele, who had been on guard, hurried into the camp and held a brief, urgent conversation with Isaias. Salim listened to their conversation with a frown, and beckoned to Luke, Nick and Elsa.

From the top of the hill, they watched a column of dust rise from the desert along the line of what Luke thought of as Solomon's Road, many miles away but clearly coming towards them.

"Gentile?" asked Luke.

"And Mochizuki," muttered Nick.

"A patrol, sent out by them to intercept us, anyway. And on horseback." Salim gave a mirthless grin. "That gives them speed, but they can't move far from water. They are probably heading here – we must leave nothing to let them know that we have passed this way."

Nick was aghast. "What about the well we dug?"

"Anyone could have done that," said Elsa. "Herdsmen, camel traders. We just have to partly fill it in again so the digging doesn't look recent."

"Will that fool them?" asked Nick.

"Hopefully." Salim shrugged. "If not, it doesn't help them much. We have several hours' start, and we will be out in the desert under cover of darkness before they reach this place."

They returned to the camels and completed their preparations for departure hurriedly and in silence. An hour later, the small band had disappeared into the desert, and in the little oasis there remained no sign that they had ever been there.

Salim called a halt just after midnight.

Luke was bone-weary and saddle-sore beyond belief, but he said, "Are you sure? Gentile and Mochizuki may not be far behind us."

"Perhaps," said Salim, "but it can't be helped. Even camels can't go on indefinitely. They need rest and so do we. Two hours."

The moon, in its last quarter, was low in the sky when Luke awoke to sounds of confusion. He threw off the blanket he had spread over himself against the night chill, and joined the group of travellers who, in English and Amharic, all seemed to be talking at once.

"What is it?" he demanded.

Salim's voice was strained. "The camels."

"What about them?"

"They've gone."

Luke gawped at him. "What do you mean, gone? They were hobbled, weren't they?" He knew that their guides were always careful, after the camels' loads had been removed, to tether the beasts' legs in order to prevent them from wandering off.

Salim made an impatient noise. "Of course they were! Either the hobbles weren't tied properly, or..." He gestured helplessly.

"Can't we round them up?" asked Nick.

"In darkness?" Luke shook his head. "It would take hours; and if we wait for daybreak, we could have Gentile and Mochizuki down on us like a ton of bricks before we even find the camels. In any case, if we just go blundering off into the desert, we're more likely to lose each other than to find the wretched beasts."

"Nevertheless, we need them. My men will not lose themselves." Salim issued a series of orders. Abele and Keshe melted away into the darkness. "I have sent them to look for the camels. I have told them to be back within an hour, whether they have succeeded or not. Then we must go."

In the event, Abele returned empty-handed. Keshe arrived a few minutes later leading a single camel.

Luke was horrified by the loss of their mounts, but Salim remained stoical. "One camel is better than no camel at all," he said. "It will have to carry our stores. We can take only essentials – water, the guns, a little food for us and grain for the camel. We will bury the rest."

A short time later, as Luke and Nick were digging a hole to bury their surplus baggage, Luke said quietly, "Someone's trying to stop us – make us go back."

Nick stopped digging and stared at him. "How d'you make that out?"

"The leaking water-skins – maybe that was an accident, though Salim said the villagers gave us the best they had – and in any case, one or two skins might develop a leak, but five? And now the camels. Isaias and his men are experts in travelling the desert, they wouldn't do something as stupid as forget to hobble their camels, or use a hobble that would break."

"So what are you saying? That one of us is a traitor? Maybe working for the Sons of Destiny?" Nick's expression was appalled. "But who? Isaias, or one of his men?"

"No idea," said Luke. "But we can't trust anyone. Keep your eyes peeled."

"Man-eating lions, and now a snake in the grass," complained Nick. "There's altogether too much wildlife in this blasted desert, if you ask me."

The remainder of the journey passed in a nightmare. Without the camels, the travellers had to walk, and their speed was drastically reduced. Each terrible mile merged into the next: heat, thirst, exhaustion and clouds of biting insects all made a contribution to their misery. To begin with, Nick almost seemed to prefer walking to the torment of riding, but soon even he began to wish they had not lost their mounts as, footsore and stumbling with weariness, the little band pressed on. The mountains that surrounded the country of the Kukuana seemed to inch over the horizon towards them, slowly, infinitely slowly.

Sometime during the third night since they left the oasis, the New Year arrived. "Do you realize," Nick said to Luke during their next brief rest stop, "it's 1935?"

Luke poured sand from his left boot. "Doesn't look like much of an improvement on 1934, to me." Nick gave a weak chuckle, which turned into a hacking cough. Dust and lack of moisture had not been kind to their throats.

It sometimes seemed to Luke, over the long miles that followed, that it was only pride that kept him going. He wasn't going to show weakness in front of Elsa, whose opinion of him was already low enough and who, in her turn, seemed just as reluctant to admit any discomfort to him. He was dimly aware that Nick was finding the going just as tough as he was, and even the Ethiopians were struggling. As the march continued to take its toll, Luke found that for long periods he was moving like an automaton, his legs shuffling onward while his mind floated in a detached haze.

It came as some surprise, therefore, when at dawn on the fourth day since they had lost the camels, their guides led them into the ruins of an old fort, and Luke, having slumped against a crumbling wall, saw the mountains of Kukuanaland towering above them less than three miles away. The cliffs were over two thousand feet high and apparently sheer. The sight took him back to his journey to the Lost World, which had presented a similarly formidable obstacle.

Salim crossed to him, and offered a water-skin. Luke shook his head wearily. "Need to save water," he muttered.

"Not a bit of it!" Salim seemed positively cheerful. "There's a well here – a deep one. This is water from it – it's fresh, and practically cold!"

Luke gazed at him dully for a moment. Then he grabbed the skin and drank thirstily. After days of drinking water half full of sand and raised to body heat by the sun, it was nectar.

After a while, Salim took the skin from Luke, who glared at him. "Not too much," Salim cautioned. "You can have more later." He passed Luke a strip of dried meat from their dwindling stores. "Chew on this, with a sip of water to help it go down. You'll feel better presently."

Luke chewed his meat, watching as Nick and Elsa were similarly recovered by Abele and Keshe. When he had finished it he found that he did, indeed, feel much better. He limped across to where Salim and Isaias were peering over the ramparts at the sheer cliff face.

"What is this place?" he asked.

"One of the Emperor Menelik's forts," Salim told him. "Menelik the Second, obviously, not the First. He set out to subjugate the warlords who ruled much of the country in the last century, and created Ethiopia as we know it today."

He pointed. "See that cleft running diagonally up the cliff? That's our way into the country of the Kukuana. We'll reach it tonight, rest up at the foot and start the climb at first light tomorrow. According to Isaias, the path up starts at the end of the valley over there."

"You mean," said Luke tonelessly, "the one with smoke coming from it?"

"What?" Salim stared and said something sharply to Isaias, who made a terse reply. Nick and Elsa, Abele and Keshe, seeing that something was up, came to join them and stared at the thin spiral of smoke rising into the morning sky.

"Gentile," said Nick, and swore.

Luke nodded. "And Mochizuki. Sitting in our way like a pair of vultures – and I don't suppose for an instant they're alone."

Isaias gave Keshe a curt order. The young Ethiopian nodded and slipped away.

Salim turned to the others. "Keshe will find out what forces they have."

"Can't we find another way up?" asked Luke.

"There is no other way up," said Salim. "Except the one Quatermain's party used, and that is too far for us to reach on foot and hunted by our enemies. I'm afraid this time, Signor Gentile and Captain Mochizuki have got the better of us. There is no way we can get past them without being seen. We are well and truly stuck."

17 ELEPHANTS

Mountains of Kukuanaland
January 1935

Keshe's report, when he returned to deliver it, was not encouraging.

"They're there, all right," translated Salim. "Gentile and Mochizuki. They have troops with them – Italian regulars. They have evidently learned not to rely on local forces – they don't want any more defections if I produce my medallion again."

They were squatting in one of the fort's remaining buildings. There was just enough of the roof left to provide some shade from the midday sun.

"Didn't Keshe say something about elephants?" said Elsa, who had been following their young guide's report closely.

"Yes – he almost stumbled upon a herd while he was circling round to spy on Gentile. He doesn't think the Italians know they're there."

The hours of Keshe's absence had given Luke the opportunity to think about their situation. The young Tigray's report seemed to him to offer an opportunity to evade their enemies – but there was something else to be dealt with first.

"I think I can see a way of getting past Gentile and Mochizuki," he said. "But before we make any more plans, there's something we need to clear up." Nick caught Luke's glance, and nodded. "We need to ask ourselves, who's the traitor in our midst?"

Salim stared at him. "Traitor?"

"Yes. Nick and I think someone in our party is trying to stop us reaching the Mines. Remember our leaking water-skins. They didn't just empty themselves." Luke turned to Nick. "You examined them – what did you find?"

"Punctures," said Nick promptly. "Each skin had several little punctures. Poor workmanship – when they were being made, someone must have been very careless with a needle."

"I don't think so," said Luke quietly. "I think someone was very careful with a needle. Don't you think it was convenient that we were left with just enough water to get back to Denebere?"

Nick nodded. Salim and Elsa exchanged a worried glance. The Tigray, not understanding the conversation but aware of the change in atmosphere, shifted uneasily.

"Then there were the camels. They were hobbled, yet they wandered off. Don't tell me all their hobbles broke at once – one or two, maybe: never all seven. The camel Keshe found didn't have a hobble. It hadn't snapped, it had been removed, or cut off."

Elsa stared at him. "Who would do a thing like that?"

"Not the guides!" said Salim stoutly.

"No," said Luke, "not the guides. Giyorgis chose them; he wouldn't have sent anyone he didn't trust. And they all believe in you, Salim, and the power of your medallion. They wouldn't have sabotaged our water supply or let our camels loose – unless you'd ordered them to do so."

Salim gave him a wintry smile. "Am I under suspicion, then?"

"No. You have at least as much reason to get to the Mines as Nick and I have. If anything can make the

Italians think twice about invading Ethiopia, losing the Spear of Destiny might, and you know it."

"That leaves, you, Nick and Elsa," said Salim. "And I take it you are not making a confession."

"No, and I'm not accusing Nick."

All eyes were now on Elsa.

"You've always hated the idea of us going to the Mines," said Luke. "Is that because you didn't believe in them? Because you'd convinced yourself you were following my mother's wishes? Because you thought it was too dangerous? Or is there another reason?"

Elsa looked him straight in the eye. "I'm surprised it's taken you this long to guess."

Nick was thunderstruck. "But...your water-skin was damaged as well," he said.

"You would have been suspicious earlier if it hadn't been," said Elsa calmly. "Sticking a needle in my own water-skin was the easy part – sneaking up behind the rest of you while you weren't looking and poking holes in yours was a lot harder. Abele nearly caught me at it."

Salim gave her a wounded look. "We could all have died of thirst."

"I wanted you to turn back!"

"And the camels?" said Salim.

"I took their hobbles off while you were asleep."

Salim sighed. "Also because you wanted us to turn back?"

"Yes! And it would have worked, if you hadn't all been so pig-headed."

Luke regarded her steadily. "Are you going to tell us why?"

"Because of what my great-grandfather did."

Luke was taken aback. Whatever answer he had been expecting, it wasn't this. "Your great-grandfather?"

The look Elsa gave him was almost amused. "Your mother always says you don't take enough interest in people. My name is Elsa Fairfax – of course, the surname is my father's name. My mother changed hers when she married – have you never heard of that quaint English custom?"

Luke cursed himself. He could already guess the rest.

"My mother's maiden name was Florence Quatermain. Her father was Harry Quatermain. And his father was..."

"Allan Quatermain," concluded Nick. "Who found King Solomon's Mines."

"I grew up with the story, and the book." Elsa's voice was low and bitter. "When I was little, I thought my great-grandpa was a hero. But then I thought about all the death and suffering his arrival brought down upon the Kukuana people, and he didn't seem so heroic any more.

"Then my father died, and I came to live in Africa. My father's family has a farm here in Ethiopia. One of the servants there was a Kukuana. He had escaped from the mountains – he wouldn't talk much about why he'd left, but it was clear from what he did say that since Ignosi's death the Kukuana people were living in terrible fear, worse than in the days of King Twala. And my great-grandfather was responsible for that! Imagine how that made me feel.

"Then your mother offered me a job, helping her dig up bones that would prove that the whole human race originated in Africa. That seemed like a worthwhile thing to do. But then, along comes her son and his friend, and they want to find the Mines, and they spin some yarn about a holy Spear when really, just like my great-grandpa, all they want is treasure – and, just like him, they have a prince with them, and why does he want to find the Kukuana if not to lay claim to the crown?"

Elsa's voice had risen; now it dropped so low that the others had to strain to hear her last words. "I would never have betrayed you to your enemies. But I did everything I could to stop you reaching the Mines. I could see it all happening again – war, death, destruction, just like it did when Great-Grandpa Quatermain came here, and I had to stop it. I had to."

Nick glared at Elsa. "So the miserable time we've been having, walking the soles off our boots and half-dying of thirst, and the mess we're in now – it's all your fault."

"No," said Luke heavily, "it isn't Elsa's fault. It's mine."

Nick stared at him. "How d'you work that out?"

Luke knew exactly how Elsa felt. He'd felt the same way when his godfather, Lord John Roxton, had been revealed as a traitor by events on the Lost World. He remembered the betrayal he'd felt on discovering that the man he'd worshipped as a hero was nothing more than a self-centred tyrant.

"I should have told Elsa what we were planning from the very beginning," he said. "I thought if I did, she would go and blurt everything out to my mother, so I kept her in the dark. And then later, after we'd talked with Giyorgis, I should have told her what he'd said, as Salim wanted me to – but I was too angry."

He spoke directly to Elsa. "I told Salim on the plane, as we were flying to Khartoum, that neither Nick nor I want any treasure from the Mines." Elsa looked quickly at Salim, who nodded confirmation. "All we want to do is stop the Sons of Destiny getting their hands on the Spear – destroy it, if we can, so they can never use it."

"And I promise you," Salim told Elsa, "that I have no

designs on the throne of the Kukuana. Luke is right. If keeping the Spear from our enemies will stop Mussolini invading my country, or even put off the invasion for one day, then I will do anything in my power to make it so."

Elsa shook her head wretchedly.

"We have to go to the Mines," Luke persisted. "What will happen when we reach Kukuanaland, I don't know. People may try to stop us. There may be fighting – I can't promise there won't be. But how much fighting will there be if the Italians invade, knowing that their leaders hold the Spear that will enable them to rule the world? How many will die then?"

It took a lot more talking to convince Elsa; but eventually she squared her shoulders, as she had in the village square in Denebere, once again having reached a decision. "All right." Her voice was defiant. "If I misjudged you, I'm sorry. But you'd better have told me everything now."

"We've told you everything we know," said Luke. Salim nodded. Nick stared angrily at the floor. He didn't feel Elsa deserved to be forgiven just like that, but he kept his reservations to himself.

"Well, I'll have to trust you," said Elsa. "It's either that or turn you over to Gentile, and I wouldn't do that. Never. You're right – we've no choices left. It's too late to turn back – so we're going to Kukuanaland. What happens there is in the lap of the gods. I won't try and stop you again."

Luke glanced at Salim, who nodded, and Nick, who gave an angry shrug. "All right."

Elsa's eyes were unnaturally bright. "Does that mean you trust me?"

"You've just said you trust us. We have to trust each other. There's no one else to trust. And you're still a better shot than any of us."

"Thank you." Elsa gazed steadily at Luke. "You said you had a plan to get us past our enemies. Are you going to tell us what it is?"

"Yes, I am," said Luke. And he did.

Kasumi Mochizuki scanned the empty desert with high-powered binoculars. "There is no movement out there – nothing at all." She lowered the binoculars to glare at Count Claudio Gentile. "Are you sure they will come here?"

Gentile was sitting on a camping stool in the shade of a large umbrella, which was held aloft by an Italian soldier wearing a long-suffering expression. The Count was snacking on a roast chicken. He waved a drumstick in a flamboyant gesture. "*Si – certamente*. Of course.

There is no other way into the mountains. All we have to do is wait, and they will fall into our laps."

"Only if they do not know we are here. The fire your fool of a cook allowed to smoulder while roasting the bird with which you insist on stuffing your face may have alerted them to our presence."

Gentile gave a shrug. "A man must eat." As his umbrella started to droop, he bellowed, "Higher, *imbecille!*" at its unfortunate bearer.

Mochizuki returned to her vigil. "We do not even know that they have taken this route."

Gentile lumbered to his feet and moved to her side. "No? What of the digging at the oasis? The shot we heard? They are on their way." He shrugged again. "Or if not, they are *morto*. Dead of thirst and exhaustion, out there."

"Challenger is not dead," said Mochizuki decisively. "Not yet. But he will not elude me again."

Gentile glared at her. "I care nothing for Challenger. It is what the Menelik boy carries that our masters want. You nearly sent that to the bottom of the Nile. Do with Challenger what you will – but only after I have secured the Seal of Solomon."

Mochizuki lowered the binoculars again and regarded Gentile with her cold, black eyes. "But of course." The Italian shuddered inwardly, and was relieved when his

Japanese collaborator took her sunglasses from their perch on the top of her head and returned them to their usual place. She glanced at the impeccably ordered camp behind them. "You are sure your men have left not the slightest gap where they might slip through?"

"*Si*. By day, we watch. At night, there are patrols, tripwires. A mouse could not sneak past my men..." Gentile broke off as a ragged volley of small-arms fire, followed by a strange rumbling noise and a chorus of confused shouts, broke out to their left. "*Che succede?*" His eyes almost started from his head as the cause of the commotion came into view. "*O Dio!*"

A herd of elephants was stampeding towards the camp like a rushing grey wave, trumpeting and shaking their mighty heads in alarm. An outbreak of shots fired into the air behind them gave added impetus to their charge. Luke and his companions had no need for further concealment. Now what they wanted was maximum chaos and confusion, and it looked as though they were about to achieve it.

Luke's party had circled around until the herd was between them and the Italian camp. Then Luke, Nick and Isaias had burst from cover, yelling and howling like dervishes, and firing Isaias's musket into the air. The herd had bolted in terror, and more yelling and firing from Salim and Abele on their left flank and Elsa and

Keshe on their right, had kept them moving in the right direction.

The Italians regarded the onrushing herd with utmost horror. They were disciplined and brave men who, when faced with an enemy they had been trained to deal with, would not have flinched. But no training had prepared them for the grey wall of death thundering towards them. They dropped their weapons, broke and ran.

Gentile tore at his hair in rage. "*Pezzi di cretini! Vigliacchi! Sparagli!* Shoot them, you cowards!"

But the soldiers had no time to regroup, or to reach their guns. The elephants rolled over their camp like a tsunami. Tents were obliterated, their guy ropes torn from the ground, their canvas and contents reduced to rags and matchwood. The field kitchen was flattened, racks of rifles scattered. The few soldiers who had tried to stand their ground, or had not been quick enough to escape, went down beneath the living tide.

Mochizuki hissed, "Challenger!" and darted forward. But she was forced back by the trampling, screaming herd and could only watch in impotent fury as the carefully-laid trap was smashed to pieces. As the last of the elephants thundered through the wrecked camp, she pointed at a small group of figures running hell-for-leather towards the valley at whose mouth it had been set. "There they are! There! They are getting away! Stop them, you fools!"

But the Italians were in no condition to stop anyone or anything. By the time the shattered survivors had pulled themselves together and found their scattered weapons, the fugitives were well above the plain, and sheltered from gunfire by the cleft up which they were climbing.

Mochizuki gave Gentile a furious glare. "'A mouse could not sneak past my men' – ha!" She pointed at the cleft. "Follow them, you idiot!"

Burning with rage and resentment, Gentile snapped orders and led his men towards the cleft.

A couple of hundred feet above, Nick snatched a glance over his shoulder. "They're coming."

"I daresay they are." Luke paused a moment, scanning the path above them. There! A huge boulder, its base eroded by the watercourse that had created the cleft, was wedged between the narrow rock walls. He pointed. "Give me a hand."

There was no need to explain what he had in mind. Nick understood instantly. He and Luke worked their way around the far side of the rock, set their backs against the wall of the cleft, braced their feet against the boulder, and pushed with all their might.

For a moment, Luke thought the task of moving the

boulder would be beyond them. He redoubled his efforts, muscles creaking, and was rewarded by a grinding noise and the sound of shifting pebbles from the base of the stone. Moments later, the boulder gave way and tumbled down the cleft. Harsh cries and screams sounded from below. Luke and Nick exchanged delighted grins and shook hands.

As the dust cleared, Luke could see that the path behind them was completely blocked. "It will take them hours to clear that lot," he told Nick. "Up we go."

The climb was long and arduous. Stones shifted treacherously underfoot, and in places the travellers were forced to cling to the bare rock for dear life while they sought minute finger- and toe-holds.

But at length, as the last of the light faded from the sky, they emerged from the cleft onto the crest of the mountains that separated Kukuanaland from the desert. They stood on a broad grassy ridge dotted with strange, cactus-like plants and outcrops of rock. Gasping for breath, they wrung their numbed fingers, rubbed life into sore calves and stretched aching muscles.

Nick gave a great sigh of relief. "Well, we made it."

"So we did." Salim spread his arms in an expansive gesture. "Welcome to Kukuanaland."

At the same moment, Keshe, the youngest of the guides, threw his head back and his arms wide. He gave a terrible cry, and fell forward onto his face. A broad-bladed throwing spear with a plumed shaft quivered in his back.

Elsa made an inarticulate noise and reached towards him. Luke grabbed her arm. In a voice like a whip, he snapped, "Stay where you are."

Warriors emerged from every available piece of cover. There must have been over thirty of them, tall and well armed, wearing plumes of black feathers and circlets of white oxtails round their waist and knees, and carrying Carcano M91 rifles. They surrounded the travellers in silence, their expressions implacable and unsympathetic.

18 KUKUANALAND

Luke tugged at his bonds and muttered blood-curdling oaths.

"You're wasting your time," Nick told him. "These fellers know what they're doing. You won't get those knots undone even if you try 'til doomsday."

Luke subsided. "In any story I've read, they'd have missed finding the knife in our pockets. Or there would have been bits of glass lying about, or cigarette lighters, or razor-sharp rocks."

"True," said Nick. "Unfortunately, they took our knives, there's no glass around here, none of us smoke, and the rocks are nice and smooth – except for the one sticking in my back but that's not razor-sharp, it's just lumpy."

On Keshe's death, the travellers' first impulse had been to throw themselves on their captors, but the odds against them were so overwhelming as to make this a suicidal gesture. Salim had taken the lead, protesting sharply in Amharic. This had had no effect whatsoever; whether the Kukuana (it seemed safe to assume that was who they were) did not understand the language, or were simply refusing to reply, was unclear. At all events, they had indicated by signs that Elsa and the guides were to put their weapons down. Isaias and Abele obeyed promptly; Elsa took so long about relinquishing the Mauser that several Kukuana fingers had tightened on triggers before she, too, laid her gun down on the grass and took several steps back.

Thereafter, the Kukuana had spoken little among themselves, and not at all to their captives. As night fell, Luke and his party had been bound hand and foot. Their guards had also lit a fire, and kept it blazing merrily to provide light. They were taking no chances on their captives escaping into the darkness.

They had also, to Luke's disgust, taken the elementary precaution of keeping their prisoners apart. Luke and Nick had tried nonchalantly wriggling into a position, back-to-back, from which they could untie each other's bonds. The Kukuana had kicked and clubbed them back into their original positions. They didn't seem to mind if their captives spoke to one another, so long as they didn't move.

"They didn't need to do that to Keshe." Elsa's voice, coming from Luke's left, was low and vicious. "I'm going to kill them all."

"That's a good plan," said Nick carefully. "Unfortunately, it does rather involve us not being trussed up like chickens."

"Oh, shut up."

"At least the rest of us are still alive," said Nick.

Luke regarded the Kukuana, standing guard like statues. There was something inhuman in their stillness and lack of expression. "Yes, but for how long?"

"You're a proper little ray of sunshine," complained Nick.

"Is Salim all right?" asked Luke.

"He's fine," replied Nick. "I was talking to him a few minutes ago. I think he's gone to sleep."

Luke shook his head wonderingly. "How does he do that?"

"He's got more sense than the rest of us. We're not doing any good lying awake fretting, though it's hard not to."

Luke shifted his weight to try and ease his cramped muscles. "Elsa, are Isaias and Abele all right?"

"Of course they're not all right – they've just seen their friend murdered. But they're alive, if that's what you mean."

Luke sighed inwardly. He still didn't seem able to say the right thing to Elsa. He closed his eyes and tried to relax, but sleep would not come.

The long night wore on.

At dawn, the Kukuana untied their prisoners' legs, dragged them to their feet and set halters round their necks. They roped these together so that the captives were forced to stand in a crocodile. Salim was first in line, followed by Luke, Nick, Elsa and the two guides.

As soon as Elsa's legs were untied she kicked out savagely at her guards. She managed to land some shrewd blows before a Kukuana wearing a leopard-skin cloak struck her across the back with the shaft of his spear. Elsa fell to her knees; but her expression when she stood up again indicated that she thought the blow a small price to pay for the relief of her feelings towards her captors.

With the sun a hand's-breadth over the eastern horizon, they began their descent from the mountains, which stretched away to their left and right, curving towards each other as if to meet in a great circle, but if so, a circle whose far rim was too distant to be seen. The twin peaks where Elsa's great-grandfather had entered the country half a century before rose sharply from the surrounding range some twenty-five miles away.

The mountain path was much less steep on the inner side, and where the going was easy and he did not have to watch where he was placing his feet, Luke managed to catch his first glimpses of the country of the Kukuana.

To begin with, the land below was wreathed in mist; but as this was burned off by the rising sun, mile after mile of rolling grassland emerged. A river flowed northwards, gathering its tributaries as it went and winding between hills and forests. The plains were dotted with herds of grazing animals; at that distance, Luke could not be sure whether these were wild, domestic or a mixture of both, though he was almost certain that the creatures striding through scattered clumps of woodland in the near distance were giraffes.

At intervals across the plain stood villages of round dwellings inside palisade fences and surrounded by fields. From most of these, smoke from cooking fires spiralled into the still morning air.

Luke would have liked more time to study the

landscape, but their captors were not inclined to dawdle. They set a punishing pace, jogging in silence for hour after hour. The travellers' march across the desert had left them ill-prepared to keep up this tempo, but stumbles were rewarded with painful blows from the butts of spears or rifles. They had no choice but to match their captors' speed, muscles aching and lungs bursting, lying where they fell during the few short breaks they were allowed and being hauled to their feet again long before they had begun to recover their breath.

Around mid-morning they emerged from the foothills and onto the plain. Now their captors actually increased the pace. The next couple of hours passed in a blur as they ran through knee-high grass, past herds of inquisitive cows, and antelopes that scattered, pronking madly, at their approach.

With the sun at its zenith, they were finally allowed a rest halt. Luke and his companions sank to the earth, exhausted, while their guards squatted on their heels, apparently quite unaffected by the arduous journey.

One of the unsmiling guards handed a water-skin around, allowing each prisoner a few mouthfuls before snatching the skin away and passing it to the next.

After a few minutes, Luke had recovered enough to take an interest in his surroundings. They were sitting in the shade of an acacia tree. A slope led down to a small stream, which chuckled between beds of wild papyrus. Along its banks, familiar-looking broad-leaved trees rubbed shoulders with date palms, wild olives and fig trees. Between their trunks grew strange and exotic species – euphorbia, red-hot pokers and giant lobelia, their domed flower heads looking like invaders from another world.

Nick, having finally managed to get his breathing under control, said, "I wonder where they're taking us?"

"Wherever they like," said Luke grimly, "and there doesn't seem to be much we can do about it."

Elsa said, "They took my great-grandfather to their capital, Leu. I daresay that's where we're headed."

"To meet their king?" said Nick.

"I don't think they have a king any more. From what my family's old servant said, these days they're ruled by a high priestess." For a moment, it seemed that Elsa had more to say; if so, she thought better of it.

Nick stirred uneasily. "Isn't there anything we can do? I bet Quatermain and his pals weren't given the bum's rush across half of Africa the way we're being! Didn't they use a lunar eclipse to convince the Kukuana that they were travellers from the stars and Ignosi really was the king?"

Elsa gave him a scornful look. "These people's ancestors were studying the stars while ours were running around in woad," she said cuttingly. "Why wouldn't they know what an eclipse was? I'm not sure I believe in any of my great-grandfather's tricks – and even if he did manage to pull the wool over the Kukuanas' eyes, that was fifty years ago. These people have bolt-action rifles now – I don't think they're going to be taken in by smoke and mirrors."

"Speaking of rifles," Salim broke in, "I wonder where they got those."

"Well, they're an Italian make," said Luke. "Do you think our friends here got them from Gentile?"

"They might be leftovers from the war we fought against Italy in the last century, but they look more modern than that. I wouldn't be surprised if it turns out that the Kukuana have already had dealings with our friend the Count."

Luke shuddered. He hoped Salim was wrong, but he had a horrible suspicion that he was right.

Conversation lapsed. Ten minutes later, they were on their way again.

They spent that night at a village, in a building that seemed to have been used as a barn. This time they were released from their bonds, but they could still find no opportunity to escape their captors. The barn's baked-mud walls were strong, as was its door. In any case, their prison was surrounded by watchful guards. Nick's attempt to find a way out via the thatched roof nearly earned him a spear in the eye.

"Even if we did get out of here," Luke pointed out, "where would we run? Where could we hide?"

"Salim could escape," said Nick. "He could pass for one of the locals – so could Isaias and Abele."

"I don't think so," said Salim with a wry smile. "The Kukuana seem to be a tall people – I am not tall. Nor are we dressed for the part." He took off one of his boots and wiggled his toes experimentally. "In any case, if Rider Haggard's book is correct in its essentials, we seem to be moving in the direction of King Solomon's Mines – and probably more quickly than we would if left to our own devices." He rubbed at a blister and winced. "Though admittedly, it's not the most comfortable way to travel…"

Luke, much as he hated his own powerlessness in their current situation, had to agree that this made sense. But Elsa gave Salim a disgusted look. "You're saying we shouldn't try to escape? We should just let them get away with the way they're treating us? With what they did to Keshe?"

Salim gave her a look that, for once, had nothing of his usual mildness. "I'm saying that there will be a time to strike at our enemies, but that time is not now." He relaxed, his customary smile back in place. "Be patient. Any insults will be repaid with interest – when the time comes."

And with that, Elsa had to be content.

The following day's journey passed in a blur of exhaustion. All the travellers had managed to get some sleep, but a few hours' rest were not enough to prepare them for another gruelling day on foot. Their captors, however, urged them on relentlessly. Sometime in the afternoon, they realized that the ground beneath their feet had become hard and unyielding; a quick glance told Luke that they were now on a wide road, which he guessed was Solomon's Road by which Allan Quatermain's party had been escorted into the heart of the kingdom.

At twilight, they paused on a hill overlooking a substantial town. The Kukuana with the leopard-skin cloak, who seemed to be their guards' officer, despatched one of his men towards the town, perhaps to give warning of their arrival. At any rate, the rest while they waited was welcome.

Luke took the opportunity to study the capital city of the Kukuana. In Rider Haggard's book, Quatermain had guessed that it was five miles round. Luke thought that an underestimation – either that, or the place had grown. He would have said it was nearer eight miles around the centre, with what amounted to suburbs – villages and farmsteads – surrounding it for a considerable distance beyond that.

But as he looked more closely, it became evident that Leu was not a prosperous place. Many of the houses he could see were in poor repair; some were even in ruins. The streets had an untidy look. The cattle on the nearer farmsteads were few in number and looked malnourished.

Then he looked beyond the city – and saw, sixty or seventy miles due north, three gigantic snow-capped mountains. Luke glanced a question at Salim, who nodded.

"The Three Witches," he said quietly. "If Quatermain's story is true, that is where King Solomon's Mines are."

Luke gazed at the distant mountains. "Let's hope we live to see them."

At length, the runner returned with reinforcements for their guards, and the last stage of their journey to Leu began.

They had almost reached the city gates when Luke glanced up – and recoiled in horror. His sudden stop nearly choked Salim, and caused Nick and Elsa to pile into him before they could stop themselves. Their guards yelled and rained blows upon Luke; he hardly felt them. He gazed, sickened and horrified, at the sight that had brought him up short.

To the right of the road, a wooden platform had been constructed at about the height of a man's head. Stretched out on the platform were human corpses in various stages of decay. Vultures and other carrion birds tore at the remains, squabbling over bones and strips of flesh, while dogs scavenged fragments that had fallen between the slats of the platform to the ground below.

Nor was this the only such platform. They ran along the road, half a dozen a side, until they reached the gate into the city, which was adorned with a grisly display of human heads. The stench was appalling.

Nick's voice was thick. "What sort of a place is this?"

"It looks," said Salim grimly, "almost as if the brutal reign of King Twala has returned."

Luke merely shook his head. He allowed himself to be pushed forward by the guards. Trying very hard not to look at the horrors on either side, the travellers entered the city of Leu.

They were hustled through streets of darkened houses, from whose shadowy windows and doorways frightened eyes watched them pass by, until at length they came to another wall, and another gate. The buildings beyond it were grander than those in the streets through which they had passed, and in much better repair.

They were brought to a halt in a substantial courtyard before the largest building they had yet seen. A ceremonial doorway led onto a wide veranda whose roof was held up with wooden pillars carved with shapes of an unsettling, serpentine quality. Guards surrounded the building, standing to attention, still and watchful. Servants scurried around them, lighting torches and braziers as the sky darkened.

"I suppose this would be the Royal Palace?" wondered Nick.

"Yes," said Salim. "It looks as if we are about to meet the ruler of this land."

The doorway to the palace was closed by curtains. As these swung apart, the guards shook their spears. *"Koom! Koom!"* The cry seemed to shiver the earth.

"Well, that's one thing that hasn't changed since your great-grandfather's day," Luke told Elsa.

He felt a blow between his shoulder blades that forced him to his knees. Looking around, he saw that all his companions were being similarly treated. The officer with the leopard-skin cloak roared a series of commands. Salim began to translate. "He's telling us to kneel. He's not being very complimentary – apparently, we are dogs, sons of goats…oh, now, really, that's a bit strong, I don't think I'll translate that. He's telling us to quail, grovel and tremble before the High Priestess of the Kukuana…" He broke off, his face a picture of consternation. "It can't be! She died in the Mines – crushed to death – half a century ago!"

But Luke had heard the name cried by the officer. So had all his companions. Even had they missed it the first time, they could not have avoided hearing it as the guards took up the cry, roaring the name of the High Priestess to the dark sky, while echoes rebounded from the surrounding hills:

"Gagool! Gagool! Gagool!"

19 THE HIGH PRIESTESS

Leu, capital city of Kukuanaland

As the echoes of the last cry died away, the hide coverings across the doorway were drawn aside and the High Priestess of the Kukuana appeared.

She was tall and slender, moving with easy arrogance as she stepped forward to survey her captives. She wore an elaborate headdress formed from the head and skin of a baboon, its paws clasped across her chest, its pelt serving her as a cape. Around her neck were many strings of beads, cowrie shells and the teeth, tusks and feathers of wild animals and birds. Beneath these decorations she was dressed in a tunic and kilt of cowhide. Her arms, knees and ankles sported bangles and beads of ivory. Her face and body were painted in swirling patterns of ochre, indigo and vermillion.

Luke understood Salim's incredulity. This woman couldn't be Gagool, he told himself. It was impossible. To begin with, the High Priestess of the Kukuana had been old even at the time of Allan Quatermain's expedition, and according to Rider Haggard's book claimed to have known not only the fathers of that generation, but their fathers' fathers' fathers. This woman was young, apparently no more than thirty. What's more, Gagool had been killed in the very act of betraying Quatermain's party, caught beneath the gigantic lifting door of King Solomon's treasure chamber, reduced to no more than a smear of blood, flesh and splintered bone on its stone doorstep by thirty tons of rock.

Nick echoed Luke's thought. "Gagool? The witch doctress? That's not possible."

Gazing at the High Priestess with fixed intensity, Elsa said, "The Gagool my great-grandfather knew is dead – but from what our old servant told me, the Kukuana believe that at the moment of her death, the soul of the High Priestess leaves her body and enters that of a newborn child. The child is then named Gagool and becomes the new High Priestess. As she grows, she gradually regains all the knowledge of her predecessors, and all their memories."

"But the Gagool your great-grandfather met died half a century ago," protested Luke. "This woman can't be that old."

Elsa shrugged. "The High Priestess lives longer than normal people. That's what the Kukuana believe."

The woman hailed as Gagool stood at her ease, watching her prisoners with a faint, sardonic smile as more figures moved into the firelight and the courtyard around the captives gradually filled. Glancing around, Luke saw that the gathering audience included warriors dressed like their captors, court officials in robes and, wearing painted faces and the skins of snakes and lizards, priests and priestesses. At the outer edges of the crowd, fearful and sullen, crept the ordinary townspeople of Leu.

The High Priestess was carrying a staff of polished wood. With a shock, Luke realized that the decoration on its end was a withered and claw-like human hand. This she raised in a lazy gesture, and the subdued murmurs of the crowd were instantly stilled.

Gagool began to speak. Her voice, though mild, was tinged with a cold arrogance that sent a shiver down Luke's spine. After a moment, he whispered to Elsa, "What is she saying?"

Elsa was frowning in concentration. "She's speaking a very old, ceremonial form of Amharic – I'll do my best." She began her translation. "*People of the Kukuana, we are visited by strangers from far-off lands. But I, Gagool, foresaw their coming.*" The High Priestess turned to address Salim, and Elsa's translation continued. "*You, who claim descent from Solomon, great King of our people – though in your throat, you lie – what seek you in the land of the Kukuana? Riches? Power? A throne?*"

When Salim made no reply, Gagool's glance flickered contemptuously over Isaias and Abele, coming to rest on Luke and Nick. Her voice became bitter and openly mocking. "*You white men, like those that disturbed the peace of King Twala many years ago – perchance like them, you also fell to earth from the stars! Seek you heavy gold and bright stones, as did those who came before you?*"

The High Priestess turned her gaze to Elsa with a look so full of venom that Luke felt his blood run cold. Elsa's voice faltered, but after a few moments' hesitation she once again picked up her translation: "*And you, descendant of my old enemy Macumazahn, the watcher-by-night, the fox who bites from behind.*" Luke remembered that Macumazahn was the name the Kukuana had given Allan Quatermain, and wondered how the High Priestess knew of his relationship to Elsa. *"'What seek you in the land your ancestor despoiled? Will you cause more death, more lamentation of women, more crying of children?'"*

Luke felt his anger rise. He opened his mouth to make a furious protest at the murder of Keshe and their treatment by their captors. But he was forestalled by Salim whose voice, though soft and measured, carried to the ears of every member of the crowd.

"'You ask many questions,'" Elsa translated. *"'Are you truly Gagool? If so, you are the murderess of times gone by, whose witch-hunts stained the land with blood and so angered the people against King Twala that they rose and slew him. You are the traitor who sought to defy your rightful lord and entrap his friends in the Treasure House of my ancestor Solomon.'"* Gagool's eyes blazed, but Salim continued unperturbed. *"'By what right do you speak for the Kukuana? You did not dare so in the days of King Ignosi.'"*

Gagool's mouth twisted into a snarl. *"'No,'"* she said harshly. *"'In those days, I was forced by the King's malice to hide myself. But in the fullness of his years, Ignosi died.'"*

"With a bit of help from our friend there, I shouldn't wonder," muttered Nick. "And that left her in charge. No wonder the place has gone to the dogs."

"'*Yes*,'" said the High Priestess, "'*Ignosi died, as all men must die – all except myself. For I am Gagool, the eternal, reborn from age to age: true guardian of this land.*'"

Salim gazed at her with superb disdain. "'*So you say*,'" he said without emphasis. "'*Yet if that is so, it seems to me that you are but an indifferent guardian. The fields of your people lie fallow, their beasts sicken, their corpses rot before the doors of your palace. These things were not so in the days of the King.*'" There was a murmur among the crowd, instantly stilled when Gagool directed her gaze over it.

"'*They were not.*'" The High Priestess turned back to Salim, her painted face suffused with rage. "'*For Ignosi was a chicken-livered fool, who cared more for husbandry than for arms, and spoke softly to his people's enemies.*'"

"'*And do you not speak softly to your people's enemies?*'" Salim nodded towards the guns carried by his captors. "'*Whence came these weapons, if it is not so?*'"

"Easy does it," Nick muttered. "Best not to rile the lady..."

Gagool's tone was savage. "'*A wise ruler knows a true friend – and a true enemy!*'"

"'*But a fool may mistake an enemy for a friend.*'"

"'*Enough! I will bandy no more crooked words with*

you. You have broken the laws of the Kukuana in bringing these strangers here. Your life is forfeit. Soon your carcass shall join those that feed the crows and dogs before my gates.'

Nick groaned. "D'you hear that now? I knew he'd go too far." He looked into the sky, where the moon was rising above the thatched roofs of the town. "Where's an eclipse when you need one?"

Salim's voice was steady. "*'You have usurped a king's power, Gagool, yet you are not a king to order life and death. Consider: would you match your power against that of the talisman I carry?'*"

This time, the murmur of the spectators broke around her like a wave, but the High Priestess threw her head back and laughed. Watching her, Luke said, "She was prepared for that. She knew Salim has the medallion."

"And she knows his hands are tied," said Nick bitterly, "so he can't produce it."

"*'What care I for any trinket you might have?'*" crowed Gagool. "*'Am I a child, to be frightened by a bauble? I say you shall die!'*"

Luke started as a rumble of thunder came out of nowhere, echoing from the clear sky. All around him, there was an outbreak of nervous muttering.

For a moment, Gagool seemed taken aback. Then she

rallied, pointing her horrible staff at Salim. "*I have wasted overmuch time on you, traitor, and on your followers! False! Forsworn!*" As the High Priestess rapped out an order, Elsa gave up her translation and said simply, "She's telling her men to kill us."

"Yes," said Nick heavily, "I thought that's what she was doing—"

He was interrupted by a perfect bellow of thunder that seemed to leap from the sky around them like the roar of some terrible, savage beast. Lightning flickered to the north; the eyes of the crowd were drawn to the flashes. Luke followed their gaze.

A murmur again ran through the spectators, swelling into fearful exclamations as a sudden storm arose – it seemed, directly over the summits of the Three Witches, the mountains guarding the entrance to King Solomon's Mines. Dark, threatening clouds erupted from a clear sky, swirling and twisting together with appalling violence. The storm gathered strength with uncanny speed. Then it detached itself from the mountains and raced across the plain towards the city, striding on legs of lightning.

Now there were shrieks and cries from the crowd; those around the edges began to melt away. The soldiers, who, on Gagool's orders, had raised their spears to strike, lowered them again, staring at each other in consternation. The High Priestess screeched a further order and the men steeled themselves. Too late – the storm was upon them.

The thunder was continuous. Rain fell in torrents, battering the nearer spectators and sweeping them back into those behind as the packed earth of the courtyard turned to mud. Lightning flashed from the swollen clouds in coruscating waves, lighting the court and palace with a fierce, eye-watering glare. Figures and buildings became silhouettes. The crowd cowered, cursing, pleading, wailing in terror, their bodies hammered by the rain, ears battered by thunder, eyes seared by lightning.

To Luke's disbelieving gaze, the storm seemed to centre on Salim. The bonds that tied his arms had apparently become loose – perhaps, thought Luke dazedly, the rain had soaked into the knots, causing them to slip – for Salim raised a hand to take his medallion from his shirt and hold it aloft. Luke felt a cold wind pluck at his clothing; a split second later, a bolt of lightning leaped from Salim's medallion to the swirling clouds, and the storm redoubled in violence.

Gagool screamed again; her words could not be heard above the violence of the storm, but their import was clear. The officer who had captured Luke and his party understood the order. As Luke watched in horror, he raised his spear, lunging forward to stab Salim's unprotected back.

There was a peal of thunder louder than the rest, a blinding flash of lightning struck the officer – and he instantly became a charred corpse, his raised spear part-melted and fused to his hand. As Luke stared in horrified fascination, the man fell, to lie smouldering. The pounding rain steamed as it struck his body, which gave off a familiar but sickening odour of roast meat.

The rest of their captors flung down their weapons and fled. The screaming crowd followed, tearing at the walls of the court and climbing over each other to reach the gates in their panic.

The lightning ceased, flickering only occasionally. The rain eased to a steady drizzle. The thunder died to a menacing background rumble. Only the swirling clouds maintained all their former violence.

The crowd had gone. The High Priestess remained where she stood, rooted to the spot and staring at Salim in shock. A few soldiers, servants and priests huddled behind pillars and beneath the veranda, too frightened either to run or to leave their hiding places.

Salim's shoulders sagged as though with weariness, but he continued to hold his medallion above his head, and his voice was steady as he said, in the language of the Kukuana, "*Release my friends.*"

Carefully not looking at their High Priestess, servants crept from their hiding places, cowering from the angry sky as they fumbled with the knots that still bound Luke, Nick, Elsa and their guides.

As Luke and his friends painfully rubbed life back into their chafed and aching wrists, Salim raised his free hand to point at Gagool. *"Now – bind her."*

The servants hesitated – until a renewed peal of thunder sent them scurrying to obey. Moments later, their task completed, they fled. Salim let his medallion fall to his chest. He closed his eyes, swayed on his feet, and would have fallen if Elsa hadn't stepped forward to support him as, with a final distant rumble and tongue of lightning, the storm died.

An hour later, Luke and Nick stood guard outside the door to the palace, standing back-to-back with a brazier between them. They were armed with rifles dropped by their fleeing guards. Isaias and Abele prowled the courtyard, guns at the ready, clearly itching for a fight. From time to time, a pair of terrified eyes would appear at the edge of the firelight, only to withdraw instantly as Luke or Nick turned in their direction. There had been no attempt on the part of the Kukuana to retake the palace or to rescue their High Priestess, who was now closeted with Elsa and Salim.

Nick said, "Lucky for us that storm blew up when it did."

Luke gave a non-committal grunt.

Nick chuckled, his laughter sounding rather forced. "That was spectacular, right enough – when Salim held up that medallion of his, and the lightning looked like it was coming out of it. I read about that somewhere – ball lightning, it's called, very mysterious stuff, does odd things, nobody really understands it. That's what it was, no doubt about it."

"Ball lightning," said Luke. "Right."

"Or St Elmo's fire. Either way, it got us out of a ticklish situation. And good old Salim, didn't he play it up to the hilt?"

"Yes," said Luke, "he did, didn't he?"

"I mean, an eclipse is all very well, but it doesn't quite have the effect of seeing someone who was about to stick a spear in one of us being struck by lightning. That really was some coincidence."

"Coincidence," said Luke flatly. "Yes."

"Well, maybe not a coincidence, exactly – I mean, there he was, in a lightning storm, waving a ruddy great steel-tipped spear in the air – I'd call that asking for trouble." Nick shot Luke a quick glance. "Wouldn't you?"

"You could look at it like that." Luke cast a troubled glance at the sky, now cloud-free and alive with stars. "I'll tell you one thing, Nick. In our time we've faced dinosaurs, rogue tanks and killer submarines. But to be honest I'm starting to wonder whether this time we've bitten off more than we can chew."

20 THE PLACE OF DEATH

As the sun rose, Nick and Luke joined Salim and Elsa in the palace, leaving Isaias and Abele on guard outside. There had been no sign that the Kukuana were preparing to attack; it seemed that they were waiting to see what would happen next.

Luke was wondering the very same thing. Ever since the events of the previous evening, he had been expecting Elsa to round on Salim and accuse him of hijacking the throne of Kukuanaland, the very thing he had promised her he would not do. But it seemed that Keshe's death, their treatment at the hands of their captors and the sufferings of the Kukuana under Gagool's reign had caused Elsa to have a change of heart. At any rate, she had made no protest at Salim's assuming command in the palace.

Luke and Nick entered the throne room to find the High Priestess, still bound, sitting hunched and silent in the middle of the floor. Elsa, who like Luke and Nick had commandeered a captured gun, was standing guard over her. Evidently her hatred of Gagool outweighed any doubts she had previously entertained about interfering in the affairs of the Kukuana.

Salim, sitting at his ease on a wooden folding chair and watching the High Priestess intently, looked up as his companions appeared.

"Luke, Nick," he said, "I'm glad you're here. I have been considering what to do with our captive. I believe I have come to a decision, and I was about to ask you to come in and hear what the High Priestess and I have to say to each other."

Nick gave Gagool a hostile glare. "I can hardly wait."

"Elsa, would you be kind enough to translate?" said Salim. "I would like Luke and Nick to understand what is being said."

Without taking her eyes from her captive, Elsa said, "It will be my pleasure."

"Thank you." Salim leaned forward to address Gagool, and Elsa began her translation. *"'What should I do with you?'"*

Gagool spat at his feet. *"'Your threats are empty, child of Solomon. You dare not touch me.'"*

"'I make no threats – yet. But why do you say I dare not touch you?'"

The High Priestess gave a harsh laugh. *"'You are but a boy! Even were that not so, you are a soft fool. You would be my judge, but you lack the strength of will to condemn me to death.'"*

"'Do I so?'"

"'Assuredly! See how you surround yourself with weaklings and women!'" Elsa scowled as she translated Gagool's last remarks, and her hands tightened on the rifle.

"'You are a woman,'" Salim pointed out.

"'But not a weakling!'"

"'We shall see. Well, I will tell you what I will do with you. I will have you show us the way to King Solomon's Mines.'"

The High Priestess gave a scornful laugh. *"'How if I do not know the way?'"*

"'If you are truly Gagool, you do indeed know the way, for you showed it to Allan Quatermain, whom you called Macumazahn.'"

"'Then how if I do not choose to show you the way?'"

Salim said calmly, "'Then you shall die.'"

The High Priestess gave him a contemptuous look. "'You will not kill me...'" Elsa broke off her translation to say, "But I would! Just say the word."

Salim gave her a gentle smile. "No. I would not have your hands stained with the blood of such carrion." He turned back to Gagool, and, reluctantly, Elsa resumed her translation. "'I say you will die. And in this manner: I shall turn you over to your people. I shall tell them I have shorn you of your powers. They shall judge you.'"

Luke gaped at Salim with a mixture of shock and respect. He had been wondering how his friend would make good his threat; this course had simply never occurred to him. He knew that he himself could never have come up with such a piece of calculated nastiness.

The High Priestess raised her head proudly, but there was fear in her eyes. "'My people will obey me!'"

"'Think you so?'" Salim took out his medallion and held it up so that it spun, catching the light of the sun's rays that lanced through the doorway to the palace. "'I think they will obey me, for I have this.'" Gagool was silent. "'Consider well,'" Salim went on softly. "'Until now, your people have done your bidding through fear. You have repaid their obedience with death and suffering. They have no reason to love you. I will ask you once *more. We seek the Mines of King Solomon. Will you show us the way?'"*

For a while, Gagool remained silent, glaring at Salim with fear and loathing. Then she lowered her eyes. Slowly and reluctantly, she gave a single nod.

The travellers stood in the shadow of three snow-covered peaks of a single great mountain, which towered above King Solomon's Road, on which they had been travelling for the past three days.

Despite Luke's determination to press on, Salim had insisted on spending the first day since Gagool's overthrow in consolidating his position among the Kukuana. He had summoned the court, the chiefs of the army and as many town and village headmen as could be assembled in the time available. Sitting in lordly state before the palace in his carved chair, with his medallion on open display upon his chest, he had made it clear to one and all that their High Priestess's power was at an end, and rescinded all the cruel laws made since King Ignosi's time. He had appointed officials to ensure peace while he completed his journey to the Mines, and on their recommendation, had assembled a bodyguard for that journey.

Luke had chafed at the delay, but he could see the

sense of Salim's precautions. It would be foolish to set off for the Mines leaving Leu seething with uncertainty or even rebellion – they didn't want a civil war breaking out behind them. And a bodyguard was a good idea, too. Luke was sure that Gentile, Mochizuki and their forces were somewhere nearby. What's more, though he had no idea what tricks Gagool might still have up her sleeve, he was mortally certain of one thing: in spite of her apparent submission, he wouldn't have trusted the High Priestess as far as he could throw her.

After three days of hard walking (though after the forced march to which the travellers had been subjected on their arrival in Kukuanaland, the journey from Leu had seemed a stroll in the park), Luke and his companions had at last reached their goal. They stood gazing at the ominous, looming peaks of the Three Witches as the evening shadows lengthened.

At Luke's suggestion, Salim had ordered the bodyguard – Isaias, Abele and the Kukuana (among whose number Luke had been surprised to recognize several of their former captors) to scout ahead for any signs of their enemies. They had found nothing.

Luke scanned the forbidding landscape. "Where are they?"

"You're not complaining, surely?" said Nick. "Personally, the fewer signs of Mochizuki and Gentile we find, the better I like it. Maybe they've given up."

"You know better than that," Luke told him. "I don't know about Gentile, but Mochizuki won't rest until she sees me dead."

"All right, but maybe they don't know where the Mines are after all."

"That doesn't make sense. They gave Gagool guns, they wouldn't have done that unless she told them how to find the Mines. In any case, all they had to do was track us from Leu. We haven't made any secret of our movements."

Nick gave a philosophical shrug. "They're probably behind us, then. There's been no sign of them since we left them at the base of the cliff. Our best bet is to press on. We can leave the Kukuana to guard our backs while the rest of us head into the Mines."

Luke considered this. "Giyorgis said Solomon built booby traps to catch out anyone who tried to break into the Mines. The fewer of us to set them off, the better."

Salim appeared at Luke's elbow. With a deferential air, he said, "Well, here we are. What do we do now?"

Luke was surprised. He had been nettled at the way in which Salim seemed to have assumed command of the expedition. "I thought you were in charge these days," he said before he could stop himself, and instantly regretted sounding mean and shabby.

Salim looked uncomfortable. "In our dealings with the Kukuana, perhaps – I do, after all, speak their language."

"And you have the medallion," said Luke.

"That is true. But it seems to me that when we enter the Mines we are likely to find ourselves pitted against the Sons of Destiny, and you and Nick have more experience of them than I do."

Luke nodded. "All right. I think we should keep Gagool on a short leash." He glanced towards the High Priestess, whose arms were still bound behind her, and who was wearing a rope collar with two lines attached, held by Kukuana guards to prevent her escape. "Isaias and Abele can take charge of her. The rest of us wouldn't kill her out of hand if she tried any funny business..." Luke thought about this and added, "Well – maybe Elsa would. But Isaias and Abele still want revenge for what her men did to Keshe. They won't let her get away with anything. And we'll need the Kukuana to guard the entrance to the Mines while we're down there."

Salim nodded. "I'll give the instructions."

Luke turned to Nick. "We'll need you to spot any booby traps – if possible, before we fall into them."

"Right." Nick rubbed his hands. "I've been feeling a bit of a spare part on this trip. No machinery to fix – you can't get a camel to behave with a screwdriver." His eyes narrowed. "Though, to be honest, there have been times when I wouldn't have minded giving it a try... At any rate, it's about time I made myself useful."

Salim gave the Kukuana their orders. There was some muttering – the guards evidently did not like the idea of their new leader going into the Mines without a proper, armed escort, but Salim was firm. More than half his guards spread out to cover every approach to the Mines. They stood, cradling their rifles, gazing down the road for any sign of pursuit and, occasionally, glancing round as Luke led the rest of the party forward.

After a few hundred yards, the road divided to run either side of an immense pit. Luke recognized this as the diamond mine workings identified by Allan Quatermain. On the far side of the pit, the two halves of the road joined again, running forwards for barely a hundred yards before terminating at the feet of three great stone figures.

Gagool, with a malicious smile playing about her lips, said something in her own language. Salim supplied the translation. *"Behold, the Silent Ones.'"

The colossal statues, two male and one female, were seated. Their blank stone eyes stared down Solomon's Road and across the plain beyond. Their countenances, though inhumanly serene, conveyed a subtle air of menace. Kings, gods, whatever they might represent, the Silent Ones gazed across the country of the Kukuana with sublime indifference to the affairs of men. Their expressions indicated that they would neither praise kindness nor condemn cruelty; peace or war, death or salvation, were all one to them. Luke gazed up at their impassive stone faces, and shivered.

Gagool noted his reaction and spoke in low, mocking tones. "*Turn back, white men,*" Salim translated. "*Is there not enough evil on the earth, that you should seek it out beneath?*"

Luke gave their guide a savage glare. To Salim, he said, "Tell her to lead on."

Salim relayed the order. Gagool's smile broadened, but as Isaias and Abele tugged none-too-gently on her collar, she did as she was bid, approaching the rock face behind the Silent Ones.

Following, Luke realized that at the base of the cliff, hidden from the road by the statues, there was an opening in the rock, like the entrance to the gallery of a mine, wide enough to admit two walking abreast. With a mocking backward glance, but without pausing, Gagool entered the dark mouth, with Isaias and Abele close behind.

"Check the entrance," Luke told Nick. Salim issued an order, and their escort opened packs to bring out oil lamps. Once these were lit, the remaining Kukuana took up positions to guard the Mine entrance. Luke – holding a rifle in one hand and a lamp in the other – took a deep breath and plunged into the darkness.

He found Gagool, still wearing her infuriating smile, and her escort waiting while Nick made a minute examination of the walls, floor and ceiling. Salim and Elsa had crammed into the narrow entrance behind him by the time Nick had completed his survey.

"Well," he said at length, "it looks safe enough."

There was a rush of wings. Luke gave a startled cry and ducked. In a split second, the whole party was swatting at rushing bodies that poured from the depths of the cave with chittering noises and the clap of leathery wings, while Gagool's laughter echoed around them.

"Bats," snapped Luke. He cast a furious glance at the crowing High Priestess. "Tell her to stop that." Elsa raised her rifle and slipped the safety catch off in a marked manner. "Politely," added Luke.

"This *is* polite," said Elsa sweetly. She worked the bolt and gave the suddenly silent Gagool a blood-curdling smile. "But I can do impolite, too."

The High Priestess, evidently understanding Elsa's tone if not her words, lapsed into sullen silence.

As the last of the bats disappeared behind them, Luke said, "On we go."

After a couple of hundred paces, the passage opened out into a breathtaking cavern, a vast underground chamber like the nave of some great cathedral. Its naturally vaulted roof was seemingly supported by gigantic, patterned columns formed of stalactites so ancient that they had grown down from the distant ceiling to meet and fuse together with corresponding stalagmites rising from the floor. The cavern was full of the sound of dripping water as the slow deposition of dissolved limestone, by which its architecture had been created, went on without ceasing, a process that might in every thousand years add to its towering structures a mere six inches of growth. The upper walls of the cavern glistened with frozen waterfalls of flowstone and hangings of stone drapery as delicate as lace, while between the pillars side caverns opened, their brooding depths beyond the reach of the explorers' lights. Luke and his companions moved slowly across the cavern floor, gazing about them in awed silence.

At the far end of the cathedral cave stood an arched doorway, with another passage beyond. Nick once again made a thorough check. He shrugged. "If there's a booby trap here, I can't find it."

"All right." Luke signalled to Gagool, who made for the doorway with a step that seemed almost eager. He followed, his heart hammering uncomfortably at his ribs. If the description of King Solomon's Mines given in Rider Haggard's book was accurate, he knew what was coming next. He made a determined attempt to control his breathing. *Forewarned is forearmed*, he told himself.

But nothing could have prepared him for the reality that he found in the next cavern. One by one, Nick, Elsa and Salim followed Luke, Gagool and her guards. One by one they came to a sudden stop, cold fear clutching at their throats.

The cavern was perhaps forty feet long by thirty broad and thirty high. Along its centre ran a great stone table. And seated at either side of the table...

Elsa gave an involuntary moan. Nick gulped. Gagool gave an evil chuckle. *"'Welcome to the Place of Death,'"* Salim translated.

Down either side of the table sat human figures: the kings of the Kukuana. Twenty-nine calcified forms, ghastly and unmoving under the dripping water that had preserved their mortal remains by encasing them in the rock from which the caverns were made. The older ones, at the far end of the table, were well on the way to becoming formless stalagmites. The two most recent additions, at the near end, had barely begun their preservation. One of these lacked a head on his shoulders: it rested instead on his knees, the sightless, milky eyes staring horribly at the intruders. The other was a giant of a man, who seemed to lack a hand. Luke realized that this must be Ignosi, Allan Quatermain's companion, the last king, and with a spasm of horror and disgust he understood where the withered claw that decorated Gagool's staff must have come from.

Then Luke raised his head, and his heart missed a beat.

Towering over the head of the table, leaning across it like a hovering angel of death, was a colossal human skeleton carved from a single stalagmite. The empty eye sockets of its grinning skull stared mockingly at the intruders; one of its bony hands rested on the table itself, the other held aloft a long white spear with which it seemed to threaten anyone who dared enter its dark domain.

As Luke and his companions gazed spellbound and appalled at this monstrous figure, there was a sudden movement at the head of the table. A hurricane lantern flared. Luke cried out and shielded his eyes.

When, squinting, he opened them again, he saw that there was a thirtieth figure sitting at the head of the table beneath the skeleton's ribcage. A figure that was not the remains of a long-dead king, but a living man, his gaunt face illuminated in lurid highlights and deep shadow by the hissing lantern.

Luke stared at him. For several seconds, he was unable to find his voice. Then he said, "You can't be here. You can't be. You're dead."

"Rather an appropriate setting, then, don't you think? Hello, Luke," said Lord John Roxton.

21 THE WAY OPENS

"Don't stand there gaping like a goldfish," said Roxton. "Where are your manners? Aren't you going to introduce me to your friends?"

Luke said nothing. Roxton's bantering tone was much as it had always been, but the voice itself was unfamiliar – weak, hoarse and hesitant, as though every word was spoken only with a painful effort. And now that his eyes were adjusting to the harsh light of Roxton's lantern, Luke could see that the old adventurer's face was some way beyond gaunt – cadaverous would be a better description. The skin that clung to his skull, liver-spotted, yellow as parchment and thin as muslin, hung in folds and wrinkles from its bones. His sparse hair was white, his moustache grey. Only his eyes, cold and ice blue, seemed to have survived the general ruin.

Roxton tutted at Luke's failure to respond to his invitation. "I must apologize for my godson. Let me see if I can supply his deficiencies myself." He gazed at each of Luke's companions in turn. "Nick, I know of course. I'm guessing that the lady with the interesting headgear would be the High Priestess Gagool, and her watchdogs look like Ethiopian tribesmen from the North – Tigray, perhaps. The charming young woman who is so very attached to that rifle would be Miss Fairfax. Which means that the remaining member of your party must be Salim Menelik, of the House of Solomon – a young gentlemen I've been anxious to meet for some time."

Elsa, her gun half-raised, said, "Who the hell is this?"

"Lord John Roxton," Luke told her. "My godfather. Not to mention a traitor."

"And a murderer," said Nick savagely.

"Harsh, boys," murmured Roxton. "I'm just a simple soldier, fighting for his chosen cause."

Luke ignored this. "How did you escape from the Zeppelin?" he demanded bluntly. "I thought you'd been blown up with your precious diamonds."

Elsa was all at sea. "What Zeppelin?" she asked. "What diamonds?"

"The last time we saw him," Luke told her, "was on the Lost World where he was helping the Sons of Destiny dig for diamonds to finance his friends Hitler and Mussolini's war preparations. He was trying to get away with the loot in a Zeppelin when Nick's dad managed to put a spoke in his wheel."

"An incomplete summary," said Roxton languidly, "but let it go, let it go."

"Let it go, nothing!" snarled Nick. "You killed my da."

"Oh, be fair, Nick." Roxton spread his wasted hands. "As you can see, he pretty nearly did for me, too."

"You haven't answered the question," said Luke. "The Zeppelin went down in flames and we didn't find any survivors."

"Oh, if you insist." Roxton began to unbutton his jacket. "They do say, don't they, that a picture is worth a thousand words." The jacket fell open and he began work on his shirt buttons. "I was with the diamonds when the – hah! – balloon went up, as you know. Hence, this..."

He opened his shirt to reveal his chest. Just to the left of the sternum lay a deep, circular depression. The flesh inside was as smooth and featureless as the skin of a balloon, and its puckered lip was surrounded by radiating lines of scar tissue. The appalling injury looked as though a crater had been lifted from the moon's surface and grafted onto Roxton's torso.

"The explosion did that," Roxton remarked conversationally. "Drove one of the diamonds right inside my chest. Damn big thing like a pigeon's egg. It's there now, right next to my heart. The doctors have tried to get it out, but they gave up in the end – reckon if they move it, it's curtains for poor Johnnie.

"It hurt like the blazes, as you can imagine. I thought I'd cashed in my chips there and then – chest full of deucedly expensive shrapnel and the whole place burning up like Billy-be-damned. But then I found myself under a thundering great flood of water – from one of the ballast tanks, I suppose – which cooled things down a bit.

"I don't know what happened after that, but when I came to a few hours later I was lying in a thicket with a couple of squareheads from the Zep crew – as unlikely a pair of nurses as you could imagine, and pretty singed and knocked about themselves – but they kept me going until you'd skedaddled and our new High Command managed to send another Zeppelin to find out what had happened to us."

Roxton began to rebutton his clothing. "After that, as you may imagine, I was definitely out of the picture as far as fieldwork was concerned, which is why I missed your little junket with the *Nautilus*. I'm still pretty much nil-by-mouth, actually, but in any case the quacks tell me I haven't got long, so I was determined to be in on the death this time. I'm not really up to desert travel these days, but some friends in the Luftwaffe were kind enough to offer me the loan of an experimental autogyro and I jumped at the chance. After all, it's not every day a chap has the chance to get his hooks on a world-conquering weapon that's been lost for almost two thousand years."

"That was very interesting," said Nick in a voice that cracked with strain. "Finished?"

"Yes, I think so."

"Good." Nick raised his rifle and aimed it at Roxton.

Luke's godfather gave a weary sigh. "Don't be so melodramatic, Nick. I doubt very much whether you'll pull that trigger, and really, you know, it would make very little difference if you did. And in any case…"

He raised an arm and made a beckoning gesture. Luke caught the sound of muffled footsteps behind him – but before he could turn, something hard and round jabbed him painfully in the back. Startled gasps to either side of him told him that his companions were being similarly served.

Luke closed his eyes and groaned. "The side passages in the cathedral cavern. We never looked in them."

A hand came from behind Luke to seize his rifle. He glanced about him. Nick, Elsa, Isaias and Abele were being similarly disarmed by troops wearing the uniform of the Italian army, all of whom looked as though they knew their business. At a signal from Roxton, they removed the collar from Gagool's neck. The High Priestess stepped away from her erstwhile captors. Confronting Salim, and wearing a ferocious grin, she spat in his face. Then she moved unhurriedly to sit on the lap of a dead king, from which position she watched the proceedings with her chin on her wrist, her sardonic smile back in place.

Roxton nodded a welcome as Count Claudio Gentile and his Japanese ally stepped past Luke and into the light. As they passed, Gentile gave Luke a nod and a wink, while Mochizuki treated him to a glare of cold hatred.

"Careless," drawled Roxton. "I must say, Luke, I'm surprised at you. Don't you remember what I taught you? Always watch your back."

"I've tried very hard to forget everything you ever taught me."

The thrust got under Roxton's guard. His eyes flashed. "Unwise."

"There has been enough talk." Captain Mochizuki drew a pistol from her belt-holster and pointed it at

Salim. "You will use your medallion to open the secret door to the Mines."

Salim stared calmly at her. "Surely, that is unnecessary. According to Allan Quatermain's account, the doorway to the Treasure Chamber lies behind Lord Roxton; that is where the witch-woman Gagool sought to trap Quatermain and his friends, and perished herself as a result. Gagool claimed that the secret of the door's opening was known only to her." He pointed to the High Priestess. "There is Gagool reborn, or so she claims. If that is so, she can open the door for you."

A muscle twitched in Mochizuki's otherwise expressionless face. "You would be most ill-advised to take me for a fool. The so-called Treasure Chamber found by Quatermain was a mere snare, baited with a few low-value gems; its sole purpose was to trap the greedy and stupid. Gagool has already opened it for us, and traded its contents for the guns her people bear. The real Mines are far greater in extent, far richer in treasure, and their entrance is hidden. You will find it, or I will kill you."

Roxton gave a weary sigh. "You see what I have to work with, Luke? Captain Mochizuki's approach is certainly to the point, but it lacks finesse." He addressed the Japanese assassin directly. "I doubt you will achieve your goals in that way. Mr. Menelik is the son of an

Ethiopian prince; I would be very surprised if he were to give in easily to threats."

Mochizuki's finger tightened on the trigger. "Then I shall shoot him and open the door myself."

Roxton shook his head. "I don't think that would work, either. Our latest information indicates that the legitimate possessor of the medallion must be the one to open the door, and must do so willingly – which would seem to imply that he should ideally be alive at the time."

"Superstitious nonsense," sneered Mochizuki.

"Oh, I daresay it is; but *after* you have killed the only person alive who could use the key to get us into the Mines would be a very bad time to discover that it was not nonsense after all, don't you think?" Mochizuki said nothing. She kept her pistol pointed at Salim. Roxton's voice hardened. "Let me be more direct, Captain. Put the bloody gun down."

With a snarl, Mochizuki thrust the gun back into its holster.

"Thank you." Roxton relaxed slightly. He turned his attention to Elsa. "I think this is an occasion for the particular skills of Signor Gentile." The Italian inclined his head in acknowledgement. "The good Count was once a wrestler, as I'm sure you know. He has made a particular study of how pain may be used to disable an opponent. Our reports suggest that Mr. Menelik thinks highly of Miss Fairfax. Signor Gentile, I would like you to hurt her a little – unless Mr. Menelik proves obstinate. In that case, I would like you to hurt her a lot."

Luke was outraged. "No!" Nick swore violently at Roxton. Salim's eyes narrowed, but he said nothing.

Gentile ignored the protests and took off his jacket, which he slung over the shoulders of the nearest king. He turned to Elsa and gave her a disarming smile, spreading his arms wide. "*Scusi.*" Then he stepped forward and twisted Elsa's arm painfully behind her back. Elsa gasped and closed her eyes. She struggled briefly, her face working in agony. Gentile's grin widened as he applied more pressure. Despite her clear intention to remain silent, Elsa let out an involuntary cry. Luke tensed, ready to fly at Gentile, and the pressure of the gun muzzle at his back increased. He glanced back. The man holding the rifle gave a slight shake of the head.

"Enough." Salim stepped forward.

Gentile twisted his face into an expression of comical disappointment. "So soon? But I have hardly begun!" At a gesture from Roxton he released Elsa and stepped back, hands raised in a gesture of surrender.

Elsa wrung her injured arm. "Shut up, Salim. You're not to help them if that gorilla breaks every bone in my body."

Gentile cracked his knuckles. "If you insist…"

"I said, enough." Salim's voice was calm. "His Lordship is quite right. I would not allow any friend to suffer if I could prevent it." He turned to face Roxton. "Exactly what is it that you wish me to do?"

Roxton croaked, "Ah, well, there you have me, I'm afraid. Our informant wasn't very clear on that point – I mean, I believe he genuinely didn't know. Signor Gentile was very diligent in seeking an answer to that particular question – he had to be quite insistent about it. Sadly, our informant at that point proved to be less – durable – than we had imagined."

The muscles in Luke's jaw tightened. "You mean you tortured him to death."

Roxton shrugged. "You can't make an omelette without breaking eggs – amongst other things." He turned his attention back to Salim. "If you wish to avoid any more unpleasantness, my colleagues and I require you to open the door. How you do it is up to you."

"Very well." Salim reached inside his shirt and held up his medallion. He bowed his head and closed his eyes.

For a while, nothing happened. Then, a faint glow began to appear in the centre of the table. It was not the harsh glow of Roxton's hurricane lantern, nor the softer glow of Luke's party's oil lamps, but a green-hued, phosphorescent gleam. Roxton nodded, as if this was what he had expected. Gagool hissed like a snake and drew back. Mochizuki let out her breath in a long, "Aaaaaaaah!" Gentile swore softly and his troops muttered; one or two crossed themselves.

Salim opened his eyes, straightened, and regarded this phenomenon with interest. In the centre of the stone table was revealed a glowing duplicate of the device on the medallion that he held – the Seal of Solomon. Nobody else in the chamber moved or made a sound as Salim, without haste, advanced towards the glowing symbol, the cogged wheel surrounding the Star of David. He took the medallion from round his neck, and with an expression of earnest enquiry, pressed it against the glowing stone. For a moment, the medallion gave off a matching glow. Then, moments later, the glow of the medallion and that of the table both winked out.

There was silence. The occupants of the chamber looked around, and at each other, with unease.

Then, a deep rumbling began. It seemed to come from the rocky floor beneath their feet, from the walls, from all around them. With a grinding roar, the chamber began to shake. Dust showered from the ceiling. The Italian troops cried out; Gentile hoarsely ordered them to stand their ground; Luke, Nick and Elsa exchanged shocked glances; Gagool shrieked like a kettle. Only

Roxton, Mochizuki and Salim gave no outcry, made no move.

Then, through the billowing dust, Luke saw that the stone table around which sat the dead kings, was slowly descending. It became clear that the table was made up of slabs of dressed stone, each about a foot thick.

The table continued to descend into a rectangular pit. The first slab came to a grinding halt about nine inches below floor-level. The rest of the table continued downwards for another nine inches before the second slab came to rest. The sequence continued.

At length, the last slab dropped into place and the rumbling stopped. As the clouds of dust cleared, Luke saw that the slabs of the table had formed themselves into a stone staircase, leading downwards. At the end of the chamber, below the place where the giant stone skeleton sprang from the rock, and where Roxton still sat, an arched doorway was revealed at the foot of the newly-created stairway. The capstone in the centre of the arch bore the Seal of Solomon.

Roxton's thin, reedy voice filled the silence. "It seems that the way to the Mines is open."

22 DEADFALL

"**G**entile." Roxton held up an arm.

Grimacing as though he faced an unavoidable but unpleasant duty, Gentile crossed the room behind the seated kings. He took Roxton's lantern and draped the sick man's arm over his shoulders. Then he returned the way he had come with Roxton leaning heavily against him, his breath an echoing rasp in the silence.

When they reached the head of the newly-created stairway, Roxton nodded towards Nick and indicated the dark entrance to King Solomon's Mines. "You first."

Nick glared at him. "Why me?"

"Our information is that King Solomon prepared at least one unpleasant surprise for intruders. This may not be true, or it may no longer work – but if it is there to be sprung, I'd sooner you found it than me. Your Tigray friends can go next."

Nick shrugged angrily. He glanced at Luke and gave a barely-perceptible shake of his head. He had seen his hot-tempered friend tense like a coiled spring on hearing Roxton's order, and didn't want Luke to get himself shot launching a futile attack, or making a protest that would do no good. He took an oil lamp, and began his descent. At a quiet word from Salim, Isaias and Abele followed. As they reached the arch, Gentile snapped an order to the Italian guards and helped Roxton onto the stairway. The guards gestured with their rifles to urge Luke, Salim and Elsa forward. Gagool made no move until Mochizuki, her face expressionless as usual, took out her pistol and made an unmistakable gesture. Snarling, backing away like a trapped animal, the High Priestess followed the soldiers, with Mochizuki bringing up the rear.

The tunnel continued downwards. The floor was uneven, with more steps in some places. Progress was slow. Nick checked the walls and floor carefully for any sign of hidden pits, deadfalls or other traps. Gentile, stooping as the passage narrowed and its ceiling lowered, had difficulty supporting Roxton, who was clearly almost incapable of independent movement. Though Luke had no cause to feel sympathy for his godfather, he found himself saddened by the extent to which the wily old adventurer's powers had been reduced by his injuries, however thoroughly deserved.

At length, they heard the thundering of water ahead. Some minutes later, they emerged from the tunnel into another cavern.

The new cave was like a gigantic chimney, the upper reaches and lower depths of its craggy walls beyond the rays even of Roxton's powerful lantern. The passage through which they had entered terminated in a broad ledge from which a spur of rock, like a bridge, leaped across the void. To their left, an underground waterfall tumbled from an unguessable height above them to unfathomable depths below. Spray swept across the rock bridge in clouds and curtains, occasionally allowing glimpses of a cleft at the far end where, presumably, the tunnel continued.

Roxton surveyed the cavern with cold, calculating eyes. "I don't know that I care for the look of this." He gestured to Nick. "Check whether it's safe."

One of the Italian soldiers stepped forward with a coil of rope, the end of which he tied around Nick's waist. Thus secured, Nick dropped to all fours, and crawled out onto the bridge. The Italian looped the rope over a projecting rock and paid it out as Nick advanced. Within moments of leaving the ledge he was being lashed with spray. His drenched clothing clung to his body but his careful examination of the stonework never faltered. Having reached a point approximately a third of the way across the bridge, his scrutiny of the stonework became more minute than ever. After several minutes, he turned with great care on the wet rock, rose into a half crouch and made his way back.

"There's something there," he reported, wiping water from his eyes. "A crack in the rock that runs all the way across, and another a few feet ahead. They could be natural – on the other hand, the slab between the cracks could be on a pivot, so that anyone standing on it will make it tilt and tip them off. Or it could be a trigger mechanism."

"A trigger for what?" demanded Roxton.

Nick gave him a cold glare. "No idea."

"Then we'd better find out." Roxton coughed painfully. "Gentile, see to it."

The giant Italian rapped out a series of orders. The soldier with the rope untied it from Nick and attached it to one of his fellows, who promptly levelled his rifle at Abele and gestured towards the bridge.

"No." Salim's voice was sharp. "I will go. If there is

danger, the medallion will protect me."

"Perhaps," said Roxton, "and perhaps not. In any case, if you cross safely, that is no guarantee that we could do the same. And then what's to prevent you using your medallion to seal the Mines to us? Thanks for the offer, but I don't choose to take the risk. We're wasting time." Roxton pointed at Abele and the roped soldier swung his rifle in his direction. "Tell him to cross the bridge."

"I will not send a man to his death," said Salim.

"You may not be. Young Nick may be mistaken – it could be safe after all. It's a better chance than a bullet, at any rate."

Salim shook his head. But Abele did not wait for orders. He gave a calm salute, then stepped firmly onto the bridge. Rather more nervously, the Italian guard followed.

Abele walked forward without hesitation. When he reached the point at which Nick had stopped, he seemed to stumble slightly. Watching intently, Luke realized that Abele had stepped on the slab Nick had identified, which had clearly not tilted as he had suggested, but had definitely moved in some other way.

For a moment, nothing happened. Then, from above there came a frightful roar. The force of the waterfall rose to a deluge, and it leaped away from the cliff, smashing directly down upon the bridge. Abele and his Italian guard were obliterated by the churning water, which rebounded from the stone of the bridge to dash into the faces of the appalled watchers. Breaking waves washed over the ledge, drenching its occupants and dousing all their lamps except for Roxton's. When the waves ceased as the deluge slackened and the waterfall returned to its original course, there was no one on the bridge. The Italian who had been paying out his comrade's safety rope hauled in the slack line and stared disbelievingly at its frayed end.

"Hell's bells!" Nick's voice was hushed. "That slab *was* a trigger – some sort of hydraulic switch that opened a sluice gate or a chute or something, up there." He stared at the empty bridge. "Poor devils."

"You must let me cross," said Salim to Roxton in a low, harsh voice, "or you must go back."

"I haven't come so far to go back at the first obstacle." Roxton's eyes narrowed in calculation. "Perhaps a lesser weight will not trigger the deluge." He gestured towards Elsa. "You will go."

"No!" Luke stepped forward. "I'll go. I have an idea."

Roxton gave him a cold stare. "And what if your idea is wrong?"

"Then you've lost an enemy and you'll need to think again."

Roxton nodded thoughtfully.

Luke took Nick aside. "Tell me what you think.

Plan A – you said the slab you found was a few feet wide. What if I try to hurdle over it?"

"No good," said Nick promptly. "They'll have thought of that if they're not fools. There's probably another trigger slab just where your foot would land if you tried to jump the first: I couldn't see that far ahead for the spray but I'll take my oath it's there."

"That's what I thought," said Luke. "Then it's Plan B."

"And what's Plan B?"

"Run like hell! There's a delay between someone stepping on the trigger and the sluice, or whatever it was, opening – only a couple of seconds, but that may be enough."

"Not if you slip, it won't be."

"Then I'd better not slip, had I?"

Without waiting for Nick's reply, Luke stepped towards the bridge. Two guards made to lift their rifles but a gesture from Roxton stopped them.

Luke backed to the mouth of the tunnel, giving himself as long a run-up as possible. He crouched for a moment. Then he sprang forward, sprinting onto the bridge.

Within moments he was half-blinded by spray and his shirt was clinging to him as though trying to hold him back, but he did not slacken his pace. He almost stumbled as he stepped onto the first trigger slab and it abruptly sank beneath his feet, but he was prepared for the movement and kept his footing. There was a second slab as Nick had predicted – and as he reached it, he heard an ominous rumbling from far above. A third slab sank beneath his pounding feet... The end of the bridge was almost in reach, but now a booming roar was shaking the bridge, the very walls of the cavern. As the flood descended like the Wrath of God, Luke threw himself forward with the despairing lunge of a batsman trying to make his crease. Behind him, the deluge struck the bridge and sent a wave to sweep him forward, dashing him against the rocks beside the far tunnel mouth and, as it retreated, clawing and sucking at his body to tear it from its precarious hold and drag it to oblivion. But his grip held. The fury of the fall abated. Gasping and half-drowned, Luke staggered to his feet and turned to face the anxious watchers on the other side of the cavern. "Throw me the rope!"

With the rope secured around rocks above the bridge on either side, the remaining members of the party apprehensively made their way across. Nick and Isaias swung across hand-over-hand, raising their legs to avoid triggering the deluge. Elsa and Salim followed in the same manner. Roxton crossed lashed to Gentile's back – the rope bowed alarmingly under the Italian's weight, but Gentile's strength made light of the task. The soldiers followed in a commando crawl, face down and with one foot hooked over the rope for control and balance. Gagool hung underneath the rope and swarmed across like a squirrel. Mochizuki came last, clambering onto the rope and walking across it, arms outstretched, like a tightrope walker. Nick gave her a savage look. "Show-off," he muttered.

The new tunnel continued downwards for some way; then it flattened out and became wider. Side caverns began to open to left and right, many of them protected by bronze doors, or what remained of them. Where the doors were rotten or missing, the vaults' contents glinted in the beams of the hurricane lantern, their one remaining source of light.

Gentile's eyes glinted greedily. "In these chambers alone, there must be enough wealth to—"

"Aagh!" The Italian's distraction had allowed Roxton to miss his footing on the uneven floor. "Mind what you're about, you great ox," he gasped painfully. "And keep your mind on the task in hand. There's only one treasure we're here to find."

"*Si*. A thousand apologies. *Vi prego di scusarmi*." But catching Gentile's expression, Luke was certain that, once his current mission was completed, the Italian had no intention of allowing the treasures of the Mines to remain in place a moment longer than he could help.

Luke realized that the walls of the tunnel in front of him were becoming visible in a flickering red glow that was not produced by Roxton's lantern. Somewhere ahead was another source of light. As the explorers moved cautiously forward, with Nick (continuing his check for traps) leading the way, the light grew stronger until it virtually swamped that of the hurricane lamp.

One by one, the members of the exploring party stepped round a shoulder of rock into the full glow of the light and halted – dazzled, fascinated, overpowered.

They were standing at the edge of the greatest cavern yet, a titanic underground chamber that dwarfed even those that had gone before. The roof was a lofty, distant expanse of naked stone. The floor in the centre of the chamber, whether as the result of a lava flow or smoothed by human hands, was level.

Their position was eighty feet or so above the floor of the cavern, which sloped away before them. At the foot of the slope stood a wall: high, square and many hundreds of feet in length, one of four arranged in a square. Halfway along its length, each wall was pierced by a huge gateway. A roof, supported by columns, ran around the inside of the walls surrounding the vast courtyard they enclosed.

The outer walls appeared to be built from dressed stone, whose colour matched the stone of the cavern.

But the next level of the temple glowed with the dull red of bronze. An inner wall, higher, more elaborate and containing within its boundaries more complex buildings, rose in the centre of the court. Ceremonial pathways linked the gates in the outer wall to grander and more imposing gateways in the inner.

In the nearer part of the inner court stood a gigantic circular basin, the size of one of the Trafalgar Square fountains. But the liquid it contained was not water – not unless its creators had somehow discovered how to make water burn. Had they tapped into some natural deposit of oil or methane? There was no way of telling from this distance; but the contents of the basin burned with a roaring, inexhaustible flame, filling the vast cavern with light and illuminating the building that lay beyond.

This mighty golden structure was clearly the heart of the temple and of the Mines themselves. A flight of steps rose from the inner court to a high doorway flanked by massive pillars and leading into a hall, several storeys high and flanked by lesser buildings on three sides. Above the pediment of the doorway rose two more great pillars, dwarfing even those that stood beneath. The whole colossal structure was as ponderous and enduring as the Pyramids of Giza.

"There it is," announced Roxton. "There it is at last. The Treasure House of Solomon."

23 SEA OF FIRE

In silence, the explorers descended the slope to the outer wall of the temple.

The gatehouse towered above them, its ramparts topped by statues of strange mythical beasts – gryphons, unicorns, winged bulls. The great bronze gates stood open. Roxton's party crept between them, casting anxious glances to right and left like small children entering a strange house for the first time.

They crossed the courtyard, their feet disturbing the dust of thousands of years, feeling themselves surrounded and hemmed in by the deep, brooding shadows of the colonnaded walkways; shadows that seemed, in that vast and gloomy cavern, to conceal some watchful, malign presence. They passed the second gatehouse, far greater and more richly decorated than the first, and found themselves before the huge basin, resting on the backs of twelve brass oxen, with roaring tongues of flame leaping from its heart.

Roxton gazed on it with rapture. "The Brazen Sea," he croaked, "just as it was described in the Book of Kings." He led the way around the flames to the wide steps leading to the great golden building that rose up beyond the basin. "And there lies the Treasure House of Solomon, the Well of Souls – and the Spear of Destiny."

He turned to face Luke, Nick, Elsa, Salim and Isaias, their one remaining guide. "I'm most exceedingly obliged to you for bringing me to this spot," he drawled. "Of course, the fact that we are here and that our information indicates that there are no further obstacles to be negotiated means that your usefulness is at an end." He gestured towards the doorway into the Treasure House. "Gentile, with me. Captain Mochizuki, you will follow us – after you have dealt with the prisoners."

Roxton leaned heavily on the giant Italian. Slowly and painfully, the ill-matched pair made their way up the steps leading to the Treasure House...to the great pillared doorway...and into the shadows of the interior.

Luke turned his attention to Captain Mochizuki. The Japanese assassin's usually expressionless face was wearing a triumphant smirk.

The High Priestess of the Kukuana gave a shriek of laughter and danced around Salim, clicking her fingers in glee, taunting him with her victory. Salim ignored Gagool's caperings and made no reply – indeed, he seemed to be hardly aware of her derision. He stood with his head bowed and his eyes closed.

Mochizuki drew her pistol from its holster and gave rapid orders in Italian. The soldiers cast doubtful glances at her and each other, but they formed an orderly line facing Luke and his friends as they stood with their backs to the Brazen Sea, and held their rifles at the ready. They clearly didn't relish what they were being made to do, but at the same time, they weren't going to refuse to obey orders.

Staring directly into Luke's eyes, Mochizuki delivered her final orders.

"*Puntare!*"

The soldiers raised their rifles into the firing position.

"*Mirare!*" The firing squad took aim. Luke heard Salim, who was standing beside him, mutter something. He wondered if he was praying.

"Fuoco!"

Luke braced himself for the bullets – but a split second later, he realized that the Italian soldiers were no longer looking at him, but at something behind him. The muzzles of their rifles wavered and fell.

The heat of the fire from the Brazen Sea had increased tenfold. The hairs on Luke's neck crisped and a crackling roar hammered at his ears. The shadows of the cavern leaped away like startled ghosts. He spun round to see that the flames pouring from the giant basin had grown vastly in size, and brightened from a dull orange-yellow to an intense white that hissed and spat like the glare of a welder's torch.

Gagool gave a thin wail and ran pell-mell from the scene. Luke threw up a hand to protect his eyes. Behind him, the Italians were doing the same, as were Nick, Elsa and Isaias. Only Salim remained unmoving. He was holding his medallion in his clenched fists, and intoning a stream of words.

Luke yelled into Elsa's ear, "What's he saying?"

"I don't know! It isn't Amharic – it could be ancient Hebrew…"

The soldiers were backing away towards the nearest refuge, the doorway to the Treasure House. Mochizuki, her face working with fury, repeated the order to fire. Two of the braver or more dutiful members of her squad raised their rifles to obey. The flames rose yet higher. There were muffled explosions from the basin followed by high-pitched whistles – and balls of fire hurtled from the heart of the flames to burst in front of the men, incinerating them in an instant.

"Lava bombs!" Nick was aghast.

Luke had no better explanation. Lava bombs occurred during some types of volcanic eruption, but he had never heard of one being spat out by a basin of fire, and certainly never of one that chose its target...

The Italians were now in full retreat, running like hares up the steps, fighting and tripping over each other in their haste. More lava bombs sped them on their way. Mochizuki, her face contorted with rage, aimed her pistol at Luke – but another bomb soared from the basin, and only her supreme agility saved her as it burst on the spot she had occupied a moment before. The assassin had lost her gun in her frantic leap for safety; as Luke watched, the lava reduced it to a small puddle of molten metal.

Mochizuki clasped her hands behind her head for protection and fled for the steps, but a bomb exploding directly in front of her forced her to turn back. More bombs rained down, always forcing her away from the Treasure House and her would-be victims until, at length, she gave up the attempt to follow her employers and ran back the way she had come, through the inner gateway and out of sight.

As soon as the court was empty of their enemies, the flames from the basin died to their former level. Salim let go of his medallion, which fell to dangle on the end of its chain. He slumped forward and would have fallen if Isaias and Elsa had not stepped forward to catch him.

Luke grabbed Salim by the shoulders. His breathing was fast and ragged, his eyes glazed. "What just happened? What did you do?"

"I...don't know..."

Luke stood up. Salim was clearly in no state to give sensible answers. "Look after him," he told Elsa and Isaias. "He can't go anywhere until he's recovered from..." He spread his hands ineffectually as words to describe the recent event failed him. "From whatever it was he just did," he concluded lamely. "You should be safe here – I don't think the soldiers will be back for a while." He turned to Nick. "Follow Roxton and Gentile. Keep an eye on them. If they look like getting hold of the Spear, come back here right away. Don't let them catch you."

Nick nodded. "And what will you do?"

"Go after Mochizuki! We don't want her skulking away behind our backs. Anyway, I've got a score to settle."

For a moment, Nick seemed about to argue. But the look on his friend's face stopped him. He gave a brief nod, and ran past the now-placid flames of the Brazen Sea, up the steps and into the temple.

Luke turned on his heel and set off through the ceremonial gateway and across the outer court, in the footsteps of his hated enemy.

He emerged from the outer gate to see Mochizuki at the mouth of the tunnel from which they had first emerged into the Treasure House cavern. As soon as she saw him, she disappeared into the cleft in the rocks. Toiling up the slope, Luke followed.

Once he was inside the tunnel, the darkness was total. Luke pressed on, feeling for the rough rock walls, stumbling over the uneven floor, while the roaring of the waterfall grew in his ears. The rock walls fell away from his clutching hands, and he realized he was on the ledge, with the bridge before him. He fumbled for the rope, aware all the time of the terrible unseen drop awaiting him if he slipped. After several infuriating seconds, his questing fingers found the rough, damp cord and he grabbed it in both hands. It was jerking and trembling between his fingers – Mochizuki must still be making her way across. Even as the thought came, the rope stilled. Without hesitation, Luke swarmed across it, past the thunder of the falls, the blinding spray.

It wasn't until he was halfway across that it occurred to Luke that all Mochizuki had to do to send him plunging to his death was cut the rope – he redoubled his efforts. But he reached the other end of the rope without incident. Perhaps Mochizuki hadn't thought of cutting it; perhaps she wasn't carrying a knife; or perhaps – and the thought didn't make Luke feel any better at all – she had something much worse planned for him.

He struggled along the tunnel to the Place of Death. As he approached the last resting place of the Kukuana kings, he realized that the darkness surrounding him was no longer absolute. Somewhere ahead of him was a light. With every step it grew stronger until, by the time he emerged from the archway and onto the stone steps, he could see every detail of his path – and of the cavern, with its huge, leering skeleton.

Moving with great caution, Luke peered over the lip of the stairwell. A lantern was sitting on the stone seat formerly occupied by Roxton – Luke could only assume that his godfather had brought a spare. Its light was blinding after the blackness of the tunnel, but it created plenty of shadows; Mochizuki could be hiding in any one of them.

Making as little noise as possible, Luke mounted the steps, darting glances to every corner of the cave, trying to peer behind every sad, stone king as he went by. Still nothing – but now, he heard a mocking whisper: "Brave Mr. Challenger. Come and find me."

Luke strained his hearing to locate its source but the echoes of the cavern made it sound as if the voice was coming from everywhere at once.

"I spy with my little eye, something beginning with C – but he can't see me..." *Mee-hee-hee-hee,* chortled the echo.

Luke snatched up the lantern and crept around the cavern. Shadows fled at his approach.

"Warm," said the voice. "Warm...warmer...ah, no. Cold...colder...freezing. Can't you do better than that?"

Luke gritted his teeth. Mochizuki was trying to make him angry, and she was succeeding, but he couldn't afford anger. He knew he was up against an opponent who was stronger, faster and more experienced than he was. He would have to find a way to take her at a disadvantage – and at the moment, all the advantage was hers.

The great stone skeleton with its dreadful spear loomed above Luke as he made his way along the side of the stairway. The spear was directly above him. He heard a flurry of movement, a rustle of cloth, and looked up – too late. Kasumi Mochizuki slipped from her hiding place inside the White Death's ribcage, leaped for the spear, and swung around it like a gymnast on a horizontal bar to deliver a two-footed kick that sent Luke tumbling helplessly over the edge of the pit and onto the stone stairs below. His head met one of the steps with a sickening impact, and the light of the lantern – all light, and sound, awareness itself – went out.

When Luke came to, he was lying in a small chamber, seemingly not more than ten feet square. His head hurt abominably, he felt weak and sick, there was a roaring in his ears and his eyes would not focus. As his vision cleared, he realized that he was sprawled at the back of the chamber, on the opposite side to the door by which he had evidently been brought here. Something was poking him in the back; turning his head (with an involuntary yelp of pain), he discovered that he was lying against a great pile of ivory – elephant tusks, four or five hundred of them, glowing pale yellow in the light of the lantern held by his nemesis.

Kasumi Mochizuki stood over him, looking pleased with herself. "I am glad you are awake, Luke Challenger," she said in low, caressing tones. "I wished to see the look on your face when you realized your fate. Do you know where you are?"

Luke shook his head, and instantly regretted it.

Mochizuki must have carried or dragged him here while he was unconscious – wherever "here" was.

That question, at least, was soon resolved. "You are in the false Treasure Chamber in which the former Gagool entombed Allan Quatermain and his friends." Without taking her eyes from Luke's, Mochizuki squatted in the doorway and held the lantern over the room's stone doorstep, on which a sinister-looking smear spread around grisly remnants of cloth, fur and splintered bone. "Here is what remains of that Gagool, crushed by the very door to their prison half a century ago." She stood again and gestured to left and right, where shallow recesses held wooden boxes and stone chests, their lids broken and scattered. "No gold or diamonds, I'm afraid – the new High Priestess commandeered them to arm her bodyguard. Apart from the ivory, you will die poor."

She pointed to a great slab of rock above her head. "When I leave, the door will descend. It cannot be opened from this side, and the secret of opening it from outside is known only to the current High Priestess, and to me. I paid her a heavy price for the knowledge, but it was worth it. You killed my sister, Luke Challenger, and you have thwarted me – but no more. No easy death for you. You will be buried alive. The present Gagool assures me that the way by which Quatermain and his friends escaped has been irrevocably blocked. You will perish here, miserably, with hunger gnawing at your vitals and thirst tearing at your throat; in the dark of the chamber and the dark of your own despair, you will die—" She broke off as a sudden grinding noise erupted from the rock, making the walls and floor of the chamber shake.

Mochizuki looked up and gave a hiss of rage. The door to the chamber was descending. Luke instantly realized that he had an unexpected advantage over his distracted enemy: she was standing, he was already on the ground. Summoning all his strength, he swept his right leg round in a powerful low-level kick. His foot slammed into the back of Mochizuki's knees and she fell backwards with a cry, cracking her head on the rock floor. The lantern flew from her hand to lie, spinning, on the doorstep.

As the assassin lay stunned, Luke rolled across the floor and over the chamber's threshold. Above him, the door continued its descent, rushing down in a cloud of dust with shocking speed in the light of the guttering lantern. He felt the moving rock brush his sleeve as he wriggled clear. An instant later, with a thunderous crash, the door completed its descent. The light from the lantern went out as thirty tons of stone crushed it to fragments.

Luke sat with his back to the door and fought for breath. Kasumi Mochizuki was trapped; the fate she had planned for Luke had become her own. What was she doing now? Screaming with fear and rage? Hammering at the door? If so, he could hear or feel nothing of it. Perhaps she was lying unconscious from her fall – or just sitting in the dark, resigned to her fate, waiting for death. Luke knew that he could not raise the door, even if he had wanted to. Only two people knew the secret of its mechanism – and one of them was behind the door, and could not tell him what it was. Only Gagool...

Luke staggered to his feet. Gagool! No one else could have set the door in motion. Where was she now? She could still be dangerous. Luke held his pounding head in both hands and tried to think. She might have gone back to the Treasure House, but he considered that unlikely; he had seen no sign that she was interested in the Spear of Destiny. What she wanted was to re-establish her hold over the Kukuana. Her best chance of doing that would be to slip back to Leu and hope Salim would never return from the Mines. Escape would be uppermost in her mind...

Luke made his way haltingly back through the pitch darkness, feeling his way through a tunnel to the Place of Death.

When he reached the last resting place of the Kukuana kings, he found that light had once more entered the Mines. Some of the guards they had left outside, perhaps becoming concerned at the long absence of their new leader, had entered the caverns. In the light of the burning torches they bore, Luke saw that they had waylaid Gagool. The High Priestess crouched at bay, hissing what seemed to be threats and imprecations at the Kukuana, who for their part were menacing her with guns and spears, clearly asking some awkward questions about the whereabouts of the travellers whose guide she was supposed to be.

There was a sudden silence as Luke entered the cavern. Gagool's eyes widened as she realized that he had not, as she had planned, shared the fate of his Japanese enemy. She gave a shriek of pure rage and snatched a throwing knife from her belt, ready to hurl it at Luke.

The officer commanding the Kukuana yelled something, raised his rifle and pulled the trigger. The shot was hurried, and missed the High Priestess, striking the base of the great stone skeleton that dominated the cavern. Shards of rock flew from the point of impact.

A crack appeared, snaking across the narrow spur where the spine of the skeleton emerged from the solid rock. With a creak of tortured stone, the White Death broke free from its stalagmite base and pitched forward. Gagool screamed, dropping her knife, which fell to the floor with a clatter. She screamed again – a scream of mortal terror as the spear in the statue's skeletal hand moved downwards in a fatal arc to strike her through the chest, impaling her, transfixing her body to the floor of the cave. Gagool, who had brought death to so many, stared sightlessly at the grinning skull as Death came to take her for his own.

24 THE WELL OF SOULS

Salim, still attended by Elsa and Isaias, was looking much better by the time Luke led the awe-stricken Kukuana warriors back to the Treasure House. "You took your time," Elsa accused him.

Luke ignored this. "How do you feel?" he asked Salim.

"As if I've just run a marathon carrying a sack of potatoes," said Salim. "Don't worry – I'm a lot better than I was. Where's Mochizuki?"

Luke told him.

"Well. When we have finished here, perhaps we will try to find the hidden mechanism that opens the door."

"If we must," said Luke. "But let's not try too hard." Elsa nodded vigorously; she would have preferred not to try at all.

Salim nodded. "And Gagool?"

Luke described the High Priestess's last moments. "Maybe Mochizuki broke something by swinging on the statue," he said, "and the bullet just finished the job."

Salim held up his medallion. It reflected the red glow of the Brazen Sea. "Or perhaps," he said softly, "the reach of the Seal of Solomon is greater than we know." He put the talisman away. "If the traditions of the Kukuana are correct," he went on, "Gagool will shortly be reborn into the tribe."

"Maybe the tradition is wrong," said Luke. "In any case, even if it isn't, it should be fifteen years or so before she grows up enough to be a nuisance."

"That is true." Salim put a question to the leader of the Kukuana warriors, and Elsa translated his reply: "'*O Father of our people, we saw Gagool perish by reason of her own impiety. Since the straw-haired one*' – that's you, Luke – '*summoned us, we took him for your messenger, and at his bidding followed him to this place.*'" She listened a while longer and added, "Salim's told them they did the right thing, and now he's explaining what happened here." As Salim's story continued, the warriors began to exclaim angrily and their leader, gripping his spear tightly, made an impassioned speech. "*'We are your bondsmen!'*" Elsa translated. "*'Sworn to protect you, and'* – oh, no you don't! They want to go in there" – she pointed at the door to the Treasure House – "after Salim's remaining enemies." She faced Salim, her face flushed and determined. "You mustn't let them! Gentile's Italians still have more rifles, and they're trained to use them. Your men's bravery won't shield them from bullets."

Salim held up his hand peaceably. "I entirely agree."

"Oh." Elsa had been expecting a fight; Salim's ready agreement took the wind out of her sails. "Well – good."

"It is Luke, Nick and myself who have brought us all to this situation, and we will be the ones to resolve it."

"Now hold on!" Elsa was back on the warpath. "The three of you brought us to this situation? And what was I doing while you were bringing us to this situation? Knitting? Baking scones?"

"You were trying to stop us; so the responsibility for what happens next is not yours."

"And what about Ali? Keshe? Abele? Do you think I'm going to sit around here while these murderers get what they want? Think again!"

Isaias made a speech, respectful but firm. Luke didn't understand the words, but the old warrior's meaning was clear enough. Isaias was going on too.

Salim regarded them steadily for a moment. Then he said, "Very well." He turned to the waiting Kukuana and spoke. Over his men's protests, Elsa said, "He's telling them they're not to follow us. They're not happy about the idea, but Salim's pulling rank. They'll do as he says and guard our backs."

"Good," said Luke.

Salim gave his last order and turned towards him. "Are you ready for this, Luke? Lord John Roxton is your godfather – are you really prepared to stop him at any cost?"

"If he gets his hands on the Spear of Destiny," said Luke, "it's curtains for Ethiopia, and maybe for the rest of the world, too. He may be my Uncle John and my godfather, but he's a traitor and a murderer and I'll put a stop to his capers if it's the last thing I do."

Salim nodded. He put a foot on the first step up to the Treasure House. Luke, Elsa and Isaias moved at the same moment. Side by side, they climbed towards the towering citadel of King Solomon.

"Sally," said Luke, "what are we going to find in there?"

"Well, treasure, obviously. But perhaps other things.

You remember I mentioned the legends about Solomon being a magician? It's said that beneath the innermost part of the Treasure House lies the Well of Souls from which he summoned the creatures that built it." Catching Luke's sceptical glance, Salim went on defensively, "I'm not saying I believe it – but we've seen some very strange things on our way here, and at this point I wouldn't dismiss anything out of hand."

"If these creatures of yours do exist," said Elsa, "I hope they're on our side."

Salim fingered his medallion. "Oh, I think they will be," he said absently. "But the legend says that, once they are summoned, they will require a reward. I wonder what they will demand for their services."

Luke shivered. "Knock it off, you two," he complained, "you're giving me the shivers – oy!" he added as Nick came pelting out of the doorway. "Watch out, you nearly had me over!"

"What's the hold up?" Nick's voice was low and excited. "There's been all sorts going on in there!"

"There's been a fair amount going on out here as well," Luke told him. "But it'll keep. What are Roxton and Gentile up to?"

"They're still inside." Nick gestured towards the shadowed interior of the Treasure House. "There are three halls and they're in the third."

"According to legend," said Salim, "that's where Solomon's greatest treasures were kept."

"I shouldn't be surprised. There's loads of valuable-looking stuff lying about – gold and jewels and whatnot. Anyway, the soldiers are with them – Gentile has them standing guard, though I must say they don't look as if they're enjoying it much. The whole lot of them look ready to grab whatever they can carry and bolt, if you ask me."

"All right," said Luke impatiently, "but what are Roxton and his playmate doing?"

"They've found the Spear – it's there all right, but... well, it's floating."

Luke stared at him. "How do you mean, floating?"

"The floor is sort of like a shallow dome, and there's a shaft of light coming from the middle of it. The Spear is in the light, just hanging in mid-air."

"That's impossible."

"I know it's impossible, but that's what it's doing. It's got Roxton and Gentile worried – they can't make out what's keeping it there. It's just out of reach and they're worried they might spring a trap if they try and snaffle it. Come and see for yourself if you don't believe me."

"Oh, we're coming, don't you worry."

"This way, then – and keep quiet. The Italians are pretty jumpy."

The first hall was little more than a vestibule – imposing in its dimensions but modest in its decoration. They crept through it, keeping a keen lookout and taking care to make no noise.

Between the first hall and the second, colossal doors rose into the shadows of the distant roof. They glowed red-gold in the light from the Brazen Sea. The doors were just ajar, with space for Luke's companions to slip through one at a time. Luke wasn't happy about showing themselves against the light, but there was no help for it. In the event, they reached the second hall without any alarm being sounded.

This hall was vast, with a smooth stone floor. Its walls and pillars were painted in striking geometric patterns and bold colours. Perhaps in the days of Solomon it had served some ceremonial purpose. Side chambers opened off the main hall. In some of these, the distant light from the doorway and high windows revealed dull red gleams.

Luke beckoned Nick, Elsa and Salim to him. "I guess those rooms are full of Solomon's treasures but we need to be sure there aren't any guards hiding there as well. Nick, you check those on the left – Salim, ask Isaias to do the same on the other side."

Salim relayed the order, and Nick and Isaias slipped away. As they peered into each shadowy recess in turn,

Luke led Elsa and Salim through the centre of the hall, taking care to keep their line of retreat open in case their enemies should appear.

About halfway down the hall, Nick suddenly stopped in front of one alcove and beckoned urgently. Instructing Elsa and Salim to stay where they were, Luke hurried to his side.

Nick pointed wordlessly. Inside the alcove was a single object – a highly decorated golden chest, with winged angels crouched at either end. Wooden poles passed through gold rings at each corner so that the chest could be carried.

Luke glared at Nick. "So?" he hissed. "I thought you'd found something important."

"Something important?" Nick stared at him. "Don't you know what that is? It's the Ark of the Covenant. Only the actual Ark of the actual Covenant! It's supposed to have the Ten Commandments inside."

"We haven't come all this way to stand gawping at a bookcase! Will you concentrate?" Luke slipped away. Shaking his head, Nick moved on to the next chamber.

Their careful check revealed riches galore, but no ambush; and at length, they found themselves at the door to the third and final chamber. Voices sounded from inside – Roxton's voice and Gentile's, apparently raised in argument.

Speaking very softly, Nick said, "There's a sort of balcony, with a low wall and pillars, all round the outside of the hall – that's where I hid while I was spying on them. If we keep low, we should be able to get in without being seen."

"All right," said Elsa. "And what do we do when we get in there?"

Luke had hoped that no one would ask that question; frankly, he hadn't a clue. But Salim seemed untroubled by their lack of a plan. "I daresay something will turn up," he said.

Luke couldn't share his confidence, but he gave Elsa an encouraging smile, which, to his astonishment, she returned. Pulling himself together – this was no time to go weak at the knees over a girl – he said, "Salim, ask Isaias to stay on guard out here." Salim gave the instruction and Isaias nodded. "All right – let's see what they're up to."

They crept in through the doors, slithering on their bellies to keep them below the level of the balcony wall. Peering around the base of a pillar, Luke realized that their precautions were hardly necessary. Some of the guards were engrossed in the argument between Roxton and Gentile, but most were staring spellbound towards the centre of the chamber. Luke followed their gaze, and drew in a sharp breath.

The Spear was hanging, just as Nick had described it, in a shaft of light coming from a hole in the centre of the domed floor, its tip pointing upwards. It revolved slowly. Luke searched for the wires holding it in place, but there were none. The Spear was simply defying gravity.

Its shaft was of ebony with a leather handgrip halfway down its length. The head was made of ancient-looking metal, bound to the shaft with coils of silver wire and, at its centre, with a sheath of gold. It looked fragile and unthreatening: yet as it hung impossibly in its shaft of light, it seemed to Luke to emanate an aura of power and menace that made him shudder.

He tore his eyes away from the Spear and tried to concentrate on what Roxton and Gentile were saying.

The Italian's voice was accusing. "You said that once we entered the Treasure House, there would be no more traps!"

"For pity's sake, Gentile, stop croaking!" Roxton was leaning against the stone wall of the balcony. His voice was weak and petulant. "We don't even know that there is a trap."

"We know that the Spear is just hanging there with nothing to hold it in place – Holy Mother of God, that is not right!"

"Damn you, stop whining. I can see what it's doing – the question is, how are we to reach it?"

Gentile spread his arms. "Perhaps if we were to build a bridge…"

"From what? And how long do you think we have? Mochizuki should have joined us by now – where is she? According to your men, the last time she was seen, she was running like a rabbit – and my tedious godson and his friends were still alive. We must secure the Spear without delay." Roxton eyed the legendary weapon with calculation. "We have already wasted precious time looking for traps, and what have we found? Nothing. It's time for the direct approach. You will cross the floor. Standing in the centre of the dome, you may just be able to reach the end of the shaft."

Gentile gave him a worried, defiant look. "I do not think so."

A pistol appeared in Roxton's hand. "I don't care what you think. You will obey orders." The Italian soldiers exchanged nervous glances. Should they interfere? If so, on which side? Gentile said something under his breath, and Roxton flushed. "I may not know much Italian, my friend, but I know what *that* means!" He drew back the hammer to cock the pistol. "Go!"

The domed floor of the chamber was surrounded by a step or kerb, too low to be called a wall. Gentile gave Roxton a murderous glance. Luke held his breath as, with infinite caution, the Italian stepped forward onto the dome.

For a moment, nothing happened. Gentile was already raising his foot to take another step when, with a sudden grinding of rock, the floor began to move. The dome broke into segments like those of an orange. As Gentile made a convulsive leap for safety, the segments drew back, sliding under the surrounding floor to reveal a circular pit beneath.

As the Well of Souls opened, the shaft of light in which the Spear of Destiny hung expanded, until it was an immense column of radiance, the width of the pit itself. Half-blinded, Luke risked a glance into the Well. It seemed to be full of roiling vapours, bursts of light, half-glimpsed forms. And, on the edge of hearing, came the sounds of running water – streams, fountains, waterfalls – and voices – angry voices and sad voices that seemed to plead and weep, wordless cries of pain, terror and heartbreak.

"Fool!" Roxton screeched. "Oaf! What have you done?" He gestured with the pistol. "Get me the spear!"

"But the pit!"

"It is only a few feet across. You're supposed to be an athlete – jump for it!"

Gentile had retreated to the other side of the chamber. "*Io, no!* What is in there? *Demoni* – devils! Creatures of perdition! I will not – it is suicide!"

Roxton's pistol spat flame, and a fragment of stone flew from the wall beside Gentile's head, cutting his ear. "Do it!"

Steeling himself, Gentile flung himself upwards and outwards. At the height of his leap, his grasping hand caught at the very end of the Spear. Clutching his prize, the giant Italian flew across the void...

But he had sacrificed too much distance for height. With a cry of horror, he fell short. A despairing hand caught at the edge of the pit and Gentile hung by his fingertips, while the vapours from the pit swirled around his legs and the voices cried out, summoning him to join them.

He held out the Spear to Roxton. "Take this – call my men – pull me out!"

Roxton seized the shaft just below the head. "And risk losing the Spear in the attempt?" He shook his head. "I'm afraid that won't do. *Arrivederci*, Gentile."

He snatched the Spear of Destiny from Gentile's hand. The straining fingers lost their grip. With a wail of despair, the self-styled Count fell back into the swirling mists, which closed around him. He was gone.

25 SOLOMON'S SEAL

There was an angry outcry from the Italian soldiers. Several raised their rifles and pointed them at Roxton. He faced them down, the Spear of Destiny in one hand and his pistol in the other.

"Put down your weapons, you idiots." Possession of the Spear seemed to have given the old adventurer new strength. He brandished the relic. "This is for Signor Mussolini – *Il Duce, è chiaro*?" The soldiers hesitated, uncertain. "Don't you understand? At last, the Spear of Destiny is ours – nothing can stand in our way…"

He broke off as the column of light from the pit first dimmed and then became brighter. It did so again – and then again, pulsing as though in anger, and changing colour – red, orange, green, blue, back to red again. The voices from the Well of Souls rose in volume and intensity, clamouring, shrieking. The soldiers stared wildly about as vapours rose from the pit to coalesce into forms – intangible, incorporeal, but threatening, full of deadly purpose.

"Luke." Salim stood and raised his voice, making no further attempt at concealment. "Nick, Elsa. To me." He held up his medallion and began to chant – slow, sonorous words. Luke glanced at Elsa, who shook her head – her translation skills fell far short of this task. In Salim's hand, Solomon's Seal glowed silver with an inner light that seemed to deflect the malign radiance from the Well of Souls.

Then, between one heartbeat and the next, the column of light from the pit exploded, filling the hall. Instinctively, Luke grabbed for Salim's arm, aware that Elsa and Nick were doing the same. The vaporous figures that had risen from the Well of Souls, freed from their confinement, swirled around the terrified soldiers. The light was blinding, the noise a cacophony. Screaming and weeping in fear and panic, the Italians fired at the impossible creatures surrounding them. Muzzle flashes erupted from every part of the hall; bullets passed innocuously through the swirling entities to whine and ricochet from the stone walls.

One by one, the rifles fell silent as their ammunition was exhausted. The frantic soldiers fumbled with bayonets, or turned the guns around to hold them by the barrel, using the stocks as clubs. They thrust, stabbed and swung at their tormentors.

Not for long. One by one, howling and kicking, the men were surrounded, lifted into the air and flung, spinning, around the hall, smashing into the walls and each other, while the voices from the pit jabbered and screeched in triumph. Luke remembered the legend: Solomon had summoned unknown forces to build his Treasure House. They had moved great stone blocks through the air to raise its walls in a matter of hours. He felt a cold wind pluck at his clothing, his hair – like questing fingers seeking a hold, clutching, grasping, seeking to pluck him, too, from the safety of the earth. But Salim's voice rolled on, and the power of the medallion surrounded him, and Nick and Elsa. The fingers could find no hold.

The Italians were not so lucky. Struggling, lashing out, clutching vainly at the empty air, they spun like leaves in a whirlpool; round and round, faster and faster, finally to plunge into the gaping pit of the Well of Souls, their screams instantly cut off as they disappeared into its seething depths.

"An army!" Roxton's voice was a triumphant shriek. "That's what the legend means – the Spear commands an army of creatures from the pit! No force on earth could stand against it." As the last of the soldiers disappeared, he looked up, suddenly becoming aware of Salim and the three figures crouched beside him. "Kill them!" he roared to the deadly creatures that still swirled, unfettered, about the hall. "Kill them, I command you! I have the Spear!" The denizens of the pit seemed to understand his intentions, if not his words. They swarmed towards Salim and his companions.

Luke felt a moment of pure terror. The medallion had shown its ability to protect Salim – at least, so far – but would its protection extend to shield him, Nick and Elsa against the malignance of the things from the pit? There was sweat on Salim's brow, and his eyes were closed, but his voice was steady as he continued to chant the words that kept the light of the medallion alive, that kept the creatures of the pit at bay.

Luke tried to think. What was happening was beyond sense, beyond reason, beyond sanity – yet it was happening, and somehow he had to find meaning in it, and form a plan that would keep the Spear of Destiny from his enemies' grasp.

All right then...the creatures of the pit had appeared when Gentile had snatched the Spear, and in light of what had happened to the Count and his soldiers it was a fair guess that they were there to protect it. But Roxton had the Spear now – would the creatures obey him? If so, what were they waiting for?

Then he understood. Roxton had the Spear, but Salim had Solomon's Seal. Both were objects of power, used in the past to subdue and control whatever force had risen from the pit; a force that may not be intelligent, but that was bound to operate according to ancient laws and obligations, laid down thousands of years ago by Solomon and his heirs.

So for the moment, the situation was in stalemate; a Mexican stand-off. The forces Gentile had unleashed could not obey Roxton without simultaneously acting against Salim, and vice versa. As far as they understood, both had called upon them for a service that was impossible to perform.

How to break the stalemate so that Salim would emerge as the more powerful? What had his friend said as they mounted the steps to the Treasure House? ...*once they are summoned, they will require a reward.* Clearly the dwellers of the Well considered themselves to have been summoned – but what reward could he offer that would satisfy creatures (if you could even call them that) with no minds and no bodies – beings that common sense told him should not, could not, even exist?

Inspiration came. With his free hand, Luke grasped Elsa's wrist. The face she turned towards him was so empty of anything but mindless horror that he almost despaired, but he gave the wrist a hard wrench, and the blank look disappeared.

"Let go!" she hissed. For the moment, Elsa's unyielding spirit was back.

Luke tightened his grip and looked her straight in the eyes. "They want a reward!" His voice rose above the yammering from the pit. "I've got one for them, but you'll need to tell them – in Amharic, they may not understand English."

Elsa's head drooped. "Tell them? Who's *them*? This is madness..."

"Then go mad, just for a minute! Elsa, I need you to do this! Tell them!"

"Tell them what?"

"Their reward – tell them, Roxton has a diamond. They can have his diamond!"

Elsa stared at him and gave a slight shake of her head. But then she closed her eyes, and Luke realized she was composing the offer in the language of the guardians of King Solomon's Mines. Luke felt the cold, insidious clutch as their unearthly assailants moved in closer. Nick groaned, his appalled expression matching Luke's own. Salim's voice rose a pitch, his chanting grew more frenzied and sweat rolled down his face. The hand holding the medallion shook as the power of the Spear of Destiny began to prevail over that of the Seal of Solomon. The creatures pressed closer still. Luke felt tendrils of fire and ice slide into his veins. A howl tore from his throat as pain and despair overwhelmed him. His mind was empty of everything except grief, terror, the numbing fear of dissolution and eternal torment.

Then, as Luke felt the last shreds of his sanity begin to whirl away, Elsa opened her eyes and swung round to face the swirling forms that circled above the Well of Souls. In a high, clear voice, she made his offer.

There was a momentary swirl of agitation among the half-glimpsed creatures of the pit. With one accord, the insubstantial, deadly forms turned away from Salim and his friends, and slowly, inexorably, converged on Lord John Roxton.

"What is this?" Roxton raised the Spear. "What are you doing? Back! Back, I say! I hold the Spear!" His voice rose to a scream. "Back, I command you!"

Awareness returned to Luke. He watched, dumbfounded, as the glowing figures surrounded his enemy. Something like a human arm coalesced from the vapour. Roxton's eyes bulged and a terrible, animal cry tore from his throat as its hand plunged into his chest cavity, through clothing, skin, ribs and all. There was a pause – and the hand was raised into the air. The clenched fist opened – and on the palm lay a single, huge diamond.

Roxton looked down at the gaping wound in his chest without comprehension. He looked up again. Just for a moment, his gaze met Luke's. Then the light faded from his eyes. His fingers loosened their grip on the Spear, which fell to the stone pavement with a clatter. His knees buckled and he fell, sprawling beside it.

With a final, triumphant shriek, the creatures of the pit swirled around the hall and plunged back into the Well of Souls, carrying Roxton's diamond with them. The segments of the domed floor slid from their housing, and came together, joining until only a single shaft of light rose from the hole in its centre, shining as strongly and steadily as it had at the first.

Salim stopped chanting and let his medallion fall. His breathing came in ragged gasps. His legs buckled and Nick and Elsa took his arms to steady him as Luke vaulted the low wall of the balcony and crouched beside the lifeless body of his godfather. From some obscure feeling of what was owed the dead, Luke closed Roxton's eyes. Then he reached across the limp body towards the Spear of Destiny.

For a moment, he felt a terrible strength flow through him. The Spear seemed to leap to his hand, an invincible weapon, straining to be used. Warm blood surged through his veins, shuddering his heart, pounding in his ears like the sound of drums. What could the British government not do if it had this? It would have no fear of Hitler, or Mussolini. *To turn their own chosen weapon on the Sons of Destiny*, thought Luke. *What power could be ours – what power could be* mine...

And suddenly he was on an ancient battlefield, in command of warriors with leather armour and long, curling hair beneath their bronze helmets, who carried spears and great curved swords into battle. He led his men as they tore into the ranks of their enemies and there was a terrible joy in his heart as he slew, and slew...

"Luke." Salim touched him on the shoulder, and the spell was broken. His Ethiopian friend took the Spear from Luke's unresisting fingers.

"Yes," said Salim quietly, "it is a powerful weapon – if you are prepared to fight on its terms. To crush and utterly destroy your enemies, without mercy, without compassion. To burn their homes, blight their crops, raze their cities. And to waste your own people's lives, to pour out the blood of your soldiers with no regard for the cost."

Luke shook his head wretchedly. "But war is coming – you know it, I know it. The Spear could turn the tide."

"I thought your only aim was to keep the Spear out of the hands of your enemies?" said Salim.

Luke fought with his conscience. "All right – but *you* could use it. Your country hasn't a chance against Mussolini unless you do." Luke shook his head. "Salim, war isn't a game – it's not *nice*. There's no room for chivalry – the Great War proved that, and the next one will be worse. You can't play by the rules because there are no rules any more..."

"That's the Spear talking." Nick's look was uncharacteristically grave. "There are still rules, there have to be."

"Oh yes? And if we play by the rules, and our enemies don't, what happens then?"

"But if we don't play by the rules," said Elsa, "we become like our enemies. And then, what are we fighting about?"

"We cannot use the Spear," said Salim. "It is a remnant of another world, a barbaric world. It is of a piece with the savagery of Gagool, the mindless destructiveness of these who dwell in the Well of Souls. The Sons of Destiny could wield such a weapon. I could not. You could not."

There was a silence. Luke glanced from face to face. He saw no support there – only understanding, and something much like pity.

He hung his head and nodded, dumbly.

Salim held up the Spear and examined it for a moment with detached interest. Then he drew back his arm and flung it into the shaft of light from the Well of Souls. For a moment it quivered, as though in recognition of its renewed imprisonment. Then it subsided to hang, as it had when they had first seen it, revolving slowly in the light from the pit; put aside for ever from the world of men, as a tool no longer of any use, as a toy outgrown.

26 PARTINGS

Before the Three Sisters
Kukuanaland

"It did all happen, didn't it?" said Nick.

"You saw what I saw," replied Luke.

"But, I mean...we're scientists, engineers, for Pete's sake...I believe in the powers of electricity, gravity, magnetism; not weird glowing watchamacallits from an ancient world..."

"Are they so very different?" said Luke. "I suppose a lot of magic might be science that we don't understand yet. Anyway, in the past couple of years we've found living dinosaurs and a nuclear submarine that sailed around the world seventy years ago. Was what we found in the Mines really so very far out of the way?"

Nick gave a moody shrug and sent a stone skimming across the still surface of the waterhole beside which they were sitting, in the shade of an acacia tree. The Silent Ones and the Mines lay behind them. No great distance away, King Solomon's Road stretched across the plain to the distant city of Leu and the even more distant mountains that had for so long isolated this land from the outside world.

The sandy ground around them was criss-crossed with the tracks of beasts that had come down in the night to drink – lion, hyena and leopard; giraffe, elephant and rhinoceros; warthog, zebra and antelope, some of which were visible in the distance, peacefully cropping the parched grass while keeping a wary eye out for predators. The Kukuana who had led Luke's party to the Mines stood or squatted in small groups. Isaias, his gun held across his chest, kept an eagle eye on the disconsolate German pilot of Roxton's autogyro. A scouting party of Kukuana had found the flying machine on a strip of level ground less than a mile away from the entrance to the Mines. Its pilot had been quietly dozing in its cockpit before being rudely awoken by a poke in the ear from Isaias's musket.

Roxton's body (and Gagool's, when it had finally

been freed from the spear that pinned it to the rock – a gory business) had been quietly consigned to the waterfall. "After all," Nick had said, "he was officially dead before he came here. I don't see why we should have to report to the coroner's office and answer a lot of tomfool questions about how the man came to die when he was already dead." Nobody had raised any objections to this view. Luke thought it likely that Roxton's body would probably wind up in some lost underground chamber. If it were ever washed down through the mountains to emerge into the light of day, it would pose a pretty problem for the authorities. They would have some trouble explaining how the body of a man who had died in South America had managed to turn up nearly two years later and half a world away.

Luke and his companions had tried, without success, to find the mechanism to open the door to the chamber in which Mochizuki was imprisoned. The secret had effectively died with Gagool, and even Nick, with his expertise in spotting hidden mechanisms, had admitted defeat in the attempt to find this one; though by his own admission, he hadn't exactly worn himself to a frazzle looking. "Anyway," he had said to Elsa (who hadn't been looking at all), "maybe there's another way out of the chamber, besides the door. Your great-grandpa found one."

Luke had shaken his head. "Gagool told Mochizuki that way had been blocked."

"Ah, well, she's a resourceful girl. Maybe she'll unblock it."

Salim, who didn't know Kasumi Mochizuki as well as Luke and Nick, had been unhappy at leaving even a ruthless enemy to such a fate. Eventually, however, even he had been forced to agree that their efforts were futile. In any case, the party was running out of supplies, and there were still urgent decisions to be made and actions to be taken. Salim had returned to the Mines to act on the first of these, while his friends, who had no wish to step out of the light of day again, awaited his return.

Nick checked the position of the sun. "Almost noon. I thought Salim would be back before now."

Luke said, "He'll be along." But his attention wasn't on Nick, or on Salim's whereabouts. He was looking at Elsa, who was sitting on a rock a few yards away, chatting to their guards in Amharic.

Nick nudged him. "Go and talk to her."

"She's busy," said Luke defensively.

"Go on – you know you fancy her. Strike while the iron's hot."

"I'll have plenty of time to talk to her on the way to my mother's dig – weeks. Anyway," Luke added with some heat, "it's none of your business."

But Nick was right. Since that moment of fleeting sympathy and understanding as they hesitated outside the third hall of Solomon's Treasure House, Elsa had been a changed person. Perhaps their encounter in the Mines had laid to rest the ghost of her great-grandfather's earlier visit, dispelling the guilt with which she had struggled for so long. At any rate, he had reason to hope that her dark moods and ill temper were behind her. Since they had emerged from the Mines she had been light-hearted, smiling at him and laughing at Nick's jokes – altogether a much more agreeable companion than the angry, resentful Elsa who had been getting his goat all the way from Khartoum. He'd always thought her attractive and now found himself looking forward to their journey together to the Omo Valley.

Greetings from the Kukuana broke into his reverie. He looked up to see Salim and his small escort approaching. The Kukuana who had returned to the Mines with him broke away to report to their officer, and Salim ducked into the shade of Luke and Nick's acacia. Elsa joined them with a water-skin, which she offered to Salim.

Salim said, "Thank you," with his usual grave courtesy, and drank. Then, gazing steadily at his companions, he said, "The Mines are sealed."

Nick sighed. "To think of all that lovely gold, those

gorgeous sparklers, just lying down there, no use to man or beast. It's a wicked shame." Elsa gave him a pitying look.

"I still think you're making a mistake," said Luke heavily. "Money talks. Some of that treasure – even a fraction of it – could buy Ethiopia a lot of friends; and right now, she needs all the friends she can get."

Salim shook his head. "Luke, it's too late for that. The treasure would be wasted. No European country will go to war with Italy over what they see as a not-very-important country in Africa, and Mussolini won't be bought off; he doesn't want trinkets, he wants an empire."

"But if he invades, some successor to Gentile will come looking for the Mines with half the Italian army at his back."

"It will do him no good. The Mines are sealed." Salim fingered his medallion. "I shall leave this in the care of someone I trust, but who has no obvious link to me; that way, if I should become a prisoner of our enemies, I cannot be tempted to give it up. It will be hidden until I call for it again. Or, if I never call, it will be kept safe – for eternity if need be." He glanced back at the Three Witches, the peaks brooding over the entrance to the Mines. "One day, it might be possible to use the wealth of the Mines to help my people. For now, bringing it out would only benefit our enemies. The wealth of Solomon – and the Spear of Destiny – can stay where they lie."

Elsa said, "You talk as if you think an Italian invasion is inevitable."

Salim gave her a faint smile. "I think it is. Before this year is out, if I'm any judge, *Il Duce*'s troops will be in Addis Ababa." Elsa held his gaze for a moment, then looked away.

"So," said Luke, "what are your plans now?"

"I shall send a message to my father, telling him where I have been and what has happened here. While I'm waiting for his reply, I shall do what I can for the Kukuana. They have suffered much under Gagool's tyranny – there is a great deal to be put right, and they must be prepared to meet an invasion. Not just from the Italians – in a world of radio and aeroplanes, this land can no longer live apart from the outside world." Salim stood. "I need to consult with our guides – everything is done here; I must return to Leu as quickly as possible. Please excuse me."

When he had gone, Nick said, "Well, I just have to go and see a man about a dik-dik…"

Luke glared at him. "A what?"

"It's a sort of antelope." Behind Elsa's back, Nick performed an elaborate pantomime, the gist of which was that Luke should talk to Elsa while the iron was hot.

Elsa, turning, caught him in the middle of a blacksmith impression. Nick gave her an unabashed grin and strode away, whistling.

Elsa smiled after him. "All the tact of a bang on the head." She turned to Luke, eyebrows raised. "Was there something you wanted to talk about?"

"Well – er – yes." Luke was back in the lobby of the Grand Hotel in Khartoum where he had first seen Elsa; he felt breathless, awkward, uncomfortable and slightly foolish. "I – that is – what I mean to say..." He gave up. "It doesn't matter. It wasn't anything urgent. Nothing we can't talk about on the way to my mother's dig."

"Luke..." It was Elsa's turn to hesitate. "I'm afraid I won't be going with you."

Luke stared at her. "Sorry?"

"I'm going to stay here. With Salim."

It still took a few seconds for the penny to drop. "You mean – you and Salim...?" Luke groaned inwardly, and then hoped he hadn't done it out loud.

"Well, sort of... Anyway, you heard what he said. There's a lot to do here. I can help. I speak the language."

"But you heard what he said, about the Italians...the invasion...it'll be dangerous..."

"I daresay it will. But I think the whole world will be a dangerous place in a few years. In any case, I'm used to danger – especially since I took up with you. Don't worry, I'll be all right." She reached out tentatively and pressed his arm. "Sorry, Luke." Then she slipped away.

"Yes – right – er, good luck!" Luke belatedly remembered to call after her. Elsa turned and gave him a brief wave before joining Salim as he discussed the details of their journey.

A few moments later, Nick, lounging against a tree trunk on the other side of the waterhole, was startled to see Luke striding past him with a face like thunder and his formidable Challenger jaw jutting like the blade of a bulldozer. "Where are you going?"

"To find Roxton's autogyro. We're flying out of here."

Nick hurried to catch up. "Are we, now? Have you ever flown an autogyro?"

"How hard can it be?"

Harriet Challenger looked up from the skeleton she was excavating as an ungainly aircraft with chattering rotors flew over the dig, banked around and made an untidy landing a hundred yards away. Its occupants climbed stiffly from the twin cockpits and came towards her, removing helmets and flying goggles as they approached.

"Luke! Nick!" Lady Challenger hugged her son and her nephew. "Where on earth have you been? I expected you to be here when I arrived – such an awful journey, the steamer seemed to have vanished into thin air so I had to hire a felucca, and when I finally reached the mule train, the drivers told me they hadn't seen you..." She broke off, looking past them to the autogyro, whose blades were still turning slowly. "What an extraordinary machine! Where's Elsa?"

"I'm afraid she won't be joining us," said Luke heavily.

"Oh, what a nuisance! She's all right, isn't she?"

"Perfectly all right, when we left her. She's with Salim."

"Oh, well, I'm sure she'll be fine. A very impressive young man, that friend of yours. Though what I'm to do without her, I don't know – my papers are all over the place, the diggers are slacking, we're short of supplies." She took their arms. "Anyway, come and have some tea – bush tea, I'm afraid, we've run out of everything else, but at least Hakim has learned to warm the pot these days. I've got some fascinating skulls to show you. Now, you must tell me what you've been up to since you left Khartoum – have you been having a nice time...?"

Look out for more of Luke Challenger's death-defying adventures

RETURN TO THE LOST WORLD

Someone is trying to kill Luke Challenger.
Fleeing the would-be assassins into the Brazilian
jungle, Luke encounters a lost world of real-life dinosaurs.
But the sinister Sons of Destiny are on Luke's tail and
they're hell-bent on destroying him...

ISBN 9781409520177

Luke learns that Captain Nemo's legendary submarine,
the Nautilus, is lying at the bottom of the Indian Ocean.
The evil Sons of Destiny are desperate to get their hands on
it because it holds the key to atomic power.
Can daredevil Luke stop them?

ISBN 9781409521426

For more action-packed thrillers, check out www.fiction.usborne.com